Baby,
Baby

Also by Liz Nickles

The Coming Matriarchy
Girls in High Places (coauthored with Sugar Rautbord)
Hype

Baby, Baby

Liz Nickles

POCKET BOOKS

New York   London   Toronto   Sydney   Tokyo   Singapore

POCKET BOOKS, a division of Simon & Schuster
1230 Avenue of the Americas, New York, NY 10020

Nickles, Liz.
   Baby, baby : a novel / by Liz Nickles.
     p.   cm.
   ISBN 0-671-72808-3 : $18.95
   I. Title.
  PS3564.I318B3   1991
  813'.54—dc20   90-25607
                        CIP

First Pocket Books hardcover printing June 1991

10 9 8 7 6 5 4 3 2 1

Printed in the U.S.A.

for Drew
with love

One

August third, she thought.

It's August third, and I haven't done it. I have to do it. Today.

She looked at her watch. Eight-thirty A.M. Was that Paris time or New York time? She looked out the window. At forty thousand feet, the sky was noncommittal. They'd be landing in half an hour—the Concorde made it from Paris to New York in two and a half hours, which meant she had thirty minutes to do something that could change her life forever.

Bolting from her seat, Kate Harrison-Weil wedged her way past her startled seatmate, who was her boss, Stanton Welch, the distinguished and now fully awake group publisher of Americana Publishing. "Excuse me, Stanton," she said as her shoulder bag smacked him in the face. There was just no room to maneuver on this plane. She hated dragging carry-on luggage, but this had been an overnight trip, and after a day at the office, she was going straight to San Francisco tonight. She'd be back in the air again by six o'clock. In her bag were: all her makeup; two extra pairs of stockings (black and off-white, in case of a run); her keys; her Filofax; her notebooks and tape recorder; two advance copies of *Childstyle,* the magazine she published; several memos; a measuring tape; the Polaroids of the last cover shoot; a framed picture of Matt for the hotel bedside—and an ovulation kit.

Kate locked herself into the Concorde lavatory. If the rest of the plane was small, this place redefined microscopic. She balanced her bag on the stainless steel sink, fished out the ovulation kit box, and purposefully prepared for action.

She hoped her timing was right. Was it fifteen days since the end of her last period, or since the beginning? It was easy to lose track. Somehow she never got it right. She, who could juggle fifty people on a masthead and give twelve back-to-back dinner parties without a hitch. She, who had a master's degree in journalism, who had defied the odds and launched her own successful magazine. She forgot. Or screwed up. And each month that it slipped Kate's mind, or she dropped the thermometer, or was out of town on business, was another month lost. She and Matt wanted a summer baby, when they both could take time off. She *couldn't* miss another month. And she wouldn't.

Kate set the plastic cups, vials, rack, and sticks on the stainless steel sink counter, like a fertility buffet. She unfolded the directions.

Mix contents of tube A with contents of tube B using stick C, stirring twenty times exactly in up and down motion, until liquid becomes clear. Wait five minutes, using timer.

Kate squinted at the words, which seemed to be written in hieroglyphics. Back in high school, which was the last time she'd seen a test tube, she'd always done fairly well at chemistry. But that was in a lab, in a white jacket supplied by Mr. Cavanaugh, the omniscient, owl-eyed teacher, not in the stainless steel straightjacket lavatory of the Concorde, hurtling over the ocean somewhere between Paris and New York City at twice the speed of sound, wearing a vintage Chanel suit that taunted, "Spill on me and I'll cost you thirty thousand francs." The whole complicated process would have been at least more convenient on the ground, without the uncomfortable knowledge that Stanton Welch was probably wondering if Kate had fallen out the emergency exit.

The problem now, as Kate saw it, was how to get the tubes and powders mixed in spite of— *Wham!* Her shoulder crashed into the stainless steel wall. It was impossible to balance with her skirt around her hips, her panty hose around her knees, and a plastic cup somewhere in between. Kate felt her palms start to sweat. No, she would not return to her seat. She'd gotten this far, and she was determined to see the procedure through. It seemed like every time she tried to really knuckle down to this pregnancy thing, something got in her way. Last month it was the trip to Cincinnati to speak at the Women's Advertising Club. You couldn't very well get pregnant if you and the man in question were in two separate cities. The month before, she'd been in such a rush she'd dropped the basal temperature thermometer, a hundred-fifty-dollar piece of techno-gear the manufacturer had hopefully labeled "The Rabbit," on the onyx tile bathroom floor and broken it, and she hadn't had time to get a new one.

Or maybe she'd had a mental block. Granted, the basal thermometer was not atom-splitting equipment, but it was, at best, damned inconvenient. It had to be used first thing in the morning, before you even got out of bed. You couldn't move, not to get up, and not even to shake the thermometer down, because any movement affected the body temperature. Kate, who was used to leaping out of bed, found it insufferable to freeze herself immobile for the requisite five minutes. Then there was the connect-the-dots chart that recorded the temperatures, and the fractional blips that signaled impending ovulation. Everything had to be recorded, studied, and acted upon, so that Kate felt more like a weatherman than a pre-parent. No wonder she'd dropped the thermometer!

The problem was, you could only get pregnant for one forty-eight-hour span occurring precisely after ovulation, and if you missed that checkpoint, you blew another entire month. So it was critical to confirm precisely when you ovulated. She wondered if her problem went deeper than the inconvenience of it all.

It was not just the physical aspects. There was the weight of the decision itself, bearing down on you from the time you were thirty, a monthly depletion of another cycle from your lifetime limit, leaving you one month older, with one less egg in the bank, one less chance for a child. There was the self-convincing you went through that you indeed had that month to spare, and the next and the next, until convincing yourself became fooling yourself, and you knew time was, if not quite up, not exactly on a K Mart Blue Light special. Suddenly, you were a reservoir about to run dry. A car with three and a half wheels. A box of candy with one piece left.

Kate vividly remembered the thrill and promise of waking up at summer camp one morning to find her underwear stained. Then she knew, in spite of her childish hips and lack of breasts, that she was a woman after all. You had forever to have a child, even as you would surely never die, because, just as no one died, everyone had children. And so would you, when the time was right.

The trouble was, Kate thought, the time was never right until time was up and you were forced to make it so.

Kate resented the pressure, but she had learned to control it by self-decree: when she decided to become pregnant, she *would* become pregnant. She would simply make sure it happened this way. And now she was almost thirty-nine years old, married two years, and successful in her career. It was the right time.

"Oh God Oh God Oh God," she whispered as she tried once more to maneuver panty hose, plastic urine cup, skirt, and half-slip while maintaining her balance. She had a wild thought: What if the plane crashed? The FAA investigators would find her here, locked in the bathroom with the charred remains of a fertility kit.

There was a polite knock on the door.

"This bathroom is occupied! *Occupée,*" she called out.

Kate took the plastic cup with the remaining urine that hadn't spilled on the floor, and, using the miniature eyedropper that came with the kit, meticulously siphoned off what looked like the right amount. She hoped this was three drops. That last one looked more like half a drop. What if she hadn't squeezed the dropper hard enough? Would the test still work? Could you flunk an ovulation test? Kate dripped the two and a half or three drops into the test tube and stirred exactly twenty times. Now the problem was where to put the test tube for the five-minute waiting period. The microscopic sink counter was a bad risk, but she'd have to try it. Carefully, she set up the cardboard stand that came with the kit. Then she readjusted her skirt and sat on the lid of the toilet, watching the test tube as intently as if she were Marie Curie waiting for mold to grow.

Another knock on the door, this one very insistent. "Please hurry up in there," a man's voice said. "I'm not feeling well."

"Well, neither am I," Kate yelled through the door. She started to sweat.

She looked nervously at her watch. *Thirty seconds*. Time was dragging. She reread the instructions. *One minute*. She reapplied her lipstick. *Ninety seconds*. Combed out her hair. *Two and a half minutes*. She used her purse-sized travel hairspray. *Three minutes*. She checked her stockings. *Three minutes, ten seconds*. The plane bumped, and some of the liquid in the tube sloshed over the side. Kate put her thumb on top of the test tube and held it. Finally, the endless five minutes was over. Then she dipped the little plastic stick into the tube and watched.

The door rattled violently. "I'm going to call the stewardess. Are you smoking in there?"

"Just a minute, *please!*" Kate cried. She was losing patience with the whole thing. But then she noticed—almost imperceptibly, shade by shade, the little stick was turning blue.

Directions! The directions! She fumbled the paper open again. Where was that fucking color chart? Which blue did the stick match? The approaching-ovulation, ovulation, or post-ovulation blue? God, who could tell? Her blue looked more turquoise; it didn't seem to match any of the patches on the chart.

The paper-thin door lurched inward, and the test tube bounced to the floor, shattering. Blue urine splashed onto Kate's shoes.

"I feel sick!" said the man on the other side of the door. There was a retching sound: he was throwing up in the aisle.

The hell with it, Kate said to herself. The stuff was some shade of blue; who needed to know more? She'd call Matt from the air-phone and tell him—what? That she would be in New York for a total of five and a half hours, between planes from Paris and to San Francisco? It was crazy. How were they going to be able to manage this? You couldn't have sex by fax.

It was going to be a bad day: first, the office. The cover meeting. The Christmas promotion meeting. The afternoon meeting with the media director of Junior Products, their biggest advertiser, who was making uncivilized noises about pulling his plan from the issue. Then the five-thirty flight. That left exactly ninety minutes at lunch.

Ninety minutes at lunch it would have to be. If Matt was busy—well, he'd have to clear his appointments. Matt was a doctor; it was true he had patients to deal with, but being a dermatologist, he saw few if any emergency cases. His partner would just have to cover for once. Usually, Matt's schedule was even worse than Kate's. As one of the world's leading authorities on skin rejuvenation, he was in constant demand for everything from a consultation with an aging movie star, to a lecture in Sweden, to an appearance on the *Today* show promoting his latest book, *Why Grow Old*. If their schedules had any coincidental convergence of free time, it was either circumstantial or accidental. Today, though, things were different. This was top priority; they'd agreed. Neither of them wanted to lose another month.

She would call Clair and tell her to cancel her lunch date. Then she would call Matt and tell him to book a room at the Waldorf—halfway between their two offices. She smoothed the white silk gardenia at the edge of her collar, tucked the blue stick into her bag, and prayed that the man outside the door would be gone when she opened it.

Two

"*W*aaaah!"

"*Waaaah!*"

"*Waaaah!*"

"Mommy! Mommy! I have to go to the bathroom!"

A hand intercepted Kate's path, thrusting a bundle at her.

It was a disposable diaper. A *used* disposable diaper.

Another typical day at the office, thought Kate, as she navigated her carry-on shoulder bag through thirty babies in various stages from infants to toddlers crawling, clinging, and otherwise packed into the red-and-white lobby of *Childstyle*. They were here, as usual, to audition for a cover, an honor that made up in prestige what it lacked in monetary compensation. Every mother in the country wanted her baby to be on the glossy cover of *Childstyle*.

Kate hopped over a yellow truck and bayoneted a sandwich with her heel. Peanut butter oozed onto her shoe as she tried to shake it off by hopping up and down until a black-eyed boy reached out possessively, yanked the sandwich free, and stuffed it into his mouth.

Most of these kids had no discipline, Kate observed. The mothers came in with them starched and shiny in little picture book pinafores and knee socks, combed and perfectly pressed to make

7

a good impression on the art director, and by the time they left the lobby, they usually looked like a tornado had picked them up and whirled them to Oz and back. Just now, three of the ones who could walk were engaged in a pushing match over by the ficus tree. Of the babies on the floor, five or six were giddily crawling loose, and one was ripping through the sample copies of *Childstyle* that were always stacked in the lobby and throwing the crumpled pages over her head. The mothers, for the most part, looked frazzled and weighted down with bags that bulged with toys. One was changing a diaper on the couch. Another actually had her baby on a little leash, like a human Pomeranian. Kate frowned, as she always did when she encountered this kind of disorder. The lobby belied her own office, which was a polished and fingerprintless symmetry of wrapping-paper-brown walls and Swedish Biedermeier. Then she smiled. It would be different with *her* child. Most of the women in the waiting room were in their twenties. This was where, Kate knew, she would have the advantage. Waiting to have your children gave you the maturity to handle them; you were no longer a child yourself.

"Hi, Kate," called the receptionist, a pretty young redhead who, in the tradition of magazine publishing, had her eye on an editorial assistant's position. She would probably make it; Kate noticed that she seemed undaunted by the surrounding scene. A smooth surface, grace under pressure, whatever you called it— the ability to *appear* to be handling it all, that was the first thing it took to succeed in this business. The second thing, of course, was the ideas and intelligence. But even that wasn't enough if you couldn't make people believe you could handle it.

Kate high-stepped her sling-back shoes over a mine field of Lincoln Logs and headed down the hall for her office, a symphony of shrieks and screams ringing out behind her.

They'd be putting the Christmas issue to bed today, although it was barely August. She'd have to go over the entire layout, coordinate all the photographs with the copy, and do a last-minute check on all the features. Christmas was their biggest issue; it was going to be a long day, and she'd already lost most of it over the Atlantic.

"Oh my God!" Kate said as she realized what she was holding.

Using two fingers, she tossed the disposable diaper into her wastebasket. Then she stashed her quilted Prada bag in a locking drawer and checked her hair in a little mirrored paperweight: blond, chin-length, pulled back from her high forehead by a black satin headband that set off the black ribbons edging the white Chanel camellia at the throat of her blouse. White blouse, pearls, black or navy skirt, signature jacket, Chanel, St. Laurent. That was Kate. She smoothed her eyebrows, which arched unevenly over gray-green verdigris eyes. At thirty-eight, Kate was still fighting a little-girl image. She was only five foot three, small enough to remember how it felt to always be the shortest person in the class. But a lifetime of making the most of what height she had gave her a bearing that could command a room simply by walking in. Her soft voice was decisive, with sentences that often ended in staccato jabs. Kate was one of those people who couldn't be called threatening, yet who left a distinct impression of a firm grip. She would have been surprised to learn that many of the people who worked for her were afraid of her. They called her "The Terminator" behind her back because if someone on Kate's staff didn't perform, he or she was out. Kate was one of that rarefied group of women executives who didn't have anything to prove, because she'd already made it. She wore her degrees and promotions with the same nonchalance that she wore the gold chains on her Chanel suit. Like Helen Gurley Brown of *Cosmopolitan* or Tina Brown of *Vanity Fair,* Kate reigned supreme, although she was so feminine and small as to appear deceivingly nonthreatening, allowing her to ambush the unsuspecting with words that could slash like razors.

Kate's manner was her camouflage. She was a good listener, and she knew it and used it, alert to the rhythms and cadences of conversation, spotting the little lapses of attention and crescendos of excitement that allowed her to read between the lines with the intuitiveness of a poker player.

Kate pulled a bottle of Evian from the minirefrigerator in her office closet, and poured the water into a brass-and-chrome electric kettle. A tray of teas and miniature jars of imported honeys, as well as a silver bowl of lemons, sat on the conference table. This morning she chose blackberry tea. It was a morning ritual that had become famous in the office, and several of the editors, writers, and advertisers had given her gifts of antique silver tea strainers, a small collection that was laid out on a nineteenth-century Limoges tray. It always gave Kate a feeling of satisfaction to see the silver spoons with their pierced handles lined up with precision, the little cloth napkins folded just so. She was not a believer in office clutter. After all, your office communicated things to your people. Kate's Steuben goblet of vintage Waterman pens, even the bowl of brass paper clips, had a cared-about air, as if awaiting a photographer from *HG* to swoop down and shoot a spread on the executive suite (an event that had, in fact, occurred).

A person who did not know Kate and her story would find it hard to believe that, just ten years ago, she had been unemployed—and, worse, unemployable.

At twenty-eight, Kate Harrison had experienced something far more humbling than being stuck in a dead-end job: she was fired from one. There was a certain dignity, Kate had tried to convince herself that day ten years ago, in moving on after being a glorified trainee gossip columnist for the *New York Herald*. It was a job that had never fit. Coming from Northwestern University with a master's degree in journalism, Kate had idolized Katharine Graham ever since she'd heard her speak at a career conference. Kate was determined to do something important, to make a difference, to be noticed. She left Northwestern with her jaw firmly set and her eyes straight ahead. But there was a recession, and the only job she could find was assistant editor of *Health Watch*, a Midwest hospital trade journal. Kate found herself writing picture captions about heart-lung machines. *Health Watch* was neither a creative hotbed nor a challenge. Kate spent most of her time hanging around the various departments, a kind of overeducated intern, filling in where she was needed and looking over people's shoulders. But she *did* learn a bit about direct marketing, forecasting, subscription economics, and financial planning. Determined to find a better job, she spent every day of her annual two-week vacations in New York, canvassing for work, and every Sunday reading the Help Wanted section of the *New York Times*.

It took three years. But finally, her opportunity came, in the form of a résumé that crossed her desk—an editorial assistant, leaving the *New York Herald*, was looking for work in Chicago. Kate took the woman's call absentmindedly.

"I really hate to leave this job—I'm associate editor of the *Metro* section. In fact, I haven't told them yet. It's a terrific place, and a chance to meet people in society, business, show business," the woman had said.

"Then why are you leaving?" Kate had asked.

"I'm getting married. My fiancé lives in Chicago, and I'm looking for something there."

God, how could she walk away from that job? Kate had wondered. *What I wouldn't give for that job!* Then it had occurred to her: maybe she could have it.

Two weeks later, having called in conveniently "sick," Kate was in New York, having wrangled a recommendation from the by-then former *Metro* editor in return for an enthusiastic introduction at *Health Watch*.

The *Herald* paid, in fact, less than Kate was making in Chicago, but that did not stop her from leaping at the job. Money was not the issue. She would be a New York journalist, a member of the working press. She would have paid *them* to give her the job.

During her three years on *Metro*, Kate was rotated from assisting the food critic to interviewing opera stars. For two years, Kate felt exhilarated every day she went to work. The paper's offices on Forty-third Street were ramshackle, her office was a broken partition, but there were press passes to every event, comp tickets from theaters, and free meals from restaurants who hoped for a good review. Kate felt like a part of something vital and significant. She felt like she was helping to define New York.

When a budget cut phased out *Metro* magazine, Kate was reassigned to the "After Hours" column. "After Hours" was the domain of society gossip columnist Harry St. James, who reported the to-ing and fro-ing, to use his words, of the *riche*, nouveau and otherwise. Harry was intensely ambitious, which may have explained his fondness for using guerilla paparazzi tactics. At first Kate didn't mind accompanying Harry to the big black-tie charity events and helping keep an eye on the rich and famous at play. Dancing for dystrophy, he called it. But Harry didn't just go to parties; he staked them out.

"You *have* to go to the ladies' room," he'd say, tugging at his bow tie with its minute pattern that, on close examination, turned out to be hundreds of tiny Mickey Mice.

"No, I don't," Kate would say.

"Yes, you do. Jackie just went in. You have to go!"

"And do what?"

"Haven't I taught you anything?" Harry would throw up his hands, showing the whites of his eyes in exasperation. "Get in there! Listen! Tell me what they're saying!"

Kate realized her career had sunk to this: she had become a human listening device fit for coatracks and lavatory stalls. Not a pretty picture. And so when Harry fired her for refusing to do the morning rounds with a celebrity dog-walker, Kate was less than chagrined. She would have quit already, but she hadn't been able to find another job.

Out of work, Kate could no longer afford her half share of her small studio. Desperate, she had answered an ad and taken a job as a summer nanny in the Hamptons for a couple named Jim and Jamie Hemphill, because it meant free room and board. Apart from the career lapse, the downside was that Kate, an only child, had had absolutely no experience with children. Fortunately, at seven and nine, the Hemphill children were not that young. They were in day camp most of the morning, so Kate's main responsibility boiled down to taking them to the beach.

"If I ever get out of this," Kate had promised herself, sitting with teeth gritted on the sand in Bridgehampton, "I will never pick up after a kid again." She hated the disorder of her own life as much as she hated the toys that tripped her everywhere she turned in the beach house. Her career had been laid out in her mind for so long. Now she was completely derailed. Without her job, Kate felt as if she did not exist. She scanned the beach; where had her charges gone now? Kids were everywhere. *Where did all these kids come from?* Kate wondered as she began walking toward the lifeguard stand, avoiding sand castles and airborne Frisbees. Just a few years ago, it seemed like nobody had kids. Now, everybody had them. There must have been some kind of baby boom. In fact, she vaguely remembered reading that there *was* a new baby boom. Certainly there were baby boutiques popping up wherever you looked, like weeds between the cracks in the sidewalk. And children's bookstores. Next thing, there'd be a magazine for kids.

Kate stopped her trudge up the beach.

A magazine for kids. Well maybe not just for kids. A magazine *about* kids, for parents. For the yuppies who spent their money on kids. A life-style magazine about kids. These new parents were well educated and affluent. They were like Kate herself, she reasoned. Except that she had no children, and right now she was temporarily less than affluent. The Hemphills spent a fortune on their kids. Every Saturday, Jamie came back from East Hampton with a shopping bag crammed with little outfits. The kids never even wore half of them. It was obvious that Jamie was buying them for herself, really, not for the children. Drawersful of adorable kids' clothes validated the yuppie existence as a mother. It all made sense to Kate. There would be a huge market for a magazine that was, say, a *Vogue* for parents of kids, where parents could peruse page after page of adorably gorgeous children's clothes and accessories. There'd be tips on kids' hairstyles. An accessories section. Nightwear. Shoes. A few features ... Kate closed her eyes and pictured the magazine, suddenly oblivious to the hot sun, the shrieking sea gulls, and the missing Hemphills. The magazine in her mind had a glossy cover, with an incredibly beautiful child on it. A girl. In a white Victorian lace christening gown. She held a bouquet of ivy and white snapdragons, and her hair curled around her face like a dark cloud. The name on the cover was *Childstyle*. She still had a good relationship with the former art director of *Metro*. If she called him, they could work up some sample spreads, on spec ...

And that had been the beginning.

Kate had managed to get the two-hundred-thousand-dollar backing for a prototype issue with typical determination. She had mailed a letter to Stanton Welch, group publisher of Americana Inc., one of the largest magazine publishers in the country. She received no response, even after two more letters. So, she sat on the floor outside his office for three days, ignoring the demands of his secretary—amusing Welch, actually, with her tenacity—until he granted her an interview.

"The thing of it is," she'd said, spreading her tissue layouts on the floor, "you'd be able to capture a big market for circulation, but that will be the gravy. The real money will be in the advertising. *Childstyle* will be a unique vehicle for advertisers."

"You know, Americana has not taken any private partners. And we are very conservative on new magazine launches."

"Mr. Welch, I do know the odds." She had looked them up in *Standard Rate and Data,* and they were indeed discouraging. "Of the twelve-hundred-some magazines that were out there last year, seven hundred and eighty have failed. But the problem is, they're all dissecting pieces of the same pie. *Childstyle* would have a unique position—the new upscale parent. An affluent, responsive market. I'm sure of it, but a test would show red flags, if any existed. All I'm asking for is a chance to prove I'm right."

It took Welch a torturous month to think it over, a month when Kate had swallowed her pride and called every day. Finally, four weeks later, Welch took the call.

"You're on to something, Kate," he had said. "I like your idea. The payout plan you worked up isn't bad either. Frankly, our people were working on something similar here, and I had to check it out, but I like your plan better. It's more upscale. Less uptight. And most important, you care about this thing. You're gonna give somebody their money's worth, and it might as well be me. We have too many corporate types here, I'm beginning to think. No push. No entrepreneurial spirit. Their idea of risk is to buy a BMW instead of a Mercedes. Good thing you came to me, though, because you're not *quite* smart enough. Because a lot of other people would have stolen it and cut you out. This has to be a leap of faith for both of us."

"I—hadn't thought of that."

"Of course you hadn't. That's why you need to surround yourself with business expertise. We can do that for you. You just deliver that magazine you described, and make it work. We'll send out a feeler. And if that does well . . . then we'll have a discussion."

The test run had done extremely well. Whether this was because of Kate's talent and ability, or simply because it was an idea whose time had come, didn't matter. One hundred thousand brochures describing the new magazine were sent to a mailing list of high-income families with children. Americana had hoped to get a thousand responses—but eight thousand flooded in. It was like dispensing an eyedropper of water onto the Sahara Desert. This market soaked up every drop of quality information that pertained to acquiring things for their children, and was left parched for more.

Kate had come in as managing editor, and within a year she was editor-in-chief—as well as part owner. She was honored by her profession with a succession of awards. Courted by advertisers. Revered by mothers, who looked upon Kate as a sort of guardian of their children's images. A frequent guest on Oprah, Phil, and Geraldo. Financially secure with the first stock offering. Kate's Sutton Place co-op was perfect down to the last soap dish. She was phalanxed by her housekeeper, personal trainer, manicurist, and facialist. Her life was ordered, routined, and successfully dedicated to maintaining her success and protecting her baby, the magazine. And then she'd met Matt.

Considering the fact that they were now preoccupied with fertility, it was auspicious, Kate thought, that they had met at a produce stand. Not just any produce stand, of course—the Third Avenue, Upper East Side produce haven Apple Annie's, where purple and green flowering kale vied with vegetables so jewellike they would have looked at home in diamond-surrounded settings. Kate had run in to buy some oil for her once-a-year pasta party, and had quickly become intimidated when she faced an international array of cans and bottles that required a linguist to read the labels. She remembered thinking that the last time she'd paid attention in a supermarket, there had been Crisco and Wesson, and that was about it. She'd loaded her willow basket— Apple Annie's would never stoop to wire carts—and was perusing the Neapolitan tomatoes when she'd encountered a man who was slowly and painstakingly picking up one zucchini at a time, examining it on all sides, then placing it carefully back in the refrigerated bin.

"Excuse me," she said. "You're not supposed to touch the produce. It's not sanitary." She reached for her tomatoes, which he hadn't handled.

"It's all right, miss," the man had said, now peering at a bunch of miniature carrots. "I'm a doctor." And he'd looked at her seriously. "Cough," he said, thumping a zucchini.

She'd had to laugh.

"I had to do it," he'd said, laughing at himself. "I saw this stuff and it didn't look biologically possible. Those tomatoes are the size of marbles! This yellow squash—I have bigger erasers. Fascinating, isn't it?"

"No," said Kate, filling her basket.

She tried not to look at him. It was never smart to talk to strangers, especially those with produce fetishes—even strangers with warm, disarming smiles and expensive shoes.

"What are all those bottles of oil?" he asked, pointing to her basket.

"Virgin, extra virgin, and triple virgin."

"Your mother must be very proud."

Kate was sure she was blushing, but somehow this man proceeded to get her to admit that she could only cook one dish—spaghetti, sometimes al dente, sometimes not.

"In that case, maybe you'll have dinner with me tonight," he said, following her to the checkout counter.

"No thanks," she said.

He handed her his business card. He really was a doctor. Or so it said. Still—

"I'll tell you what. Think about it. Give me your card, and I'll call you. And if you'll see me this weekend, we can stay in the broad daylight and I'll bring chaperones. Two of them. Okay, Miss Extra-Extra Virgin?"

The man had charm.

"Can I give you a lift home, at least?" he had asked. At the curb was his car: a navy-blue Mercedes limousine.

And when he'd called, Kate had agreed to meet him, and her life had never been the same, and within a month she had a new routine—one that made her feel loved and safe and important and beautiful, all at once, and his name was Matt Weil.

"Jingle bells, jingle bells," sang Margo Stern as she knocked on Kate's office door. "Ho, ho, ho. I hope you're in the holiday spirit."

"It's ninety-three degrees outside, I think," said Kate as the group filed in. "I hope Santa hasn't melted." One of the art directors shook a little snowstorm paperweight over his head. Everyone was used to working months ahead of the actual publication dates.

"Okay, what do we have here?" Kate asked, as five people, including Margo, the managing editor, and Tina Compton, the sales marketing manager, spread tissue layouts around the huge round conference table with the burled wood top. Both women were dressed like Kate—not in Chanel, but in Chanel-like variations, with gold chains.

"Don't you love these shots, Kate?" said Phil Corbusier, the art director. "We have five choices. Here are prints of the picks, and Polaroids of the backups."

Kate glanced quickly through the stack of shots, then pulled one from the Polaroids.

"I like the redhead twins. Full-length shot. Yellow taffeta dresses."

"Are you sure, Kate? The velvet is so festive."

"I like the yellow. It will pop out at the newsstands, when the rest of the world will be a sea of red and green. When they zig, we zag. What about metallic silver type? I thought we talked about a fifth color."

"Over budget. We cut it."

"What? We made our ad pages, didn't we?"

"Well, that's questionable, Kate. At this time."

"There is no other time, Tina. The issue is closing. Is there a problem?"

"Junior products. Again. They committed last month to a ten-page insert. But they backed out."

Kate nodded tersely. This was the reason for her trip to San Francisco. Since the Japanese bought the Junior Toy company

17

six months ago, the account, a key account, had been shaky. She needed to check things out in person.

"Okay," Kate said, scanning the layouts on her table. Everything looked good, except for one layout, which featured children's-theme Christmas trees. There were four trees, and Kate thought every theme looked a little tired. Not much—but the freshness, the unexpected, slick yet romantic look *Childstyle* was known for was slightly off. The headline treatments, for instance, were more mundane than usual. The casual reader would not have noticed, but Kate did. She was not the type to wait until something she did not like got out of hand; she moved instantly rather than let a situation fester. Kate eyed the art director. Phil seemed to have lost his edge lately; his intensity and focus seemed to be drifting.

She had heard he was having marriage problems—maybe that was why. He was losing his grip on the work. It was possible Kate would have to replace him, bring in someone who could give a hundred percent. It was too bad, because she liked Phil, but marriage problems or not, the pages needed to be better. That was the bottom line.

"Phil," Kate said. "Can we reshoot these trees this week? Maybe rearrange the look a little? Give each one a storybook look, something more upscale. Romantic upscale—you know, the Brothers Grimm meet Madison Avenue?"

Phil's chin tilted forward, but he made no response beyond a noncommittal shrug. He knew Kate's "maybe" meant "do it." Everyone still remembered the time that someone had suggested breaking format and putting a mother instead of a child on the cover. Kate had calmly said that would be fine, when the person making the suggestion had his own successful magazine. "Or, when circulation is down, we might consider it," she'd said.

"Dr. B's column is late again, Kate," said Margo.

"What's his excuse this time?"

"Conference in Hawaii."

"I think we'll get him some help. A ghost writer. Look into it for next month, Margo. He always puts us behind schedule."

"Maybe we should get somebody new? Somebody younger, more with it?"

Kate frowned. Dr. Hugo Bronsky was not just any pediatrician. He was an icon. A fading icon, true, but ten years ago it had been a coup to attach his name to the magazine. He had never been associated with another publication in his fifty-year career, but he had believed in the magazine, and in Kate. She wouldn't forget that. "Call Dr. Bronsky wherever he is," said Kate. "No, I'll call him. I'll tell him we know how busy he is, and we've got someone in mind to help out if he's crunched for time." She made a note. "Next?"

"The feature on homeless children that Marcia Eliott sent in. It's a very hard-hitting piece. Did you read it?" Margo asked enthusiastically.

"I did, and it's good. But not for us."

"But it's such an important issue. It'll be in the news when the issue breaks."

"It's *not* for the holidays, Margo. Too down, depressing."

"I just thought . . ."

"Listen, you're not wrong here. It's a very significant issue, even if it is a little off our format. Maybe we could run a small news-type sidebar. Let's revisit this later in the year—spring or summer. Maybe then. Anything else?"

"Roy Guardino of *Finance* was over here yesterday. He wants to do a joint circulation package to executive mothers," said Hal Radia, the circulation director. Hal was the oldest person in the room, but, Kate thought, the smartest. He had come out of semi-retirement to consult on the magazine's launch, and Kate had persuaded him to stay. He was totally connected with all the major distribution channels, and he had delivered wonderful newsstand positioning. This, combined with his knowledge of direct marketing and the fact that he was a virtuoso with mailing lists, made Hal a key member of Kate's team. She always took his advice.

"Is this a good thing, Hal? *Finance* is way off. Roy's been discounting everything on paper over there. They could pull us down with them."

Hal blinked slowly, the folds of his upper eyelids almost obscuring a turtlelike gaze. "You know, I'd go for it, Kate. As long as our friend the Slasher keeps his rates where they belong."

"I just wonder if we're equal partners."

"No, not right now. But . . ."

Kate nodded quickly. She understood. If they did this favor for Guardino, he'd owe them a favor. At no real downside to *Childstyle*. It never hurt to have people owe you favors. "Okay, let's do it," she said.

"You know," said Tina, looking through the page layouts, "I don't see the J and J spread at the front of the book."

"That's because it's not at the exact front," said Phil.

"They bought that placement," said Tina. "I promised it to them."

"They were out of context," said Phil. "The Revlon ad looked better. It's just a two-page difference."

"Two pages is a continent, Phil, and you know that."

"*You* know that, aside from the covers, we only promise the *approximate* placement of an ad. You said front of the book, this is front of the book." He overemphasized each consonant, as if driving stakes with his tongue.

"Kate," said Tina, exasperated, in search of a referee.

Kate was looking out the window.

"Kate?"

I wonder if we'll finish the nursery renovations before the baby is born, Kate was thinking. The contractors had sworn a blood oath, but she knew better than to believe them. Kate had already ordered ceramic tiles in pink, blue, and yellow gingham glaze from France, and Laura Ashley wall fabrics and curtains. When the decorators had remodeled the huge, prewar co-op, with its terraces and views of Central Park, a warren of prisonlike maids' rooms had been gutted, opened up, and combined into a large suite. Ostensibly this was for Gregory and Kim, Matt's children from his first marriage; but, in Kate's mind, it was for their future baby. Kate had made sure that an intercom system had been wired into the walls before they were replastered. She had installed a huge, tublike sink with a swivel faucet that would be ideal for bathing a baby, and she had put a little fenced and awninged play area on the terrace. When the time came, Kate had known she would have her hands full, and she had not wanted the additional hassle of blueprints, estimates, and plaster

20

dust in her life. Yet, almost a year later, the tiles had still not arrived from France and the white-lacquered custom cabinets remained uninstalled. She'd have to call the contractor today and apply some additional pressure.

"*Kate?*"

"Wh— Yes?" She jolted back into the meeting. God, what were they discussing? She had completely tuned out; her mind was really wandering. It wasn't like her.

"Kate, this Revlon ad. Does it get priority or not?"

"Hm. Whatever you guys decide is fine with me. It's your call."

The phone buzzed. Kate picked it up. "Your car is downstairs," said Clair. "Should I tell them to wait?"

"What time is it?"

"Five to twelve."

"No! I'm on my way." Kate turned to the roomful of people. "Everybody, stay here and finish up, please—use my office—but I have to run." She grabbed her bag and was out the door before anyone realized that it was the first time they had ever known Kate to abdicate a decision on anything.

Kate got to the Waldorf before Matt. She'd asked the driver to wait. *Childstyle* had a car with a driver on staff and she had access to it, but somehow it didn't feel right to use a company car for the purpose of sex—even if it was procreational sex.

For five minutes, Kate sat in the huge rococo lobby, looking at her watch, ticking off the precious minutes. They couldn't afford to waste time, but traffic was snarled, and she knew that at any rate Matt would never walk out on a patient, even if he was running late. She had to admit, that was one of the things she loved about him. Unlike Kate, who always gave the impression of being in a rush, with somewhere more important to go than wherever she was at the moment, Matt always gave the sense that every encounter, every conversation, was the most important of his life. Where Kate would rush in, coatless, a limousine idling at the curb, poised to sweep her off to her next tactical strike, Matt would dismiss the car and driver and walk—stroll—ambling in with the air of a man on a perpetual vacation, even if he was running two hours late.

Kate supposed she should go to the desk and check in, so they could go right up to the room when Matt arrived. She flipped her platinum card onto the counter.

"I'm Kate Harrison-Weil. You should have my reservation."

"Oh yes," said the clerk, consulting the computer without looking up. "Here it is. Do you have any bags we can help you with?"

"No. No bags."

"And how long will you be staying with us, Ms. Weil?"

"Oh. Um. One hour."

The clerk's eyebrows shot up to his hairline.

"I'm afraid we don't have an hourly rate, madam." He emphasized the word *madam*.

God! Kate realized. *He thinks I'm a hooker renting a hotsheet hotel room!*

"I mean, we'll only be in the room about one hour. We'll take the room for the day, of course." She found herself babbling.

The clerk eyed her suspiciously. She supposed he was wondering if hookers had platinum cards. There was a sudden silence, as if he were contemplating calling a supervisor.

Kate started to sweat. "May I have my receipt?" she asked through gritted teeth. "And the key? Please."

Grabbing the key, she spun away from the desk, imagining that all eyes in the lobby were on her. And someone's eyes *were;* across the room, a man was waving energetically. In the intensity of her aggravation, she almost didn't recognize Jerome Kravis, the publisher of *Manhattanite* magazine, rushing across the lobby with his raincoat slung over his arm.

"Kate! Kate! Hold up! Are you going to the magazine association luncheon here in the ballroom? So am I! Wait, I'll join you." He waved a *Manhattanite* folder at her, hustled up, and grabbed Kate's arm.

"Jerry, hello."

Kravis twisted and motioned to three other men to join them. "Did you folks buy a table?" he asked Kate. "Bill! Ted! Look who's here!"

"Uh, sorry, Jerry. I'm not going to the luncheon."

He frowned, confused, still holding her arm as the other men approached. "But—well, what're you doing here, Kate? Just

22

passing through?" He looked down and noticed the key in her hand. "Are you—checking in? Don't you and Matt live just up Fifth?" Everyone in New York knew about Kate and Matt's new penthouse, although only a few people from the business had actually seen it. They had purchased it for a record four million dollars from the widow of a deposed dictator, and it had gotten a lot of press. There was very little excuse for Kate to be renting a hotel room. Kravis looked confused, paused, then dropped Kate's arm, a purplish flush creeping up his neck.

"Yes, gentlemen, I am checking in," Kate announced to the group of men, raising her voice over the din in the lobby. "I am meeting a man for a mad, passionate affair. Now, if you'll excuse me." She walked away as they stared, slack-jawed, after her. *I think I know what his table is going to be discussing at lunch,* she thought with a smirk as she got onto the elevator. Matt would get a kick out of this.

In the room, she took off her jacket and shoes, sat on the bed, and wondered if she should order anything. Hot tea? Wine? Champagne? They probably wouldn't have time to drink it. The desk clock said twelve-thirty. She just hoped they'd have time to *do* it. Kate took off her blouse and skirt and hung them in the closet. She flicked on the television to a soap opera. It might as well have been a message from aliens; Kate had absolutely no idea what she was watching. She couldn't remember the last time she'd watched daytime television. She was certainly never home during the day. About once a year, she came down with a cold or flu, but it never put her out of commission. She just went to work with a fever. *So this is what women who don't work watch,* she thought. Dostoyevski, it wasn't. She turned off the set.

Where was Matt? Kate knew she couldn't be late getting back to the office. It was going to be close, especially with the routine the doctor had recommended: lying motionless on her back with a pillow under her hips for fifteen minutes after they made love to ensure the most aerodynamically favorable angle for the sperm. Suddenly she wished she had skipped the whole thing and had lunch at her desk. But then the phone rang. She grabbed it on the first ring.

"Hello?"

"Kate. Sorry, darling. The traffic was horrible. I'm downstairs."

"I'm waiting."

Kate hung up. She pulled off her slip, which was one of those Maggie-the-cat, satin, lavender, and lace delectables. Kate believed in *lingerie,* as opposed to underwear, and she collected it like other women collected purses or shoes: underwire push-up bras embroidered with silk rosettes and transparently sheer soufflés of lace bikini panties; garter belts frothed with Point d'Esprit, silk stockings from Fogal. Her lingerie was expensive French, Swiss, or Italian, fragrant with the scents of her sachets and Fracas perfume. Even if no one knew what she had on under her business clothes, Kate knew. And Matt knew. In the satinwood armoire in Kate's dressing room at home, each piece of lingerie was wrapped carefully in fragranced white tissue by Helen, the laundress, then placed in the white-piqué-lined Lucite drawers. It was Kate's favorite indulgence.

But today, no lingerie. There would be no time for Matt's ritual unhooking of her bra and garters, no time for the civilities of a slow, sensuous strip. She pulled off her stockings and dropped them on the bedside table. Her panties went onto the chair, on top of her purse. Naked, Kate dragged back the heavy quilted bedspread, then yanked off the sheet, which she wrapped around herself like a trailing white gown.

She felt a little like a bride, dressed in strapless white, embarking on a new romantic adventure. Their wedding had been like that—Kate remembered putting on the Carolina Herrera white silk suit, holding gardenias, waiting to be married under swagged garlands of pale green and ivory ribbons on the deck of Stanton Welch's 60-foot teak sloop, anchored off of Sag Harbor. Kate had never wanted to wear a wedding gown with a train, or have one of those capital-W Weddings. By the time she reached her thirties, she'd come to envision her wedding as a no-nonsense coffee-break affair, getting married in a business suit, at lunchtime, at City Hall. But meeting Matt had changed all that. Matt was the one man who made Kate reprioritize her life. His evenness, gentleness, and incongruously childlike air both cushioned and jolted her, shaking her out of her self-involved cocoon. He had opened emotions she hadn't wished to acknowledge, and then had respected her vulnerability.

"Do you mind if I bring along another couple?" Matt had asked, the first time he had called Kate. And he had appeared at her door with eight-year-old Gregory and four-year-old Kim, who were adorable and charming the entire day at the Bronx Zoo. They had all stuffed themselves on cotton candy and popcorn and peanuts, and as Kate listened to the kids talk about school, she had felt, for the first time, what it might be like to be part of a real family, a family that could be hers. Matt had been so loving to the children—infinitely attentive and patient, following them with his eyes, laughing at their terrible knock-knock jokes. It was ironic, Kate had thought, to work every day with children's issues, children's clothes, and yet have no children of your own in your life. And while she didn't feel completely ready just yet for children, she knew from that first day that Matt was a different kind of person from the other men she knew, a man with the right priorities. Not his office—although he had an internationally acclaimed career. Not himself—although he was one of the nicest-looking, most intelligent men Kate had known; the kind of package that until now seemed to go hand in glove with egomania. Matt Weil's priority was clearly, happily, his family. In fact, once she got to know him, Kate was surprised that Matt ever went through with his divorce, in spite of the fact that his ex-wife, Elise, had virtually wrenched the children from him. Elise had, he said, left him in a flurry of accusations about his being overinvolved in his career, his books, his patients, his lectures and appearances. The marriage was over, but Matt never spoke disparagingly of Elise—only about himself. And the children were clearly his lifeline. That was the kind of priority that impressed Kate. And Matt was taken by the fact that she was *not* impressed, as other women were, by his money, his status, or the fact that he was Dr. Matthew Weil.

On their second date, Matt had arranged for them to go horse-back riding in Central Park. Kate was not quick to agree.

"I haven't done this since I was ten and there was a pony at the block party. I can't," she said.

25

"Yes, you can. I'll reserve old Caraway. He's barely mobile," Matt had replied.

And she did it, after all. On the ride, Matt stopped on the bridle path near the Plaza to buy from a park vendor a bouquet of roses, which he threaded haphazardly through the bridle of Kate's horse.

"There," he said. "The Queen of the May."

Riding with Matt, Kate wouldn't have minded falling off—she felt he'd be there to catch her. And for the past four years, he had been. A child now seemed to be a natural segue into the next phase of their lives.

When she heard a tapping on the door, she ran to it.

I hope this isn't the bellboy, she thought, as in one quick move she opened the door and dropped the sheet.

Kate lay across her husband, using his legs to pillow hers, watching the hotel's bedside digital clock flip its numbers until the prescribed fifteen minutes, the optimum time for conception-friendly immobility, was up. Luxuriating in the muskiness of the sheets was not on the agenda, tempting though it was. She dragged herself out of bed, as did Matt, dressing as he placed a call to his answering service.

Assuming again their professional clothes and selves, they paused at the door of the room.

"I forgot to ask," Matt said. "How was your flight?"

"Fine," said Kate.

"Here, I have a present for you." He handed her a paper bag. Inside was a box, which she opened. It was a world-time-zone aviator's watch.

"Perfect," she said, strapping it on.

"There's only one time that's not on here," he said.

"What's that?"

"Our time."

"Yes it is. It's here." She pointed to a minute wedge on the face of the watch. "Right between Eastern Standard, Pacific, and Paris time."

Kate kissed his cheek briskly. "See you Thursday," she said.

San Francisco was already on her mind.

Three

By eight A.M., the sonogram waiting room was packed. Kate could barely find a seat among the rows of women, all of whom chugged white cups of water from a large cooler in the corner. Kate had brought her own liter bottle of Evian.

"So," a frizzy-haired, bleached-blond woman named Angela turned to Kate and asked, "what's your cycle?" Angela, Kate quickly learned, was a veteran of four in vitro fertilizations. Eggs and tubes, hormone counts and sperm counts. It was all they talked about, *they* being the thirty-five-plus women who were down to the wire on getting pregnant. They recognized each other with the sure instinct of a flock of homing pigeons, at cocktail parties, in gynecologists' waiting rooms, at business lunches. In the more advanced stages, they spoke the high-tech language of reproduction, their sentences crammed with buzz-words like *GIFT, ZIFT,* and *TET,* encyclopedic in their know-how of laboratory miracle techniques.

"Well," Angela said authoritatively, tapping off the options on French-manicured nails, "there's in vitro, but it's a real long shot. Eight percent. Then there's GIFT—they harvest your eggs, mix them with the sperm *outside,* then they surgically return them to your tubes right away, so it's more natural. You've got a better chance there—thirteen percent. Of course, all this costs five thousand a shot. You'd better be sure you really have the problem

27

down. It turned out Stan had a low sperm count. What's your husband's sperm count?"

Kate almost dropped the bottle of Evian. Was it possible to discuss your husband's sperm count in public, with strangers, as casually as you would mention the chance of rain for the weekend? She couldn't imagine it, but in a strange way she was fascinated. Kate was standing on the threshold of an alien planet, and it actually felt good to have someone to discuss the situation with, someone who had been through it herself.

"How long have you been—at this?" Kate asked Angela.

"Four years, total," Angela said. "The first three were the worst, because we were on our own. We didn't know anything about anything. We were stupid enough to think that all you had to do was do it, and you got pregnant." She laughed, a short, tense laugh. "Yeah, just do it. Right. That's a fairy tale around this place." She flicked her hazel eyes across the waiting room, where ten women sat clutching their paper cups and bottles of water.

"I'm beginning to realize," Kate said. And she was.

Angela touched Kate's arm. "Don't get discouraged. It's attitude as much as anything. You have to think, *This could be it, this could be the month*. That's what keeps you going. Otherwise, you'll go crazy. Believe me."

"Oh no," said Kate. "I'm totally optimistic. After all, we just started trying, really. This is just a preliminary test, to be sure I'm ovulating. It's just, I never thought it was something you had to *work* at."

Angela laughed. "Welcome to the Baby Game. Behind door number one we have tubal surgery. Door number two—artificial insemination. Door number three—in vitro. Take your pick, and take your chances, ladies."

They laughed then, and exchanged business cards. Angela worked at the Pink Scissors, a beauty salon, as a cosmetologist. *That's how she can devote her life to her ovaries*, Kate thought. *She has a low-pressure job. But what about me?* The nine-to-five was the least of it, she knew. For Kate, there was travel, late nights, advertiser breakfasts, publishing lunches and dinners. There were weeks when she fell into bed, too tired to dream, much less make love. Last year, she'd broken so many dental appointments she'd been fired by her dentist. How could she even think she could keep pace with these fertility pros? Because, Kate decided, that's what they were, these women who read every article, asked every question, knew every statistic. Maybe *they* could afford to devote their lives to getting pregnant, but Kate wasn't sure where she would have to draw the line.

That night, she told Matt about Angela. "All she does is go from doctor to doctor, test to test," she said incredulously, picking the pea pods out of the order-out Chinese. Kate and Matt had a brand-new, custom-designed, state-of-the-art kitchen with restaurant equipment, but they rarely so much as made instant coffee. Entertaining consisted of a fleet of caterers swooping down upon the apartment. "The woman is compulsive. It's amazing. And she's not the only one. It's an entire subculture."

Matt was nonplussed. "I can see how it becomes an obsession. I mean, look at us, when we did the remodeling; it was all we could talk about for months."

"Gaskets and bathtubs."

"Kohler and Sherle Wagner."

"Steam versus sauna."

"God, how could anyone stand us?"

"Because the world is dying to know what is really, truly, the ultimate faucet. I believe that."

Matt smiled and stirred his coffee. "Honey, we aren't going to be boring about this. We can't; it's too personal. For all anyone knows, we're trying *not* to have a baby. After all, we have Kim and Gregory."

"*We* don't have Kim and Gregory! *You* have Kim and Gregory. I love them, Matt, but they're your children. This baby will be *ours*. There's a difference. To me. To Kim and Gregory. And, believe me, to your former wife, there is a *very* big difference." Kate choked out the words so fiercely she bit the inside of her lip. It always infuriated her when Matt did this—implied that because he had Kim and Gregory, her own child, *their* child, was less necessary; a luxury item, as it were. Matt was so intelligent in every other way, this attitude was even more exasperating. "Tell me right now, Matt," she said, the belligerent thrust of her chin doing a poor job of hiding her anxiety. "Tell me if you don't want this baby, because it's not going to be a cakewalk. It might be hard, real hard, and I'm going to need you one hundred percent there for me. For us."

He caught her hand. "Sweetheart, calm down. I love you, and of course I want this child. I was just saying that we already have everything; this will be icing. Relax." He stroked her wrist with his thumb.

"A baby," he whispered, and suddenly he pulled her across the couch and held her, stroking her hair, pulling off first her head-band, and then her blouse, until she sat half-naked next to him.

He took her face in his hands and said, "Kate, we will have our baby. We will," he said, with a seriousness of purpose that made Kate certain that this time, making love on the couch in front of a "Honeymooners" rerun, would be *the* time. This time, when he put his softly moving lips between her breasts, he was coaxing the beginning of a new life within her. When he whispered a hot breath on her throat, he was calling her the mother of his child. This time, when he traced the damp creases at the tops of her thighs and the soft folds between them with his fingertips, he was sealing their baby inside her.

Afterward, they both had a feeling of connection, an intuitive and primitive sureness that, yes, this was the time their lovemaking would create a new human being, a soft little soul Kate felt she already knew, as if he or she were hovering unseen above the bed, awaiting entry. There was a nearly magical quality to her skin, Kate thought later that night; an opalescence that seemed to light a path for the soul she hoped would shortly make its presence known by settling in her womb. It seemed inevitable that a baby was being made, that this particular unison of their bodies was purposeful and predetermined in a way that had never been before, a way that could only mean one thing.

Kate believed this with all her heart. However, her body did not believe it; she started her period that weekend, bitter blood that stained her white-embroidered voile underwear. It was as if her body was saying, *You cannot control me;* flaunting its refusal to cooperate yet again.

* * *

30

The metal slab of a table, pressing against Kate's spine, was cold. Her fingers felt as if tourniquets had been applied at the wrists. Her feet, their peach-lacquered toenails incongruously cheerful in the stirrups, were chilled to the bone. Still, Kate was determined to distract herself by thinking about something pleasant. She tried to concentrate, but the first thing that came into her mind was her temperature chart. That was what happened when you immersed yourself in your problem, she thought—there was no way to detox. It took over your subconscious, like the time she'd dreamed about ectopic pregnancies three days in a row. It was sick. There must be something more pleasant to think about, like—her mind thrashed desperately—*potpourri*. That was pleasant. Dried flowers, fragrant scents. Kate tried to focus on rose petals, lemon peel, and cinnamon sticks.

"You may feel some discomfort." The technician's voice broke in. Kate's eyes flew open, and suddenly she was staring at the pockmarked ceiling tiles again. She tensed, knowing that the radiologist was about to insert a wicked-looking tube with a rubber gasket into her uterus. She tried to reconjure up the rose petals, but instead visualized her womb, a soft, pink living fruit, and the tube, a stake in its heart.

Why was it, she wondered as a metal speculum tugged between her legs, that the medical profession had a different scale of pain than the rest of humanity? The minor but undeniable sting of a shot was a "pinprick," excruciating pain was "discomfort"—euphemisms laid on you from childhood by men like your own father, who would earnestly promise that "this hurts me more than it hurts you" as he whacked you with a hair brush. It wasn't that she distrusted the medical profession, Kate thought—after all, Matt was an M.D.—it was just that all this doctor-speak and false hope made her suspicious. She used to trust doctors, back when doctors were Marcus Welby, Jonas Salk, Dr. Spock. Now they were Dr. Strangelove. Literally.

For the past eight months—ever since she and Matt had started trying to figure out why she hadn't conceived—doctors had controlled when and how they made love, what time Kate got up in the morning, whether she could or couldn't exercise, and when she could travel on business.

31

Now that the initial jolt was over, Kate noted that the test really didn't hurt, at least not much more than a moderate cramp. Still, she felt like a deer trapped in the headlights of an oncoming car, in spite of all her textbook knowledge of the procedure. Dr. Warneke had explained it in detail, diagramming her reproductive system from Fallopian tubes to cervix with a yellow chalk illustration on the blackboard in his office, demonstrating the finer points with a fist-sized model of the uterus, which, Kate had noticed, doubled as a desktop paperweight.

No; what Kate was feeling was an entirely unfamiliar sensation that had nothing to do with the fact that a syringe was now pumping blue dye into the microscopic regions of her reproductive system—she could see it happening on the television monitor above the table. Kate was feeling what she had never felt when she uprooted herself from the Midwest and moved to New York, what she had never felt when she put multimillions of Americana's money on the line to launch her new magazine. It was a novel sensation, this internal tightening and knotting that had nothing to do with the test—a feeling, a misfiring, that made her want to climb off the table and run.

It was *fear*.

Of the procedure itself, Kate had no fear. *Hysterosalpingogram*. The name sounded like a medieval torture, the kind you saw in sepia woodcuts, where patients with eyes rolling out of their heads were assaulted by giant pincers. But Kate wasn't afraid of the hysterosalpingogram, any more than she'd been afraid of D and C, the endometrial biopsy, or any of the battery of procedures she'd undergone since—after all the disappointing months when she'd been catapulted between hope and failure, when her period came and came and came like clockwork until she thought she'd scream from frustration—they'd finally decided to find out why.

Now she was afraid of the answer.

"What we're getting here," said the specialist, hidden behind Kate's left thigh, "is a picture of the uterus and tubes. If there's any obstruction there, any abnormality, we'll spot it."

Kate knew the statistics. She'd been thoroughly briefed by both Dr. Warneke and Matt. Fifteen percent of all couples experienced some degree of infertility. Fertility declined with age. In her twenties, a normal woman had only a twenty percent chance of conceiving in any one month. By her late thirties, the probability plunged to eight percent in one month. The average time for conception after age thirty-five was twelve months. But the averages couldn't be relevant to her, especially now; Kate had never considered herself "average."

Kate remembered hearing stories of fibroids as large as tennis balls, twisted tubes, ovarian cysts. That was the thing about the Baby Game. Once you joined the ranks, you heard all the war stories, the horror stories, the sob stories. There weren't too many happy endings, but those that existed, you heard about over and over: the cousin who had a baby after menopause; the sister-in-law's neighbor who got pregnant after she adopted; the woman in the sonogram waiting room who'd had her tubes tied, then reopened, and got pregnant. Those were the stories that kept you going, the ones you clung to, thought Kate. It was like watching the lottery winners on TV—somebody out there hit the jackpot; it could just as easily be you.

Kate was afraid the test would show she'd never be one of those lucky women, that her reproductive system had double-crossed her; maybe back in her thirties, maybe—she didn't want to think about this possibility—maybe after, or because of, the one thing Kate could not face: the abortion four years ago, when she and Matt had first started seeing each other. The abortion she had never told him about. The abortion she had convinced herself was right, then tried to forget, had forgotten, or had filed away under Things It Is Best Not To Remember.

That was the hell of it, Kate thought. If something was really wrong, whatever it was, it would probably be her fault. Matt had fathered two perfect children. True, their values were distorted in a way that Kate was sure *her* and Matt's children's would never be, but she had to admit they were smart, good-looking kids. He was above suspicion, if *suspicion* was even the right word when it came to making babies. But what other word was there? She *suspected* she couldn't get pregnant anymore. She thought of the abortion, all the years she'd been on the pill, all the years she'd worked sixty-hour weeks as her estrogen slowly seeped out of her. All the time she'd wasted, not taking care of herself, postponing, believing you could turn on a pregnancy like a light switch, living on false assumptions. She conjured up a crazy image—the blue dye as a runaway shopping cart, racing down the supermarket aisles and crashing head-on into a dead end at the produce section, artichokes, eggplants, cucumbers, lettuce, and peas tumbling in slow motion to the floor.

Suddenly the test was over. Getting up off the table, Kate felt dizzy.

"Are you all right, Mrs. Weil?" asked a young nurse, grabbing her arm. She quickly unwrapped a hard peppermint candy. "For your blood sugar," she said. "If you feel faint."

"No, thank you. I'll be fine." Kate wondered why she'd said that. She didn't feel fine at all. But a peppermint candy wasn't going to change things, and she couldn't afford to not feel fine. She had completely missed a meeting with Accounting and was backed up for another one with Legal. As she shrugged off the crinkly blue paper robe, Kate wondered if they would be sympathetic if they knew why she'd pushed back the time for the meeting with Legal. Probably not. The bottom line—that's what counted. That was life and death in the publishing industry these days. *Real* life and death—that was something to be downplayed, if it came up at all.

The truth was, Kate was finding it increasingly harder to walk into meetings, on time or not. There was something pathetically demoralizing about trying desperately to have a baby, having sex the night before practically standing on your head, with five pillows under your hips so the sperm would hit at precisely the right angle, lying in the dark hoping against hope—and then, eight hours later, being surrounded by pictures of literally hundreds of peach-cheeked, angelic infants. Just last week, Kate had stopped in on a cover shoot, where she'd been enveloped by forty infants, all crawling, cooing, smiling, crying, grinning two-toothed smiles, and she had been paralyzed by their fragrant baby powder scent.

She hadn't planned on this.

Kate buttoned her silk blouse as fast as she could, but not without noticing that her fingernails were a mess. She used to

34

have a manicure every week, but lately, she barely had time to brush her teeth. Her hairdresser, her masseuse, her weight-trainer, her leg-waxer—all were figments of an increasingly dim past. She couldn't even recall the last time she'd had breakfast with Matt, or even an extended conversation with him about anything but Getting Pregnant. It seemed like all her spare time, and an increasingly large chunk of her working hours, was spent in doctors' offices: three blood and urine tests last week, and, later this week, the consultation about the results. Just thinking about it exhausted her. Kate put on her tweed jacket, plucked her black crocodile shoulder bag off the hook, straightened her skirt, and dashed out.

It only took ten minutes to get to the Americana offices, but when Kate walked in, the meeting was already in progress. The lawyer's blank stare in Kate's direction was enough to let her know they were angry. And what was she going to say? "Sorry I'm late. I was having a hysterosalpingogram, and now I can't get pregnant?"

So Kate said nothing as she slid into the last open chair in the executive conference room.

"Kate, we have a small problem here." Arthur Kent, the head of the legal department, was the master of cool understatement. Kate could read his face: they had a *major major problem*. The mere fact that Kent was sitting in on this meeting indicated the priority level involved. Kate still recalled—actually, she would never forget—the first time she'd been in a meeting with Arthur. As she was discussing legal liabilities for unauthorized photos, an editorial assistant sitting next to Arthur had been rustling through some papers. Arthur had taken one sideways glance out of the corner of his eye, as if the distraction were a fly buzzing the table. Then, almost imperceptibly, he'd picked up a pushpin from the table and with a sudden *thwack!* flipped his arm in an arc and nailed the papers to the table. All conversation had stopped abruptly. "Someone was speaking," Arthur said, straightening his French cuffs to underscore his point. That was Arthur.

Richard Zane, a Harvard MBA handpicked by Kate for her sales marketing team, held up the new *Childstyle* bus poster and pointed to the picture of the mother and smiling baby. The fluorescent overhead lights flickered across his wire-rimmed glasses, hiding his eyes. "It's the mother. We have a potential problem on our hands."

Kate knew that if Richard, who had viewed Chernobyl as a marketing opportunity, was calling this a "potential problem," the situation must be approaching a nuclear meltdown. The ad agency's creative director, who had chosen the model from a head sheet, studied the weave of the carpet.

"Celebrity Search has revealed that she is not as white bread as she appears." Richard handed a bound report to Kate.

"Let's not mince words, she's a porn queen, for God's sake," said Margo, her short black hair moussed into a wave in front, offset by huge silver Paloma Picasso earrings. "Triple-A porn."

"What?" Kate couldn't believe it. The clear-skinned woman looked like a cross between a milkmaid and the picture of all-American motherhood. Kate glanced at Richard. This was unusual. The ad agency routinely did a thorough check for what they called "C's and P's"—cocaine and penitentiary.

"*Condominiums of Babylon*. That's the name of her film. She made it under another name. A photo spread is coming out in *Playboy*. Good God, and she's going to be on buses all across America representing *Childstyle*. . . ." Margo rubbed her eyes, smudging her mascara.

"This could be an image problem," the creative director admitted.

Arthur nodded. "Well, we've seen worse. I'm sure we can handle this."

"Kill the mother," Kate said, meaning, of course, drop her contract.

"What? And lose all that money?" Margo stared at Kate.

"We pull the posters and donate the money we save to homeless families, then publicize that," Kate said. "Do it before any word gets out on the model. Everyone will be so busy with the press on the homeless, they'll overlook the model. We'll get more publicity than any ad campaign could generate."

Arthur nodded. "That's it—capitalize on a potential problem. Good thinking, Kate."

"We can even make a media event out of it," she added.

"Make it a yearly thing. Plus, it's a tax writeoff. We'd have to ditch this campaign, anyhow."

"What's that?" said Arthur Kent.

"What?"

"That sound."

"What sound?" Kate asked.

"Tapping. Quiet, everybody."

There was a persistent tap on the parquet under the conference table. Suddenly Kate realized it was her right foot.

"There. It stopped."

"Now," said Arthur. "Let's analyze the repercussions of all this."

Kate found her pen drifting. It was writing names on the corner of her pad as if it had a life of its own. Emily. Audrey. Charlotte. James. Jason. Thomas. Emily was a great name. Solid, yet feminine. Emily Weil. For boys ... *God!* What was she doing, mooning about baby names for a non-baby. Still, Dr. Warneke had assured her that everything seemed to be in order. The test today was just a double check. Wasn't it? Kate dug the pencil into the pad, snapping the lead point. What if the test found something? A tumor. A blocked tube. What if she were infertile? It couldn't happen, and yet ...

"Kate?"

She snapped back to the meeting.

"Yes!"

Margo was looking at her. The room was quiet. She hadn't even noticed that the meeting was over.

"Anything else on the agenda? Arthur is leaving town for a few days."

"No. We're finished. Have a good trip, Arthur."

He nodded slowly. No one had ever seen Kate's attention wander.

"Thank you, everyone." Kate rose from her chair, and the meeting was officially over. *I wonder when the doctor will have the results,* she thought, and went to her office to phone him.

"Hold my calls," she told Clair.

The doctor was busy. Kate told his secretary she'd wait, held on for fifteen minutes, then called back twice more. Finally she left her name, then told Clair specifically that if the doctor called, she was to pull her out of any meeting. This was top priority. By four-thirty, she was nervous. Had they found a problem? God, what if she had a tumor? Or worse. Kate couldn't imagine what was worse, but she feared she had it. At five-fifteen, she called again and this time she got through.

"Kate," said Dr. Warneke. "How can I help you? Are you feeling all right, after this morning?"

"Yes, fine. But—I don't suppose you have any results yet?"

"As a matter of fact, I stopped by the lab myself, after rounds at the hospital. Didn't Matt tell you?"

"Matt?"

"I ran into him and gave him the full report."

"Oh, I see. Well, I've been busy. We haven't touched base today."

"Well, in layman's terms, Kate, you need a minor plumbing repair."

"What?"

"Now, nothing major. We'll clear it up with a laparoscopy."

"What is a laparoscopy?"

"An endoscopic test. We'll use a belly-button incision and go in for a look-around. You'll only have to stay in the hospital overnight, and the incision can be covered by a Band-Aid. It's nothing. Matt can reassure you."

"If it's nothing, why do I have to have it?"

"Well, if there's any endometriosis, it will show up, as will adhesions or closure of the fimbriated ends of the tubes."

"One night in the hospital." Kate was wondering how she'd fit this in. She hadn't planned on any hospital stays.

"Yes, and of course, if possible, one or two days of rest at home before returning to your normal activities."

A bad idea. A very bad idea. One or two days at home! She might as well take a cruise on the *QE II*! Kate glanced down at her calendar. Every square, every hour, was filled with minute writing. She flipped three pages: same.

"When can we schedule you, Kate?"

Of course there was no good time. Kate quickly calculated rearranging her schedule, but it was impossible. It was like dominoes; one change collapsed everything around it. She picked up a red marker and drew an X through three arbitrary days.

"Next week." Why not? Any week was equally bad. She might as well get it over with as soon as possible.

The minute she hung up, Kate called Matt.

"I'm with a patient," he said.

"Then just listen, don't talk," she stormed. "Dr. Warneke tells me he told you the test results before he talked to me, and I think that is totally unprofessional."

"Really, Kate. He was trying to be helpful."

"What about doctor-patient confidentiality? Don't I have any rights? What am I—just a walking womb? You're the brains and I'm the uterus, is that it?"

"Kate, you're overreacting."

"You didn't even call me. I sweated it out here . . ."

"Kate, there is no problem. Except the one you are creating. Will you please relax?" His voice was even, as if he were lecturing a child, which infuriated her.

"I'm not some patient with a pimple, I'm your wife, who is trying to get pregnant and is very, very concerned."

"So am I. But now I can't discuss it."

"Oh, you could discuss it with Dr. Warneke, but not with me?"

"We'll talk about it later."

Kate sighed. It was pointless. "Forget it," she said. "Just give me at least the same courtesy you give your patients. I want to be informed. And not last."

"Fair enough. Talk to you later."

She hung up. Why did she get the feeling that Matt thought he was doing her some kind of favor? Wasn't it her body, her right to know first?

That was the thing, Kate thought. She felt like her body wasn't hers anymore. It was a rented room, where people threw parties, didn't invite her, and then left her with the bill.

Kate could always spot her mother in any crowd: she was the one wearing the hat. Like a member of the British royal family, Janet Harrison seemed to wear a hat in lieu of a crown. Her bearing was regal, her posture impeccable. Kate had never seen her mother's spine touch the back of a chair. She frequently wore Jackie Kennedy gloves—one-button length—even in warm weather, and she was always immaculately dressed in simple, tailored styles.

As a teenager, Kate had taken to calling her mother by her first name, Janet. It seemed to be the most appropriate label for a woman who bristled at any suggestion of matronliness. "I want us to be best friends," she frequently told Kate, although, of course, that could never happen. So Janet Harrison abdicated both positions—that of friend, and that of mother.

Instead, Kate had taken her mother under her wing. Her father's death when she was in ninth grade had left them well enough off financially, but her mother, who had never even made a plane reservation, was at a loss. It was Kate who showed Janet how to refinance the house, how to pay the bills and plan a budget. It seemed to Kate that her father's death had abruptly terminated her childhood, and marked the beginning of a search for security that had evolved into her intense ambition. Janet had never understood this, and Kate wondered if she would now understand her fierce desire to have a child. Somehow, it seemed important that Janet, her only link with her own childhood, be part of this magical loop. And so, on one of her two days off following the laparoscopy, she had scheduled the rare luxury of a lunch with Janet. She had invited her mother to Arcadia, where the paneling and anemones seemed appropriate to the restful pace of the day. Only in her life, Kate thought, would surgery seem like a vacation.

"What do you think, Kate?" asked her mother, delicately fishing a color chip book out of her crocodile Kelly bag. "Willow blue or cerulean blue for the ceilings? In this light, it's hard to tell." Janet Harrison was the kind of woman who carried her life in her purse. If you had a question, she could be counted on to materialize an encyclopedic batch of neatly trimmed magazine clippings; if you had a paper cut, she had every size and shape of Band-Aid; if you needed dental floss, you had your choice of waxed or unwaxed. But there the efficiencies stopped. Her own opinions, unlike Kate's, seemed stunted by uncertainty; revealing that her confidence was merely a veneer of proper etiquette and decorating ideas, a holdover from a world where spotless white gloves got you where you wanted to go.

"Really, don't ask me to pick a color," said Kate. "I can't process one more piece of information right now."

Janet laughed, sipping her tea. Kate wondered how she could wear so much lipstick and not leave an imprint on the cup. "What's this great news, darling? Let me guess. You're pregnant!"

"No. Not exactly. Not yet. But—we're trying." It felt good to get that out, to share the decision.

"Trying?"

Kate wondered how she would explain the state of Trying. Trying was neither pregnant nor not. It was the hazy midpoint, after the decision had been made but before results had been achieved. Trying was a psychological state with rules and laws and its own set of truths and commandments. In the world of the Trying, you had tests, you had surgery, and you had hope, and that, for now, was enough. "Yes," she said. "We're trying."

"Well, I think that's wonderful."

There was an awkward silence, and Kate resolved never again to discuss her reproductive status with her mother.

"You know," said Janet, "I think it's a good thing. Your career is wonderful, darling, and you're so talented, but all that stress isn't good for your skin, and the skin is a window to your health, you know. I was talking to my friend Jessie—you remember Jessie, fabulous red hair, so-so tennis—well, Jessie looked positively *gray,* and wouldn't you know, she had a circulatory problem. Waiter, I'll have the lobster club sandwich."

"Well," said Kate. "We'll let you know how it's going."

"Oh my God," said Janet, waving her hands. "Please don't, darling. When you were born, I said to the doctors, 'Spare me the details. Knock me out and wake me when it's over.' And they did."

Kate twisted the inside of her roll into little pills. She'd had a dream of how Janet would respond, and this wasn't it. Actually, she'd expected too much; she'd expected the baby-to-be to close the family loop that had been broken by her father's death. She should have known better; had she thought Janet would leap up and run out and buy a complete layette at the Wicker Garden?

"You know, speaking of such things, Marian Dreshler's daughter had twins last month," Janet said, adjusting her napkin. "Imagine that."

"So how's your belly button?"

"Ouch, CeCe. You have a real way with words."

CeCe MacGraw frowned over the spatterware bowl in which she was mixing buttermilk-pecan pancake batter. "Well, I'm not trying to rub it in—for God's sake, you're spending the weekend here to recover." Ever since CeCe had quit her job as an editor at *Glamour* and moved upstate to Bedford, after her first child was born, Kate had periodically managed to drive up for weekends. It was not so much to retreat to the white-porched clapboard Victorian house, which, with three kids, two dogs, and CeCe's husband Steve, was never peaceful; but because CeCe was someone Kate could talk to. She had seen the publishing business, marriage, and motherhood, and she was objective, if not brutally frank, about them all.

"I didn't really need much recovery," Kate said. "But they were right, I was too sore to go to work. Three days, wasted."

"I wouldn't say wasted, all things considered." CeCe ruffed her short, spiky auburn hair.

"You and Matt went through this together. At least sometimes people get closer when they face things together."

Kate's laugh was brittle. "Right. We faced it together for a whole two hours. Then he had to leave for Geneva to deliver a paper."

"Two hours, huh?" CeCe frowned. "Well, it was probably quality time."

"The thing is, I asked him not to go. You know, I've never asked him not to do anything since we've met, but this time I was just feeling . . . I don't know, I guess I had visions of Matt bringing me breakfast in bed or something, some acknowledgment that I'd had surgery, that this was not fun."

CeCe handed Kate a plate of pancakes. "But you're one step closer to being a mom. Isn't that your priority?"

Kate poked at a pecan. "Yes, it is. It's just taking so long. It's so discouraging."

"Why? You've been trying less than a year."

"I only *have* two or three. Maybe more, but one year, one *month,* is a big percentage."

"Tick, tick."

"And things are absolutely falling apart at the office. I missed the budget meeting. Arthur was there, asking where I was. God."

"Well, we all know you can be everywhere," CeCe jibed, cocking her head. "Cindy! What's going on down there!" she shrieked. Then her voice returned to normal. "It takes one to know one."

"You're the maternal type. You can handle it."

"Maternal!"

"Well, three kids and a station wagon is maternal to me."

"It's not a station wagon. It's a Range Rover."

"So what. It has two dogs and a car pool in it."

"What's maternal, anyhow? It's a matter of semantics."

"Let's see; what's maternal? Hmmm. The Madonna for one. And that dress you're wearing."

"Hey, lay off! It's a maternity dress. I just can't get back into my size eights yet."

A yellow Labrador lumbered up and made a lunge at the pancake batter.

"Down!" CeCe waved him off with her spoon, fanning the air with batter.

"Point taken. But CeCe, you know, I think this whole motherhood thing can be organized from day one."

"*Organized?* Like a closet? And before you jump all over me, let me remind you that I have *seen* your closets. An art museum would not do them justice."

Kate always had to hold herself in check at this point when she got into discussions with full-time mothers, even CeCe. She didn't want to seem so unsympathetic to their choices. But in reality, she and CeCe were opposites. That was, she supposed, why they got along so well—they were opposite in similar ways.

"I'm not competitive," CeCe would shrug, meanwhile using tweezers to construct a scale model of Westminster Abbey in toothpicks for a fourth-grade geography project.

"No," Kate would say, as she sat across the kitchen table, editing a pile of papers from the briefcase that seemed handcuffed to her wrist, even on weekends. "No. Clearly not. You spent the last week shaking the leaves off deciduous trees for Cindy's science scrapbook because you're a nature lover."

"That's not competitive for me, it's competitive for *her*. There's a difference."

"Let's not split hairs. We're both nuts. I just get paid for it."

CeCe's husband, Steve, walked by, carrying four-year-old Kevin under an arm.

"Come here, Kevvie. Come to Aunt Kate." Kevin airplaned for a landing on Kate's lap, dropping a lollipop out of his mouth onto the floor, where it was quickly retrieved by the dog.

"Garden, Mom," called out Steve. "See you."

" 'Bye, Dad," CeCe said.

"Mom? Dad?" Kate hated this idea.

CeCe shrugged. "Habit. Now. What did that doctor say?"

"Slight scarring in one tube. No problem. It's nothing a little microsurgery can't clear up."

"Microsurgery? When?"

"Ten days. I just want to get it over with." Kate sagged. Her whole body felt as if the bones had been removed. "You know, I never thought it would be like this. It's such a drag. The calendar, the thermometer, the doctor, the surgery. There is no part of me, no matter how deep inside, that has been left unprobed. Sex used to be beautiful and private and romantic, and now it's public domain. You get up there and spread your legs and the world looks in with a microscope. I could deal with it if I could do more about it. I have never not been able to handle a problem." Kate picked angrily at her cuticles. "Work harder—okay! Work longer—fine! Be smarter—I will! But this—fertility never-never land! Nothing I do makes a difference. I'm trying, I really am, but I feel so . . . helpless." Kate's eyes blurred in tears. The stress was getting to her.

CeCe shook her head. "Honey, *relax*. That's what it takes. The first time I got pregnant, I was so relaxed I was unconscious. You and Matt should take a trip, get away."

"When? Before or after the microsurgery, or between the hysterosalpingogram and the laparoscopy, or before the microsurgery and after the laparoscopy?"

"Matt's a doctor. He'll think of something. Don't let it get to you."

"Oh, it may kill me. But it won't get to me."

"Good. Now in the meantime, maybe you'd like to take one of my kids. If the price is right."

Kate knew CeCe was joking, but she didn't see any humor in that remark. She knew CeCe loved her children. Why did otherwise sensitive people make comments like "You want kids? Take mine" or "Relax, it'll happen"? Oh well. Kate supposed you only could understand something like this if it happened to you. Even Matt didn't really understand it.

She felt her connection with Matt was drifting, like they were reaching out, straining for each other, but their fingers couldn't quite connect. Right now, when Kate most needed him to empathize with her, Matt was withdrawing. Maybe it was just a coincidence, but he seemed to be spending an inordinate amount of late nights in the library, working at his desk on his next book. Of course, his career was important, but wasn't having a child important, too?

She couldn't wait to be pregnant—at least *that* was a state people understood. She wanted to be huge and swollen, to complain about her weight, to get stretch marks, even varicose veins. She wanted to eat right. Take vitamins. Drink milk. She'd already called Families Together to get their prenatal exercise class schedule; she could go Thursdays at seven A.M. She was looking forward to rubbing vitamin E cream on her swollen watermelon-belly. She wanted to experience morning sickness, maternity dresses, to eat breakfast off her belly in bed, and watch the baby kick off the plate. She had been trying for over a year now; she wanted to be *pregnant*. There was no name at all for what she was now, Kate thought. Well, there was one, but she hated it: *infertile*. *Infertile* was a term that applied to the Nile Delta in a drought, not to a woman in her thirties who could do two hours of aerobics and beat men at squash.

She *hated* it. Just hated it.

Four

Kate pushed her way through the aisles of the second floor of
F.A.O. Schwarz, using two huge red-and-white gift-wrapped
boxes as battering rams to get through the crowd. No matter
when you went to Schwarz's, it was a mob scene. She had hoped
to run in, pick up two toys, and run out, but somehow she'd
spent an hour in the store. It was her thirty-ninth birthday, and
she was anxious to get home, but she didn't want to be the only
one receiving presents tonight. She'd found a doll with waist-
length hair and a rock-polishing kit fit for a professional geolo-
gist. She thought the gifts would help with Gregory and Kim,
who never seemed too thrilled with anything connected with
Kate anymore. While Kate and Matt were dating, the children
had seemed wildly enthusiastic about their relationship. Kim,
especially, had been caught up in the romance of it all, chattering
on and on about brides and Princess Diana's wedding, which she
had on videocassette. At the ceremony, no one had been more
angelic than the Weil children, Kim in her flower girl organdie,
Gregory in his little white suit. But once the reality of the marriage had sunk in, things had changed. Kate was not Princess
Diana. She was Kate, their stepmother. She was married to their
father. She lived with him; they did not. Kate was now an interloper, a fifth wheel.

Kim in particular had not adjusted well to the divorce, that much was clear. She'd become sullen and waiflike, pulling on her hair in a wistful sort of way if Kate looked at her too long or too head-on. She was polite enough, but, if Kate took her hand, it went limp, as if touching her stepmother drained off her energy. Maybe this doll would spark something. Kate hoped so, but right now all she could focus on was the endless chorus of "It's a Small World" that chanted nonstop over the speakers.

Kate negotiated the escalator, peering over the top of the boxes to the lobby below, with its swirl of toys, window full of stuffed pandas, and giant toy piano keyboard. She wondered when, or if, Matt's children would ever totally accept her. She'd tried all the approaches: "I know I'm not your mother, but we can be such good friends" ("No, we can't," Gregory had retorted). "I'm new at this, and I need your help" (blank stares). "Will you play this game with me? I can't seem to figure it out" ("She's stupid," Kim had hissed). "Believe me, children, I'm not trying to take your father away" ("You already did," Gregory had said). Still, if Kate had not totally melted the children's defenses, at least there were no overt hostilities, if you overlooked the borderline case when Kim had "accidentally" magic-markered Kate's white suede jacket. It was the subtle things that bothered Kate the most. Simple things she couldn't even bring up, like going for a walk and having to walk alone behind the three of them as the children clung to Matt. Or finding herself excluded from conversations about people they had known before, as another family.

Unlike his sister, Gregory was not withdrawn, but he never said what he really thought. He had adopted a deceptive, miniature-adult persona. He was always smiling and full of flattery in a twisted sort of way ("That's a beautiful necklace, Kate. Who paid for it?"). If he was unhappy, he showed it by acting out destructively; he had to be rushed to the doctor when he swallowed an action figure "to see how it tasted." With a wit and sense of humor beyond his years, he reminded Kate of a stunted Woody Allen.

Matt had custody this weekend, and, if past scenarios were any indication, it would not be restful. Kim would be overexcited about Kate's birthday. Gregory would try to steal the scene. Kate was already gearing up to have a headache when she walked into the elevator that opened directly into their foyer.

She went into the entrance hall, with its arched, curved ceiling, sponged faux clouds dotting the ebony-blue rotunda and tiny lights forming the pattern of constellations that marked Kate and Matt's zodiac signs—a touch of Kate's whimsy. She and Matt never told anyone about this; and unless you knew, it looked like a random bunch of recessed tiny lights. Only Gregory had noticed immediately. "Sooo, what's this? Pisces and Leo. Uh-oh, astrological disaster." Leave it to Gregory.

Kate dropped the box from F.A.O. Schwarz on the inlaid marble-and-onyx floor and rushed into the living room, her heels echoing. Sometimes the vastness of the apartment made her feel like she was passing through a hotel lobby. Where was Matt? If they were going to make it to dinner, she had to hurry and change.

Kate wandered through the boiserie-paneled living room and into the raspberry-glazed library, where Matt stood silently, staring at the far wall, where a fifteen-foot-long fish tank was recessed. The tank was a living work of art, a miniature coral reef with jewellike live corals and tropical fish in gemstone colors. "Shh," he said. "They're courting."

"Who? Anybody I know?"

"The *Syngnathidae*. The sea horses. Finally. Look at them. See how they're floating side by side?"

Kate peered into the tank. Matt's coral reef, ostensibly bought and maintained for Gregory, since the boy was allergic to animal fur, had become his own pride and joy. A major concern when they moved into the apartment was ensuring that the pH and nitrogen balances of the tank remained intact. Matt had flown an aquarium scientist in from Holland, and for the past two years he had focused on restoring the corals. Kate had to admit the aquarium was beautiful. Graceful anemones and velvety leather corals, invertebrates and tropical fish, formed a jewellike seascape that bore no resemblance to a pet shop aquarium with the prerequisite plastic coral and goldfish. Each week Matt calculated the lighting, the nitrate content, and the pH balance of the water with the absorption of a child, determined to create his own undersea world.

As Kate backed away from the tank, a mini-school of damsel-fish scattered, led by a pair of white-collared clownfish.

"Gus was here," Matt said, touching her shoulder.

"Oh no! I completely forgot!" Kate had a standing Wednesday six P.M. appointment with her personal trainer. They worked on floor stretches and free weights in Kate's exercise/dressing room three times a week. On Mondays and Fridays, Gus came over at seven A.M., but lately Kate had been missing the Wednesday sessions, and this week she'd even canceled Monday. She felt terrible. It was rude to not show up or call, but she'd been so distracted with all the doctors' appointments, and then buying the gifts for the kids . . . She'd pay Gus regardless—he sent a monthly bill to the accountant's office—but her workouts were obviously slipping in priority. Well, so be it. She couldn't be two places at once.

"Well, it's not the end of the world. Hey, look at this," said Matt excitedly. "The anemone fish are spawning, too."

"How can you tell?" She couldn't even tell the males from the females.

Matt pointed to two opalescent orange fish. The pair were locking jaws, as if they were kissing. "This is what they do before they spawn."

Kate wasn't quite sure how she felt about fish spawning in her library, unless they were going to start growing their own caviar, but Matt's obvious enthrallment with the aquarium made her smile.

"Beautiful," he said quietly. He seemed mesmerized, the under-sea shimmer reflecting blue on his face like a neon moonglow. He was staring intently into the tank, a barely contained smile and curly dark hair giving him the look of a boy who was about to be bad. His hand stretched toward Kate, and she took it. For a moment, the two of them stood silent, watching the dynamics of the marine population.

Kate stroked Matt's wrist, underneath the cuff of his shirt. "Look," he said, pointing at the tank. Something was sparkling in the coral. He took a little net from a shelf hidden under the tank. "Something fell into the tank." He fished with the net. "I can't seem to reach it, Kate. Can you try?"

"The kids will be here any minute; shouldn't I go change?"

"You look fine." He handed her the net. Kate made a swooping pass at the foreign object, netted it, and pulled it to the surface. It was an old gold coin, set in a wide gold band.

"What do you think this is?" Kate wondered.

"Oh, maybe a nickel. From five hundred B.C."

Kate stared at the ring. Matt knew she didn't wear much jewelry, but this was different—it was a piece of history. She loved it.

"It's beautiful," she said.

"Happy birthday, sweetheart." Matt plucked it out of the net and put it on her finger. "We can tell people we found it diving on the reef."

"The fish are jealous," said Kate, kissing Matt and rubbing his cheek. "It's wonderful."

They stood holding each other, the faded hum and bubble of the aquarium the only sound. Kate wished they could make love now, following a real impulse, instead of by appointment on a calendar, as they'd been doing for months. But it never seemed to work out that way. Sex by medical decree left so little time or inclination for real affection. And now, when Kate would have liked nothing better than to let this particular kiss take its course, they had to brake and behave not like lovers but—and the irony of it was outrageous—like parents, because Gregory and Kim were due to arrive any second.

Kate admired the ring on her finger.

"You should have seen the one that got away," said Matt.

The house phone rang, and Kate knew it was the kids. She opened one button on Matt's shirt, reached in and tickled his chest. "Later," she said.

A familiar noise sounded from behind the front door: the kids were fighting. Kate winced. She had hoped to have a peaceful dinner, the kind that was always pictured in her magazine. There was something about playing referee that took the edge off being the birthday girl, she had to admit. Luckily, she was ready for them.

"Presents for everyone," she announced as she opened the door.

"Ouch! Da-deeeee!" Kim's screech broke the sound barrier as she raced toward the library, eluding her brother.

Gregory was small for his age, a precocious preteen with curly reddish hair and mahogany eyes. He looked nothing like either of his parents. Kim, on the other hand, resembled her mother to such a degree that Kate felt as if she were looking at a miniature of Elise, whom she had only seen in person four or five times. Most of their contact and arrangements for the children were made by phone, and although she didn't have a job, Elise delegated much of the child-rearing to a revolving series of British nannies, imported to stand an impeccable but hopeless guard. Kate couldn't understand why children this age still needed a nanny. She blamed Elise for keeping them in a perpetual state of immaturity. It was obvious—if you treated children like infants, they would act accordingly.

Like now, for instance. Gregory had netted a damselfish and was chasing his sister around the aubergine silk couches, the dripping net inches from the neck of her new pink eyelet party dress.

"Stop it right now," Kate said. "You'll kill that poor fish, if you haven't already." She dashed over, grabbed the net, and dropped the fish back into the tank where it floated belly-up. "Matt, this is not cute. Not at all." Why did he never do anything about the kids' wildness? He seemed afraid to discipline them, or do anything to risk their approval, even at the expense of his precious aquarium. Kate saw his face tense. He was upset. And it didn't look like she was going to get a chance to change for dinner. Well, it didn't matter. The main thing was to get the evening off on the right foot.

"What's for dinner?" said Gregory. "Fish sticks?"

"Whatever you want. We're going to Le Cirque."

"I'm hungry," said Kim. She started to sing to the tune of "It's raining, it's pouring": "I'm hungry, I'm hungry, I'm hungry, I'm hungry."

It was only six-thirty. Early for Le Cirque, a restaurant where the international crowd gathered and children were rarely seen.

51

"I'm sure Charles can be persuaded to let us have our table a little early," Kate said. She was sure that once they had ordered dinner and opened the F.A.O. Schwarz packages, the kids would relax and enjoy the evening. Didn't all kids like birthday parties?

"Here, honey, your laces are loose, let me tie your shoe." Kate bent to tighten the bows.

"Ouch!" squealed Kim as Kate tightened the ribbons. "Daddy, she pinched me!" Kim ran into her father's arms.

"What happened?"

"Nothing! I was just tying her shoe—"

"Well let's go, before there are tears."

Kate sighed.

On the ride to the restaurant, Kim and Gregory sat flanking their father, leaving Kate alone on the facing seat of the limousine. Somehow, whenever the four of them went out, the group sorted into "us" and "her," and Matt went along, just to keep the peace.

At Le Cirque, they were welcomed enthusiastically by the maître d', who fussed over the kids as if they were celebrities.

"Ah, *mes enfants,*" he said.

"Eurotrash," muttered Gregory under his breath.

Menus were distributed, orders were placed, and Kate settled in to enjoy her birthday dinner. For a few minutes, conversation revolved around the expected: school, vacations, grades. Matt smiled at Kate and nodded. Was he going to propose a birthday toast?

"So," he said, as Kim licked the sauce off a shrimp. "What would you kids think of a new baby brother or sister?"

Kate stared, speechless. Matt must have lost his mind. She wasn't even close to being pregnant yet. He caught her look.

"Well, we're a family here. It's good that the kids be part of the decision." He smiled in a paterfamilias way that Kate wanted to slug off his face. Why did the kids need to be involved at this point? So they could feel threatened? So they could run back to their mother with the news? When the time came, before the baby was actually born, it would be fine to tell them, but *now* . . .

"Personally, I do not buy into the concept," announced Gregory, twirling an artichoke leaf. "I think it's a terrible idea. You might say it sucks."

"Gregory!"

"What are they talking about, Greggie?" Little Kim was wide-eyed.

"Replacing us. They want to replace us, that's what."

Matt leaned forward. "No. Never. You are always my children. And Mom's. And Kate's."

"We're not! We're not Kate's children!" Gregory shrank away, closing the subject.

"I don't wanna be replaced," wailed Kim. Big tears splashed onto her pink party dress.

Matt stood up and went over to take her in his arms.

"Shh, sweetheart . . ."

Well, what did he expect? thought Kate. The children were not ready for this.

"Starship log: Today, I was tossed out by my own flesh and blood, like a used Kleenex, intergalactic waste in the flotsam of mankind."

"Kim, Gregory. Listen to me. There is no baby now. Your father was just being . . . theoretical. Calm down. Your dad loves you, you know that. I love you, too."

Kim sniffled. Gregory looked at Kate with pity.

"Now. I know it's my birthday, but we're all celebrating here, so I brought you guys presents." Kate cheerfully hauled the huge boxes from under the table. As the children ripped open the paper, Kate leaned over to Matt. "Please. Nothing more on any future babies," she hissed.

He looked helpless. "I thought they'd be thrilled."

Kate rolled her eyes. For a brilliant man, Matt could be maddeningly obtuse.

"Later," she mouthed.

Kim had unwrapped the doll and was combing its hair with her fork. Gregory was staring at the rock polisher.

"What kind of rocks am I supposed to find in New York City? Broken glass? Chunks of concrete?"

"We'll go to a geology shop together. They'll help out," Kate said.

"Great." Gregory showed an enthusiasm level of point one on a ten-point scale.

"What do you say, Gregory?" cued Matt.

"Thank you."

"Thank you," echoed Kim, petting her doll.

Suddenly Gregory brightened. "I have something for you. First, open the card I gave you before." He seemed genuinely excited for the first time.

"Oh, I will. Right now," Kate said. It was a lacy old-fashioned card. Probably picked out by Elise, from a drawerful she kept for any occasion. Elise was always organized about social things.

"This is wonderful! What a pretty card," Kate enthused.

Gregory produced a four-inch rectangular box from inside his jacket.

"I couldn't wrap this. You'll see why."

Kate took the box, opened it, and was startled as a laser-fast green thing whiplashed out of the box, onto her lap, and onto the floor, running her stockings on the way down.

"He's getting away!" squealed Kim. "Ninja, come back!"

"Ninja is a chameleon," said Gregory, scrambling from his seat. He dove headfirst under the tablecloth, where Ninja was launching an epic crusade across the carpeted floor of Le Cirque.

"Matt, do something!" Kate hoped they wouldn't get thrown out.

To Kate's right, a chair fell over as a rattled diner leaped up. "Waiter! Something crawled across my foot!" A woman in a veiled cocktail hat let out a little shriek.

The maître d' raced over and flapped at the floor with a napkin. "Everybody sit down," he said pointedly to Gregory and Kim. "The excitement is over."

"You'll hurt him. He'll suffocate!" said Gregory, grabbing the napkin. He commando-crawled through the tables. "Here, Ninja. Here, boy." His sister followed.

The maître d' searched the ceiling fruitlessly for divine deliverance. "Ms. Harrison-Weil," he said, his deference still in evidence only because of Kate's numerous business lunches at the restaurant. "Madam. I beseech you. This is a—well, an unappetizing disturbance."

Across the crowded room, a table seemed to levitate as two geriatric diners dropped forks and knives in unison.

"Oh my, oh my . . ." The maître d' rushed to their assistance.

"There he is!" yelled Gregory, scrambling out from underneath. "Ninja! Get out of that salad!"

The chameleon cooperated by springboarding into the air and again disappearing.

"I didn't know those things could move like that," said Matt, shaking his head.

Kate tugged at her napkin. "We're creating a spectacle," she said, teeth gritted. "We *are* a spectacle. Gregory, come back over here."

"Kate, relax, will you, honey? Nobody's getting hurt. It's just a harmless little lizard."

"So was Godzilla."

Gregory walked back to their table, clenching his fists. "I don't see what's so funny. This is an actual, cold-blooded reptile. He could die from the air-conditioning. He could starve." He kicked sullenly at the rock polisher.

"Luckily, he's in a four-star restaurant," said Kate.

"Let's finish our dinner," announced Matt. "Kim, come over here."

"I can't find him, Daddy," said Kim.

"He'll turn up," Matt said firmly. "You'll see."

The birthday soufflés came and went, untouched by the children, and the chameleon had not reappeared.

"That's it," said Gregory. "I'm not leaving."

"Me either," said Kim. "I'm not leaving."

"Is there an echo in here? They'll find him. When they clean up and shake out the tablecloths." Matt shot Kate a look, and she knew that he was planning to race out before the children woke up in the morning and buy a replacement.

"That's right," said Kate, signaling the maître d'.

"Charles will look out for him, won't you, Charles?"

"Of course." Charles stood rigidly at the back of Kate's chair, anticipating their soonest possible departure.

On the way out, by the entrance to the restaurant, Kate stopped to check herself in the mirror. Out of the corner of her eye, she saw the chameleon, frozen absolutely still—now camouflaged yellow, clinging to the mustard-colored molding. Her first instinct was to call out to Gregory, but she instantly reconsidered. Quietly opening her purse, she pulled out a hundred-dollar bill and pushed it into the fist of the shell-shocked maître d', who stared at her, his face a frozen veneer of barely contained professional courtesy.

"If the chameleon turns up," she said, "find it a good home."

Kate wondered if there was one chance in fifty of getting dried chocolate soufflé out of silk chiffon. Gregory had found it hysterical when he smashed her arm into his dessert. ("It's cold! I want to send it back! Kate, you feel for yourself.") Of course, she had walked right into the trap, but that was the point. What kind of children set traps for people? Elise's approach, or lack of approach, was a disaster. The kids were running wild. She and Matt would have to step in—if only Matt would let her take them in hand.

At least now they were sleeping peacefully in the guest rooms.

Matt came into Kate's dressing room and sat on the ottoman. It was an old-fashioned, wantonly feminine room, a real boudoir with a flounced dressing table and a fireplace with old roses on the mantel, flanked by a Venetian putti screen. It was the kind of room where a man seemed out of place, except by specific invitation.

"So," he said. "It's not too bad, is it, turning thirty-nine? I don't remember feeling much pain when it happened to me. At least not compared to forty. That one was tough, I admit."

Kate wrapped herself in a Carole Lombard–style thirties satin dressing gown.

"No, thirty-nine isn't bad, under two conditions. One, you don't look it, and two, you're married to you."

"Well, you're in luck on both counts." He pulled a rose from the vase and flicked it under her chin.

Kate resisted the temptation to say something about her biological clock. That would just be too trite. She was sick of hearing about women's biological clocks; it was as if everyone had a set of gears that was pretimed to sound off an alarm at thirty-five, then grind to a halt at forty. Everywhere you went, it seemed, women were discussing the innermost workings of their biological clocks in the way that, ten years ago, everyone discussed real estate. It seemed to Kate that women were sentenced to a lifetime of cycles and syndromes, all centered around ovarian functions—menstruation and menopause, PMS and ovulation—feeding and building themselves like some hormonal food chain. For most of her life, Kate had accepted it all as a matter of destiny. Now she was starting to resent it. The fact was, Matt could still have a child in ten years, or twenty or even thirty. His cycle was not so much a cycle as a continuum. It wasn't fair, when you looked at it that way.

"Matt," Kate said suddenly. "What would it be like if women could have children as long as they lived, like men?"

"Well, I suppose we'd have to initiate a new subspecialty—geriatric obstetrics."

"Seriously. Science might make that possible some day. They've even done some post-menopausal fertilizations recently. Look what you're doing with your own work, making people look younger. What if that extended to reproduction?"

"You'd be pushing baby carriages with one hand and us guys in wheelchairs with the other."

"But at least women would be able to have their children whenever they wanted, as part of a plan for their whole life."

"But would anybody in their right mind plan it that way?"

"I guess you're right. But nobody thinks it's so terrible when a sixty-some-year-old man has a child. Then it's charming."

"I don't think that's so charming. When Kim and Gregory were born, I wasn't even forty."

"But when our baby is born you'll be over forty."

Matt pulled open Kate's robe. "Do we have to talk about this right now?" he asked, tracing a line from the bridge of her nose to her breasts.

"Well," she said, "we could stop talking and do something else."

"For the record?"

"No. Three more days till it's time. Tonight's a freebie."

"Whew. The pressure's off." He pulled Kate's satin hair ribbon until it fell off.

Don't I wish, she thought.

Making love that night began lazy, sticky and sweet, like a lick of molasses, blissfully without the lockstep purposefulness that had taken over their babymaking sex. Matt's touch, his kisses, his scent, reminded Kate once again of why she'd married him, why her body and his had reason to seek each other out, why she felt this place was hers. She sank back into the lusciousness of it all.

Knock-knock-knock-knock-knock, knock-knock.

"Daddy!" piped Kim's voice through the bedroom door. "My brother needs to talk to you."

Matt and Kate froze.

"Daddy, it's really important!"

Matt climbed over Kate's hip and out of bed. "I'll be right back," he whispered. "Don't go anywhere."

It seemed like hours later that Kate felt Matt's warmth back beside her. Hazily, as if from a great distance, she was aware of his arms around her waist. He seemed very far away, and Kate did not feel up to rousing herself to lessen the distance. It was easier to drift in sleep.

"I'm asleep," she mumbled, as his fingers moved in lovemaking patterns along her back.

"I bet we could do it now—make a baby."

"Asleep," she mouthed.

"Honey . . ." He tugged at her, insistent.

Kate flopped onto her back. She had to get up for a breakfast meeting tomorrow; she felt exhausted, but she cooperated, or rather her sleeping body did, by lying there. It was really all she could manage.

That night, Kate had a dream: she was eighty years old, wearing a maternity dress, pushing a newborn baby. The infant was in a carriage. Kate was in a walker. She was struggling up a very steep hill, to the tune of "It's a Small World." The carriage kept slipping backward. Finally, when she was almost at the top, Kate lost her grip and fell down the hill. She was powerless as the carriage careened backward, rolled over her, and squashed her flat.

Kate was a list person. Lists, in her opinion, were the key to accomplishment, the means to all ends. At this moment, there were two lists in the yellow section of Kate's Filofax. They were:

Department
1. announce promotions
2. make new hire in Editorial—call recruiter
3. check new floor plan with Building
4. computer seminar
5. press release for Stanton Welch
6. talk to Nina
7. reservations to Washington
8. note to Marilyn Quayle re: child welfare speech

Home
1. assemble catalogs for mail order
2. call landscaper re: terrace bulbs
3. call calligrapher
4. remind Alicia—touch up linens
5. call Glorious Food re: party menus

As she sat in the bleak, basement-level office of the nurse coordinator of Mount Sinai's in vitro fertilization program, Kate turned to a fresh yellow page and got ready to make a new list. What would be the appropriate heading, she wondered. Baby? Pregnancy? Fertility? How could she distill the past five months of discouragement into one abbreviated word? She decided on I.V.F., the acronym for the program, and wrote it at the top of the page. Just writing the letters made Kate feel slightly relieved; at least she was doing something.

The nurse coordinator gave Kate some forms to fill out and literature about the program. Kate had already read everything she could about in vitro fertilization, starting with Xeroxes of every article published on the subject in the past two years, and she had jotted down a list of questions. Matt, being a doctor, had a better fix on the subject; Kate had to admit it was hard for her to assimilate all the information. She remembered the headlines when baby Louise Brown, the first in vitro baby, was born a decade ago. Test tube babies had seemed so surreal. Now Kate hoped to have one herself.

"Based on my history," Kate began, facing the interview desk with paper poised, like a student, "what kind of options do you see for me?"

"Well, that depends." The nurse looked earnestly at Kate. "There are several procedures. Simply stated, in vitro fertilization is the process by which mature, healthy eggs are removed from a woman's body and fertilized in the laboratory with her husband's sperm—or donor sperm. The fertilized eggs, which by that point are actually embryos, are then transferred back into the uterus to continue their development. The eggs can be retrieved endovaginally, using sound waves, and aspirated from the follicles through the vaginal wall by a needle. Or a laparoscopy may be performed in which the eggs are aspirated directly from the ovaries. That is a gamete intrafallopian transfer, or G-I-F-T, and general anesthesia is used."

"Gift," said Kate, scribbling as fast as she could.

"Your doctor and you will decide which is the best procedure for your circumstances."

"What is the success rate?"

"Overall, for in vitro, twenty to twenty-five percent. With GIFT, the natural environment raises the rate to thirty percent. We have a very high take-home baby rate with our program."

"High take-home baby rate," Kate repeated, not missing the fact that the phrase had a certain disturbing resemblance to *takeout Chinese food*. She envisioned a drive-through window, where you pulled in, ordered a boy or girl with blue or pink condiments over the microphone, and received the appropriately wrapped bundle for home consumption. She shook off the thought. Matt always accused her of being overly cynical about the medical profession. She had to take this seriously, and she knew it. It was probably their last chance. They had planned for Kate to be pregnant by now, and so far, the only occurrence had been her period, relentlessly on schedule, month after month. Because of Kate's age and lack of success, Dr. Warneke had put Kate on the accelerated program and sent her to an endocrinologist, Dr.

Street. Dr. Street in turn had run his own battery of tests, then had sent her to the I.V.F. program for a consultation, so Kate would understand her options.

"Exactly what steps are involved in the program?" Kate asked. "And how much time will it take?" She felt ignorant. It was strange to be so uninformed. Matt knew more than she did, but, of course, he was a doctor. With one fast phone call to Kate's specialists, he was able to shortcut every aspect of Kate's treatment far better than she ever would, in spite of the fact that it was her reproductive organs that were on the table.

The nurse had obviously had experience with this question. She handed Kate a twenty-page Xeroxed brochure. "Let's break it down," she said.

Kate dutifully readied her pen.

"First, there's the initial consultation, which we are now having. Your operation reports and lab records are now consolidated with the program. Next, you'll have a medical consultation with the doctor. He or she will review your records, explain the plan, and give you orientation. Plan on two hours. Then you'll call the center with the onset of menses, which, for discussion sake, we will place at Day Three. On that day, you will arrive at seven A.M. at the center for blood work, which will take an hour and a half. There's usually a backup in the waiting room. Days Three to Seven, you'll have pergonal injections at home every night for five nights running. Fortunately, your husband is a doctor, so he'll be involved, but even if the partner is not, we encourage him to give the injection. If he's not available, we'll teach you to inject yourself. Day Eight: arrive here at seven A.M. for preoperative blood samplings and ultrasound of the follicles. You'll have your pre-op physical and sign the consent. That's three and a half hours, roughly. Of course, you'll be coming by every day from then on for blood samples to check your estrogen level, and to monitor the ovum development on ultrasound. On the day the eggs are confirmed mature, we retrieve them and you'll arrive at seven A.M. and spend six hours in the recovery room. That day your husband will donate his sperm. The day after, I will contact you and schedule the embryo transfer forty-eight hours later. That's an all-day procedure. Day Ten, you'll return for blood work to check your estrogen levels. Day Twelve, a pregnancy test." The coordinator held up a picture of a smiling baby. "We hope this is the end result."

Kate sat stunned. Suddenly her mind was totally blank. She had taken no notes at all. This was not a procedure, it was a life-style. When would she be able to go to the office? "How can I travel?" she asked.

"Well, you can take your injections with you on short trips, assuming you learn how to self-inject. But the egg monitoring and retrieval of course will be done here, in town."

"What if it doesn't work and I don't get pregnant?"

"You start the cycle again."

Kate shifted uncomfortably in her seat.

The coordinator nodded sympathetically. "I know. It's tough. It will be the toughest thing you've ever done. But we find it's best if you're totally aware of what can and will happen. Your friends and spouse, too. And necessary professional associates. If they're told ahead of time, they will cope better."

Kate couldn't imagine Stanton Welch coping with any aspect of her reproductive system.

"There is a lot of stress. You must be here by seven, alter your work and travel schedules, be available for phone calls from nurses, and time the injections. And there's the waiting."

Kate took a deep breath. "But it's worth it, we hope?"

"Well, there is a failure rate."

Kate nodded. The statistics were not overwhelming, but they were not discouraging. This was one of the best programs in the country. Her hormones were functioning. She'd conceived once before; she knew she could get pregnant. According to Dr. Street, the problem was minor scar tissue in the tubes, which was proba-bly correctable, but if it wasn't, the in vitro fallback plan would bypass the problem area. She had every chance of success, as she saw it. No, she would not be a bad statistic. There would be a baby. She tried to focus on the baby picture on the coordinator's desk. *That's my goal. Objective: baby.*

"From my record and your experience, what do you think my chances are?"

"Well," said the nurse coordinator, "we all grow up believing having a child is our right, but it doesn't enter our mind that we won't be able to achieve a successful pregnancy."

Kate laughed bitterly. *So true.*

"Mostly, it's hard to come to grips with something you can't control. Science can only do so much."

Yes, Kate thought. *But we will control it.* Matt was a doctor; she was determined. They were fortunate; they had the resources for a program that could cost tens of thousands of uninsurable dollars. Whatever needed to be done, they'd do it. God knew how she'd explain herself at the office. This nurse had no idea of the reality of the workplace. You couldn't waltz in and say, "Excuse me, I'll be late tomorrow. I don't know how late; I'm having my eggs retrieved."

But Kate supposed she'd work it out. First things first. She looked at the few notes she'd made:

Day One.

Day Three.

Day Seven.

It sounded like Dan Rather reporting on a hostage siege. Of course it did. Because, Kate realized, she was about to become a hostage.

Five

"*P*hil, I'm sorry. Believe me, no one hoped this would work out more than I did." Phil Corbusier had been chief art director with *Childstyle* since the beginning. As part of the original group who used to call themselves the Four Musketeers—Kate, Phil, Margo, and Tina—he had always been considered part of the core management team. His work had been good—they both knew that. At the beginning, when he had designed the original format, it had been a spectacular statement. Nothing on the market could approach Phil's clean use of white space, combined with joyful primary colors and innovative, almost European use of type. But ever since Phil's personal life had fallen apart, so had his work. Kate had hoped that he would work through his problems and return to his former level of performance, but that hadn't happened. In fact, recently, Phil had cut back dramatically on his hours. In his position, Kate felt, Phil was doing worse than a bad job—he was setting a bad example. Now it was time to do something.

Phil shook his head slowly, sadly.

"This can't be a surprise to you, Phil. We've gone through this. We went over your evaluation. You know the problems." They had talked before. Six months ago, one month ago, two weeks ago—every time a problem came up, Phil had failed to

64

meet expectations. But since his divorce, he'd been too preoccupied to take positive action. Nothing seemed to change, and now the magazine wasn't looking as fresh as Kate expected. She'd already contacted a brilliant young German designer who could step in. Now, Phil had to go. In her career, Kate had fired many people, and she knew it was never easy. But it was hardest of all when a friend was involved, and Kate considered Phil a friend. He was one of the few people she had lunch with regularly, one of the few with whom she had shared confidences. That only made it worse now. Kate suddenly felt like crying, but tears were totally inappropriate. Standing up and crossing the room so that Phil would not notice, she struggled to control herself.

"God, Phil, what happened? You just seemed to stop caring about this job. I don't know how else to explain it."

"Maybe so, but you know what was going on in my life. Sara and the boys moving out . . . I had a lot to contend with. So, in a way, you're right. By comparison, any job is less important. But isn't that the way it should be? At least that's what I'm finding out. I guess what I'm saying is, I don't regret it, if that's the way it goes."

"I'm totally sympathetic, believe me. But you can't expect me not to apply the same professional standards to you as to everybody else, just because of our relationship. God, Phil—how can you do this to us? It's so competitive right now—you know what's going on. The magazine market is a mess. Ad pages are down everywhere. We need one hundred and ten percent." As she said this, Kate felt the hollowness of her words. How could you compare magazine ad pages with the loss of a marriage, of two children? Now, for the first time in her life, Kate knew that if she had two children, she would give up everything for them. She couldn't believe she was virtually standing here telling Phil Corbusier she was firing him for paying more attention to his family than to her magazine. She hated herself, but she knew she had to do it.

"I can't say things will change, Kate," said Phil, his voice soft but firm. "My eighty-hour weeks are over. I let it get in the way with Sara, but I'm not going to be an absentee father to the boys. And if that means leaving *Childstyle,* well, then that's what it means."

Kate couldn't turn around. "This stinks," she said, her nose running.

Phil laughed. "No it doesn't, Kate. It's just a magazine, not brain surgery. We'll both be okay." He walked over to her and put his arm around her. "Actually, I'd say right about now, you're in worse shape than me."

He was right. She was a mess. Ever since she'd started on the pergonal shots, Kate had been on an emotional roller coaster. She felt as if she were possessed by an alien being, half Bambi, half Hitler. The pressure was terrible enough, but these hormones left her feeling jagged and raw, ready to burst into tears any time and anywhere. She had to pull herself together.

"Phil," she said, trying to muster a sympathetically enthusiastic tone. "We're old friends. And, thinking it over, I think this is best for you, I really do. Actually, you have the best of all worlds. You got what was best out of the magazine. You were there from the beginning. And maybe that *was* the peak. We all need a change.

"Let me know if there's anything I can do for you. And we'll keep in touch." But she knew they wouldn't. She could barely keep in touch with her own husband these days.

He handed her a Kleenex. "Thanks, Kate." Then he was gone, off to pack his office, she supposed. Kate remembered all the times she'd fired people before, and how pat the routine had become. You fired people on Friday afternoons, late, when it wouldn't demoralize the rest of the office for the whole week. You went through the severance routine, the reference offer. It was all very professional; she'd never shown a shred of emotion. But this was not the same.

Kate had to admit, as she sat wiping mascara smudges from under her eyes, that there was more than sympathy to Phil in her reaction. In a way, she saw herself in him—not that her performance was falling off. But her priorities were shifting, that much was clear. Her desire to have a child had encroached on her professional self like a parasite feeding for survival. It was harder to get excited about whether ad pages were up this month versus last year when your mind was focused on something as primal as having a baby. Was she really any better off than Phil? She didn't know how much longer she could juggle so many agendas.

Clair buzzed on the intercom. "Sorry to disturb you when your door is closed, Kate, but it's Mr. Welch on two."

Kate punched the blinking button. "Hello, Stanton."

"Kate, you've been on my mind. How are things? I missed you last week when I stopped by. I'd hoped we could have lunch."

Last week. The sonogram session had run late that day. "I've been running, Stanton. We'll set something up for sure next time."

"Good. Breakfast on the twelfth?"

The twelfth. She was scheduled to be inseminated at eight o'clock that morning. "Gosh. The twelfth doesn't look good. How about the thirteenth?"

"I'll be in Toronto. Why don't you fly out with me?"

Kate wasn't sure if she could fly then, but she figured she could check with the doctors. "Fine. Toronto. Anything specific I need to be briefed on?"

"Actually, yes. But it has nothing to do with *Childstyle*. *Finance* is experiencing some serious losses, and I want your input on some marketing suggestions. I want to kick them in the rear end, to be precise. Ad pages are down. And Roy Guardino and his gang of stiffs have just gotten too carriage-trade in their mentality. I'd be interested in your perspective. I'll fax you a briefing package."

"I'll get right on it, Stanton. This will be very interesting."

Hanging up, Kate was pleased. It was important to be included in the big picture, to be consulted about *Finance*. She'd always felt she could apply her abilities on a broader scope, and this would open the door. But, more than that, Kate was sure she could come up with some innovative ideas. Certainly more so than Guardino, whose only idea was always to slash rates. She made a note on her calendar to block out the time.

Kate wanted to think more about this new opportunity, but her head was splitting. She took two Tylenol and fixed herself a cup of herbal tea. The ritual relaxed her, and she decided to go through some paperwork to clear her head. The correspondence was mindless, easy. The upcoming issue of *Childstyle* was on the corner of her table, and she leafed through it. A sidebar on child abuse caught her eye. At first, she was irritated because it didn't seem to fit in with the rest of the book. But the subject drew her in. There was a hot line number for a support group, and some horrifying statistics. The piece startled Kate—and the fact that it was opposite a picture of a beautiful, peach-faced, six-month-old baby modeling a little lace bib gave it even more impact. *It was hideous. Despicable.* The abuse of an innocent child was so senseless. Especially when such a child would have been so wanted elsewhere, in other homes, homes where children were desperately wanted. Homes like . . . hers. She, who so deserved to have a baby, was childless, while other women, women who didn't deserve to raise houseplants, were tormenting precious children. She grabbed the phone and pounded Margo's extension.

"Margo, the child abuse piece—why wasn't it given more prominence?" Kate's voice was breathless.

"I thought our editorial policy was minimalize the less-than-upbeat."

"I said that?" Her mind was blank.

"Yes, if I recall."

"Well, you must have misunderstood, or else I did. It's up to us to keep the important issues out front for our readers. And to run a mouse-type sidebar like this! It degrades the subject! If we're going to run anything, we should think about how we present it!" She was shrill, almost screaming into the phone.

Margo said nothing.

"Are you listening?" Kate demanded.

"Yes, Kate."

"Well, expand on this piece and get back to me with ways we can deal with this issue within our format. Do it now!" She crashed down the phone, then stopped short.

What's the matter with me? she thought. Her perspective was shot. Kate put her head down on top of a stack of magazines and sobbed senselessly, ignoring the buzzing and blinking of three phone lines.

When she lifted her head, she did not look at the cover. She could not look at one more picture of a smiling baby. Smiling baby faces were everywhere. Even the halls were lined with huge, life-sized blowups of smiling babies. But there was no escape on the street, either. There were babies in strollers. Peering out of backpacks. Sailing along in nanny-captained buggies. Every other Christmas card seemed to have a new-baby variation of the family picture. Babies were everywhere, except in her life.

Wearily, Kate dictated a memo to Margo.

"To: M. Stern; From: K.H.W.; Re: child abuse piece. Margo— Let's flesh out this piece and run a more in-depth feature A.S.A.P. You did a super job on this. I apologize for the misunderstanding."

There was so much more Kate wanted to put in the memo, but, as editor-in-chief, she couldn't afford the personal luxury of letting out her feelings. She had long been accustomed to the pyramid effect, which meant that there were lots of people to send for coffee, but no one with whom to share a problem. Kate sat listlessly in her chair for the rest of the afternoon, aware of nothing so much as the fact that just being there had suddenly become excruciating.

Matt was still at the office when Kate got home. His schedule was as bad as hers lately. Maybe they could do something together, just the two of them. Something they used to do before these fertility rites had begun.

Next week was the egg retrieval; her third time through the cycle, and it was already October. The end of the year was in sight, with no new beginnings for her. It was so frustrating. Twice, she'd been certain that they would succeed. There was every hope for success, according to the doctors. Twice she'd gone through the ritual of daily shots, and then the trip to the twentieth floor of the Stratton Pavilion, to the sonogram waiting room, where all the women circled in a holding pattern, white-knuckled. Twice there had been the unpleasantness of the vaginal sonogram, and then they told you how many eggs and their size, which she had written down like the measurements for a new rug: this one was nine by twelve, that one was eight by ten—or at least that was how it sounded to Kate. Twice, Matt had had to go into what he disparagingly called the Sperm Shop and leave sperm to be inseminated into her. Twice the procedure had failed; this time, the doctor had decided to try the in vitro technique.

They needed a break.

She called Matt. "Honey, let's go out."

"Sure. Whatever you want."

"The Rainbow Room?"

"Why so fancy? Is this an occasion?"

"Just us together."

"No other doctors in the room? That *is* an occasion."

"Eight o'clock? Can you get out by then?"

"It's a date."

Kate changed into her black silk St. Laurent spaghetti-strapped dress with matching tuxedo jacket. She pulled off her velvet headband and replaced it with a black satin ribbon. Picking up a plump sable brush from her dressing table, she fluffed fresh powder over her face. Then she clipped on the yellow sapphire earrings Matt had given her for a wedding gift, picked up her purse, and glanced at herself in the mirror. How long had it been since they'd dressed up and gone out, alone together? It was going to be a good night.

When she got to the Rainbow Room, she raced to the elevator, knowing Matt would be waiting. Meeting him like this reminded Kate of their early dates, when she would rush in, breathless, straight from work, and he would be there, anticipation in his eyes. They really needed to regain some of that sparkle, Kate thought. All the fun seemed to have been sapped out of their relationship lately. Anticipation was such a delicious feeling to Kate, almost better than reality. Reality rarely lived up to your hopes. How much of your life was spent making reality more palatable, she wondered.

Reality had never seemed more stark, however, than when Kate saw Matt in the cocktail lounge of the Rainbow Room. With him was a woman with the blond meringue hair that was rampant among New York society women. Kate recognized the back of her shellacked head: Elise.

Well, Kate thought, *how civilized we are.* She extended her hand. "Hello, Elise."

Matt jumped to his feet. "Kate, darling. Something urgent about the children has come up. Elise thought it was important to discuss this in person, as soon as possible. I figured the three of us could talk over drinks, before you and I have dinner."

At least they would still be eating alone.

Elise sat nervously smoking a cigarette, a pile of half-smoked stubs accumulated in the ashtray in front of her. Her skin was rice-powder pale, her smile outlined by perfectly applied red lipstick, the kind of shade that left stains on linen napkins. She had a long, heart-shaped face with a widow's peak and slightly puffy eyes. Kate thought she looked like she could use a good night's sleep, but otherwise she was thin, the bones in her perfectly manicured hands standing out in relief, and beautifully put together in what looked like a couture gabardine pantsuit shot with gold threads. She blinked cautiously at Kate. "I apologize for disturbing your evening," she said politely. "But as parents, Matthew and I must discuss our son's problem immediately. Things are already quite out of hand." She stubbed out her cigarette to emphasize the urgency.

"Well now, Elise," said Matt calmly. "I admit it's serious, but, let's face it, the fact that Gregory has been trading is not going to hurt anybody."

Kate was confused. "Trading? Trading baseball cards?"

Elise gave her a glance of supreme condescension. "*Insider* trading, Kate. Stocks. It's absurd, I know, but children are so much more sophisticated these days."

"I see. But I don't understand—"

Matt cut in. "Up at Cranston, his prep school crowd—I guess a number of them have fathers who are key men in important companies, or on boards, and some of them, well, you know kids, they bragged about their dads, and talked about the companies, and who was going to take over whom, or merge, or be acquired, and who was going to be richer, and Gregory picked up on all this insider talk and bought stock."

"Who paid for it?" asked Kate.

"He leveraged his five-hundred-dollar savings account."

71

"No one would take stock orders from a child."

"He called Elise's father, who is an investment banker. Gregory told him it was a class project."

"He overindulges him," said Elise. "It's a problem."

"Well," said Kate, "if he lost all his money, he'll learn his lesson."

Elise snorted. "Really, Kate. Gregory is much too intelligent to lose five cents. He made twelve thousand dollars."

"What!"

"He bought options." Matt shook his head. "I don't know whether to punish the kid or hire him as my broker."

"I fail to see the humor in this," said Elise. "This is your only son you're talking about."

Kate ordered a Lillet and kept her mouth shut. She'd been there before—when Kim wanted to wear makeup; when Gregory mail-ordered a BB gun and had it Fed-Exed collect to his school; when they both refused to go to sailing camp and the deposit was lost. She had discovered that she was in a no-win situation. Gregory and Kim, of course, could do no wrong—or, if they did, Matt would not risk losing them to admit it—and Elise, the single mother, deserved a supportive attitude. Kate wanted to tell Matt the facts as she saw them: those kids were begging for attention because their mother was too busy dancing for dystrophy, or whatever the charity of the moment was. Elise was always in the society columns. The time had to come from somewhere. She didn't work outside the home, yet she was allowing her kids to drift. It was pathetic.

Elise flipped open an enameled cigarette case, and Matt, as if on autopilot, jumped to light her cigarette. Kate noticed that she leaned toward him and touched his hand with the familiarity of people who had rehearsed this gesture a thousand times. "I can see we are heading for trouble," said Elise. "Matt, you're the only one Gregory will listen to. You'll have to step in."

"I'll have a serious talk with him." In spite of his serious expression, Kate could tell Matt was more amused than concerned.

"Not good enough. What kind of talk—a phone call between appointments and lectures? The boy needs his father."

Kate saw the anguish on Matt's face. Elise was playing her trump card—guilt.

"That is totally unfair, Elise," Kate said. "You know how Matt feels about Gregory and Kim. He'd do anything for those children."

"They are his children and mine, Kate," said Elise calmly. "Please stay out of this."

"Elise, give us all a break," Matt said. "Kate has a terrific interest in the kids. She's concerned, and that's the way it should be."

"Fine. She's concerned. Now. I propose this: a study date with Gregory two evenings a week. Just you and him, Matt. He needs the individual attention."

"That's a good idea. He can come over right after dinner, and . . ."

Elise shook her head. "Don't you see? His life has been so disrupted already. This behavior is a cry for help. He needs the familiar surroundings of his own home. Matt, you will just have to come over to our apartment for this. How difficult can it be? You did live there for twelve years."

"We've got a very comfortable library where Gregory can study." Kate spoke evenly.

"Well, that's encouraging," said Elise. "Especially since Gregory tells me you've eliminated his and Kim's rooms and put them in the guest suite while you're renovating a nursery." She stared pointedly at Kate's flat stomach.

"Now just a minute, Elise," Kate said hotly. "Their rooms are beautiful. They have park views, and—"

Elise cut her off. "Children don't need park views and Egyptian cotton sheets. They need security, familiarity, routine. A boy needs his father. I realize this is not your territory, Kate. You're a career woman. But my children are my career. And I do expect both of you to understand and cooperate." She picked up her purse, slipping the gold chain handles over her shoulder. "And one more thing. The children were terribly upset when the news was absolutely *dropped* on them that you are thinking of having a child. Kim cried herself to sleep for a week. It was needlessly traumatic. So I'm telling you both that according to the child

73

psychiatrist I consulted, we will have to work together to prepare for future half brothers or sisters. Sensitivity is the key."

"Elise," Kate said, "I can assure you that there is no baby on the horizon at this moment. We have plenty of time to orient the children."

Elise gave a wry half smile. "Well, you never know once these things get started. Don't you remember, Matt? It seemed like every time I turned around, I was pregnant."

Kate sat frozen, stung. Elise was a vapid egocentric, but she was right. She had been successful where Kate had not. She had her children to prove it; Matt's children.

Matt stood up. "I think our table is ready, so if you don't mind, Elise. Thank you for coming by and meeting us. I will call Gregory tonight, from the restaurant. We'll make plans. It will all work out—you'll see. And Kim, too—I'll make more time for her, one-on-one. Now, where's your coat?"

Straightening her skirt, Elise bestowed her best charity party smile on Kate. "Good to see you both. Bye-bye, now."

"Good-bye, Elise."

As the maître d' led them to their table, Matt shook his head. "I'm sorry, Kate. Elise has the capacity to be abrasive, I will admit. But we have to think of the kids." He laughed. "Not that I really believe Gregory needs any help. It's us who need to be saved from him. He's just too smart for his own good."

Kate noticed the view of New York at night, spangles against black velvet. The dance band was playing a rumba. It was a beautiful Deco setting, but it was hard to muster any vestige of romance.

"Let's dance," she said suddenly.

Matt was not a particularly good dancer, nor was Kate, but they always loved dancing, along with their particular sport of satirizing the other couples on the dance floor.

"Ex–prom queen, nineteen fifty-four," said Matt as they passed a couple on their left.

"She dropped the football team captain and ran off with him," said Kate. "He was the class ring salesman."

They both laughed and started to relax.

"You won't mind if I spend a little extra time with Gregory?" Matt asked.

"Of course not. You're a wonderful father." But Kate was wondering how Matt was going to find several evenings a week to spend with Gregory, and it went without saying that those would be evenings spent away from her, slicing their rare and precious time together even more thinly than it already was. She was not the kind of woman who had to have her husband around all the time—quite the opposite, in fact. But recently she'd felt a new neediness for Matt. She wanted him there to reassure her, if only by his presence, and to hold her after her shots and on the awful days when her period came. They were a team now more than ever—at least, that's how she saw it. But she couldn't say this to him, not in the face of a little boy who so obviously needed him more. So she said, "I hope I'll be as good a mother someday myself."

"I'm not worried."

"I just wish it would happen."

"It will."

"How can you be so sure? I used to feel that way, but now . . . I don't know. I really wonder."

"I spoke to the endocrinologist on Tuesday, and he assures me we have a better-than-average chance. The PK test was fine. The baseline FSH, LH, and estrogens are fine."

"He never discussed those things with me. I think he's condescending."

They danced more slowly.

"He's the best. The chief of the department."

"But he only talks to me in generalities, as if that were all he thought I could understand. Then he picks up the phone and calls you with the details. I wish I had a woman doctor."

"Kate. It's just professional courtesy. It's not chauvinism, believe me. I just have the medical background to ask those kinds of questions, and he answers them." Matt patted the small of her back. "You have the A-team here. Now you're in the in vitro program. It will increase our chances by twenty-five percent. Unless of course you have some problem we haven't found yet, which can always happen."

"What do you mean, *I* have some problem? I thought it took two to tango. You're part of these procedures, too, you know." Kate felt completely exasperated. She was on a short fuse tonight, admittedly. "I think they're doing one more sperm count before they let you off the hook," she joked, but her voice was brittle.

He took it the wrong way. "There's nothing wrong with my sperm!" Matt barked, yanking away from Kate in a reflex reaction.

Heads swiveled in their direction from all over the dance floor. A couple dancing beside them froze mid-spin.

"I have two children. What could possibly be wrong with my sperm?" Matt's teeth were gritted.

"Who knows? Maybe your sperm can't penetrate my eggs. Maybe your sperm count dropped. Maybe you went through too many weapon-detection devices at airports." Kate knew her voice was rising, but she couldn't help herself.

"Jesus Christ, now she's a doctor." Matt pushed his way past the other couples on the dance floor, his shoulder butting into a twirling woman and sending her reeling off balance as he stormed back to the table.

Kate caught up with him and grabbed his sleeve. "Matt, please. You are the doctor. You know as well as I do that any-thing could happen. Why are you taking this personally?" Kate felt like crying again. *Those damned hormone shots! She should have known that when it came to male vanity, there was nothing that was not personal.* She took two deep breaths. Was she get-ting hysterical in public? "Honey, let's not fight. I love you. Let's have a nice dinner. Okay?"

He sighed. "Okay. Truce."

During appetizers, they talked about seismic disturbances. For the main course, interest rates. Dessert brought a stimulating discussion of fabrics for the couch. It was worse than dating, thought Kate as she searched for neutral topics, when you weighed every word to give the right impression. Suddenly every sentence was a potential mine field. But the innocuousness of the conversation gradually salved their nerves until, in the cab ride home, Kate and Matt kissed and made up.

The minute the elevator door closed, Kate started pulling off

Matt's clothes. They left his jacket on the entrance hall floor, his shoes and suspenders in the hall. His pants disappeared somewhere near the bedroom. And they never made it to the bed. Kate's skirt was pulled up around her waist, her garters loosened, her tiny panties crumpled on the carpet beside her satin hair ribbon. Matt pulled her to him and she stretched beside him on the floor like a languid cat. She rubbed her leg along his and waited for him to push into her.

But he didn't.

The moment broke. What was happening? Was Matt waiting for her to make the next move? She reached for him and trailed her hand along his open shirt and down between his legs.

"Don't." He twisted away.

And then she knew; Matt couldn't. Kate was startled. This had never happened before. Was it the argument? Maybe his masculinity had been threatened. Maybe he'd had too much wine.

"Want to take a break?" she whispered into the back of his neck.

"No," he said, standing up abruptly.

"What is it? Are you mad at me?"

"No," said Matt. His voice sounded weary, as if he'd been deprived of sleep for a week. "No, I'm not mad." He pulled off his shirt and flopped onto the bed, arm over his face.

Kate sat on the floor and stared at her husband until he fell asleep, which was, in fact, within minutes.

Kate had known longing before. Longing for love, for instance, was a bittersweet experience; longing for sex was lustful. Longing for a ripe nectarine to bite into on a hot summer day was sweet, longing to own a painting was wistful. Longing for a baby was just an ache. *When had this happened?* she wondered. Kate wasn't sure when her rationally grounded desire to become a parent because the time and circumstances were right had become a relentless passion.

She knew she had become a bore, because CeCe told her so.

"Kate," she said one Saturday afternoon as they window-shopped their way down Madison Avenue, "I think you should forget about this pregnancy quest for a while, because your friends, specifically me, have noticed that this is the only subject you discuss."

"CeCe, if I can't talk to you, who is there? Besides, you talk about your children."

"For one thing, they exist. I'm worried about you, Kate."

"All I said was that I couldn't believe it didn't work. The embryos looked so good. They really did. Cells dividing and everything. We could have had triplets. Or twins. I thought about buying a double stroller. But instead—nothing."

She didn't tell CeCe the whole of it; that she had secretly named the embryos Emily, Sara, and Steven. She was convinced there were two girls and a boy. That she had talked to them, told them each how much they were wanted, how she and Matt were waiting to welcome them. That she had envisioned them at their first birthday party, with three identical cakes. That the petri dish embryos had seemed like living children to her. That the fact that the implantation procedure had not worked had left her bereft, almost as if she'd had children and they had died. When she had had the abortion, when a real fetus was involved, she had felt sadness, but not this grief. Did wanting a life to exist make it more valuable? Was this the same as a death? Kate wasn't sure, but she felt the grief, just the same, and it was grief she could not share, or even show. Not even to Matt, who had assumed a professional attitude: a medical experiment had not worked out. She actually understood; it was similar to the way she had felt after the abortion. But her own pain was no less.

"Well, Katie. You know what they say," said CeCe.

"I never listen to Them anymore."

"Be that as it may, they say that when you stop trying, that's when it happens."

Kate thought again of the three embryos, tiny, failed cell-chips of what might have been. Honestly, she didn't know if she could take another failure. Because that was how she felt—failed, drained. She averted her head as they passed Lady Madonna, the maternity boutique. Maybe CeCe was right. Maybe if she blocked it out for a while, it would happen.

*   *   *

Kate decided to refocus on her work. This was difficult, since focusing on her work meant focusing on the one thing she did not want to think about—children. Fortunately, Stanton Welch had provided her with a window when he asked her to come up with some suggestions for *Finance*. She gathered every piece of information on the financial market and dug in with her sleeves rolled up. As she studied the details of *Finance*'s readership survey in Stanton Welch's briefing package, the problem became clear to Kate. *Finance* was right on target to the financially oriented reader—if you assumed that reader had the interests and investments of a fifty-year-old-plus man. The editorial format was geared to an older, stodgier investor, someone who was on the verge of retirement. The problem, as Kate saw it, was that the most vulnerable market was not these older men, but younger men and women, thirty to forty-five, the yuppies. True, they had slightly less money to spend, but more of them were actively spending it. And, most important, since they were more active consumers, they would yield higher-quality advertisers. The key was to reposition and reformat *Finance* to attract this market.

As when she conceived *Childstyle,* Kate worked alone. She couldn't write fast enough to get all her ideas down. Her adrenaline kept her afloat for late nights and ordered-in lunches. Work piled up for *Childstyle,* but she pushed it aside. She was onto something and she knew it. She felt good about it; better than she had felt about anything in a long time.

Within a week, she had an action plan on paper, and the plan in her head had evolved into something beyond even that.

Kate called in Hal Radia to bounce her ideas off him. She knew that while she was editorially strong, he had a lock on the financial end of the business.

Hal nodded slowly, cracking his knuckles as he thought about her plan. She trusted Hal. He was one of a rare breed; an old-timer who stayed fresh and current. His instincts were impeccable. If he thought her ideas wouldn't work, she'd scrap the whole proposal before she even showed it to Stanton Welch.

"Makes sense to me," Hal finally said. "But I have to ask you—to what end? I mean, a plan is all well and good, but why do you have this plan? And what about Roy Guardino? Where does he fit in?"

Kate folded her hands in her lap and leaned forward intently. "I really think a lot could be done with *Finance*. It's been such a problem child for Americana. Stanton Welch is looking for answers, and I'd like to give them to him. I guess I'd like to be involved with the future of *Finance*."

"As?"

"I don't know yet, Hal. I'm just walking through this very preliminarily, at the moment."

His eyes narrowed. He knew Kate too well. "Yeah? I smell something. Like blood."

"Come on, Hal."

"You want Guardino's job, that's what."

"Hal! I'm not even thinking in terms of personalities." Kate was offended. It wasn't a position she was interested in—it was the work.

"All the same, there is no other job. Not for you. What're you gonna do, get his coffee? Give me a break. All I can say is, watch out for Guardino. Right now, he owes you one, but if you're talking about his home turf, I warn you, the man will defend. He's tough."

"The truth is, I'm just giving Stanton some suggestions. That's all he asked for." She sighed. "But to be honest, Hal, I wouldn't mind the change, on one condition. Hypothetically speaking, of course."

"What's that—hypothetically speaking?"

"You'd come with me. We'd do this together." She spoke excitedly. "I know we could turn this thing around, Hal. It's just a matter of repositioning the magazine. Giving it appeal to the yuppie market."

A thin smile inched across Hal's face. "I like this. Hypothetically."

"Some neat ideas, huh?"

"No, the big idea, turning *Finance* around."

"Is it possible, from a distribution point of view? Will the trade ever think of *Finance* in another way, or is it impossible to change the current mind-set?"

"Kate, if there's one thing I've learned after forty years in this business, it's that nothing's impossible."

Clair stuck her head into Kate's office. "Can I get you guys some lunch?"

"Maybe that would be a good idea. It looks like we'll be here for a while." Kate paced in front of the couch. She had a million ideas. She felt refreshed and exhilarated, as she had when she started working on *Childstyle*.

She couldn't wait to call Stanton Welch.

When was the last time she had felt this enthusiasm about work? she wondered. It was a physical relief, most notable for the fact that she was not to be thinking about children, or looking at their pictures. She was dealing with a concrete business issue that did not carry an emotional depth charge. For the first time in months, Kate left the office anticipating, rather than dreading, the next day.

She knew it then, on the way home in the car.

She wanted to leave *Childstyle*. No; she *had* to leave *Childstyle*.

"You want to leave *Childstyle*?" Matt was incredulous. "Why? You have one of the best positions in publishing. That magazine is your creation, honey. Sometimes I think it's your life."

"That's exactly why I have to leave." It was amazing, Kate thought, as she lay on the fringed cashmere throw, her bare feet in Matt's lap. Amazing how, the more she mulled it over, the more positive she was that this was the right thing to do. It was the kind of decision, she was sure, that only seemed sudden. In reality, the elements had been building up for months. Not that she hadn't been tormented by ambivalence—the initial notion had been both liberating and agonizing. But it boiled down to the fact that when you dreaded going to the office, for any reason, it was probably over. Just like a relationship.

"I just can't do it anymore," she said. "It's been a lot of years, and the magazine is more successful than I ever had dreamed, but right now the pressure is just too much."

Matt massaged her ankles. "Isn't it mainly pressure you've been putting on yourself, though? God knows, I don't blame you for feeling it—we both do. I'm just saying, maybe if we weren't so caught up in this baby thing, you'd see it in a different light."

Kate stiffened. "It's not 'this baby thing,' " she snapped. She hated it when Matt depersonalized what they were going through. "*We* are trying to have a baby."

"Okay, okay. Sorry."

Kate looked around the sitting room. Just a year ago, she'd been so proud of it—the carved mahogany paneling, the gleaming brass wall sconces, the faded but perfect Kilim rugs. Now none of that seemed to matter. What difference did it make what fabric you put on your couch? Having nice things tricked you, she thought—deceived you into thinking you could have anything you wanted, if you worked hard enough and could pay the bill.

"Matt, *Childstyle* was a challenge, a wonderful, once-in-a-life-time challenge. But I've thought this through—it wasn't the day-to-day running of the magazine that I loved, it was the creating of it. The conceptualization. I want to be able to do something like that again, and I actually think there may be a chance with this *Finance* opportunity."

"That's not the whole reason," Matt said. "I know it isn't, because we both know the real reason."

Kate could hardly believe it. Matt was inferring that she would let her feelings about not getting pregnant dictate a career decision of this magnitude. "Matt," she said carefully, "the real reason is the opportunity. Believe me, I'm not going to throw away my career or do anything foolish. I think I can turn *Finance* around, I really do. It's something that could let me use my conceptual capabilities again, the part of the business I really love. Don't you see that?"

"Yes, I see that. But I also see you running—whether it's to one thing or away from another, I'm not sure." He patted her shoulder. "I just want to help you think this through out loud."

Kate sat bolt upright, tossing off the cashmere blanket. "I'll sort out my own logic flow, thank you," she said testily. She hated this condescending attitude of Matt's, even though she rationally realized that it was only a result of his concern for her.

"I'm just trying to help." Matt's voice was tense. "Really, Kate, don't think I don't feel the pressure, too. You know, last week when Jack and Lori asked us to that christening, I really didn't want to accept. At first I thought it was because I didn't want you to get upset—I thought a new baby might, well . . . at any rate, I realized that it was upsetting me. The baby is too real to me. It's getting to me. Believe me, we're going through this together." He leaned over and held her.

"I'm sorry," said Kate. She should have seen his side of it. It must be awful to know that once a month, on demand, you had to go to the Sperm Store, sit in the windowless room with the "helpful" copies of *Playboy,* and ejaculate into a white plastic cup. It must be humiliating to have to perform like a mechanical stud machine whenever your wife's calendar dictated it. No wonder he had this perspective. If those were the facts, they had to deal with them. It was senseless to keep up this constant barrage of torture. But Kate really wasn't interested in *Finance* simply to escape the dynamics of a fertility problem. She saw an opportunity, just as she had with *Childstyle.*

"You're leaving *Childstyle!*" CeCe cried. "No! You *are Child-style.* You can't leave. What will the press say? Is it a done deal?"

"Shh!" Kate cautioned. "The tablecloths have tape recorders at this place." They were lunching at Mortimer's, where it was not unheard of for reporters to be mixed in with the society regulars. During Kate's gossip column days, she and Harry often ate there for the explicit purpose of eavesdropping for juicy tidbits.

"CeCe, I'm really excited about this. I know it's the right move. And it's not as if I were leaving the business; I just want to do other things. Look at Anna Wintour. They brought her in and she's virtually relaunched both *HG* and *Vogue.* It's not unheard of." Talking to CeCe, Kate felt excited about her decision. It was true that her emotions had led her to this, but she was becoming convinced it was the best business decision. At least, in her own head, she had constructed an ironclad fortress of pros.

"So enough about me. What brings you to the city? This is a landmark event—you in town for lunch, and me actually having lunch with a friend."

"I'm doing some publicity work for a new gallery."

"Hey, that's great." It had been years since CeCe had done anything professional.

"I figured I should keep my hand in. You know what, Kate? I looked in my wallet a while ago, and Steve's name was on all my credit cards." She grimaced. "When did that happen? Anyway, this new gig should bring me into town at least once a week."

"You needed a break from all that fresh air."

"Among other things."

"What's that supposed to mean?"

CeCe shrugged and poked at her crab cakes. "They make the best crab cakes here, don't they?" She wasn't looking at Kate.

"CeCe?"

"I guess I need a break from a few things. The good mother routine is starting to get to me. I'm not complaining," she added quickly. "It's just time to look at myself again."

They smiled silently at each other, knowing, of course, that each had what the other wanted, and that neither would be happy if they traded places.

On the trip to Toronto, Kate wasted no time in laying the groundwork for her plan. Before she and Stanton Welch had even ordered coffee at their first breakfast meeting, she put the issue on the table.

"Did you have a chance to go over my proposal for *Finance?*"

"Yes. It was damn good. Cross merchandising! What a way to bring the magazine to the mass market. Guardino would never have thought of that. His idea of a big time is to straighten his tie." Welch chuckled. "Now, Kate, let's talk about something concrete here. Maybe you could go on the board of *Finance.*"

"Stanton," she said, "I'd prefer to go on staff at *Finance.* I think my perspective could bring a lot to the business. Of course, I'd like to involve some key people to bring about these ideas." She handed Welch a bound report. "Read this over and see what you think. It's a complete plan for repositioning *Finance*. I think it could work, with your support, and the contribution of a few key people, like Hal Radia."

Welch looked intrigued. "What about *Childstyle?*"

"I was thinking, Stanton. My mission there is really over. The format is in place, the magazine is successful, the people are humming. They don't really need me. It's just a matter of repeating the pattern and keeping the right people involved. I believe I have a lot to bring to another situation within the Americana group. I'm serious. Please consider me for *Finance*."

"Kate, I'd have to say it would be a pretty unorthodox move. Or at least unexpected. How would you see your role?"

"I'd be responsible for revitalizing the magazine and increasing its relevancy to the twenty-five to forty-five's. It wouldn't work unless I had a mandate from corporate to do that. But if I had it, I wouldn't care what title I had."

"What about Guardino? He's historically been very important to *Finance*. He'd have to be there for continuity."

Kate knew Welch was worried about losing advertisers. Advertising revenues were what kept magazines afloat—newsstand sales were just the gravy. She smiled confidently. "I could work with him," she said.

Six

Why don't doctors' waiting rooms ever have any magazines that are less than four months old? thought Kate as she flipped nervously through a frayed vintage copy of *Time.* Even more incredible was the fact that everyone, herself included, actually read this ancient history as they waited interminably for their names to be called. Kate had become somewhat of an expert on doctors' waiting rooms, having been in fourteen of them in the past year.

"Kate Harrison-Weil," announced a nurse, and Kate sighed with relief. She nudged Matt unnecessarily. This particular fertility specialist, Dr. Pitcarin, had insisted on seeing them both. He had a world-renowned reputation and had been suggested by Kate's endocrinologist, who, in turn, had been suggested by her gynecologist. Kate had come alone a week ago, for the preliminary lab tests and blood work. Today, the doctor would give his opinion.

"Basically, Kate, I think you have a slight endometrial infection that may be interfering with conception." He scribbled something on a prescription, ripped off the sheet, and handed it to her. "Three weeks of this antibiotic should do it."

Matt intercepted the prescription. He glanced at it. "Actually, Doctor, wouldn't Kate be better off on adriamycin? My associates tell me that's been working well for them."

Dr. Pitcarin frowned. "That's fine, Doctor. Kate can take adriamycin. But tell me—why are you here? Do your associates handle fertility problems?"

"No, they're infectious disease specialists."

"I see. Well, if your wife doesn't wish to be in this program . . ."

Kate stiffened. "I do want to be in the program!" What was Matt doing, questioning the doctor's competence? Dr. Pitcarin was highly recommended. It had taken three months to get this appointment. And now, she was being shut out before he had a chance to try to help her?

"I do want to be in the program," Kate repeated, more firmly this time.

She leaned over to Matt. "I made a decision and you made a decision that we would come here," she said, her voice low.

"We're here," he said. "Now. I'm not questioning the validity of your program, Doctor, I'm just questioning this antibiotic."

Dr. Pitcarin closed his notebook. "You know, I don't have to be your wife's doctor," he said.

Kate felt deflated. She felt tears well up. "I can talk myself," she said.

Pitcarin frowned at Matt. "Look how you're starting my afternoon," he said, "with your wife crying in my office." He turned to Kate. "Mrs. Weil, I don't have to be your doctor."

"I want you to be. I want to be in your program."

Matt stood up. "Well, *I'm* not in your program."

Walking out of the brownstone office building, Matt fumed. "The man's irrational. He hasn't read the current literature. I don't know how Warneke could have recommended him."

"I feel terrible," Kate stormed. "But not because of that. Both of you practically ignored me! It was like I didn't exist!" She whirled upon Matt. They stood at the curb, glaring at each other. "Now I don't know what to do." Kate felt panicked. If she didn't go along with this doctor, would the endocrinologist drop her? Would the gynecologist absolve himself of responsibility? Would there be a doctor domino effect? She couldn't afford to start over. Every week she didn't get pregnant was another week lost. To choose the wrong approach, the incorrect doctor, the flawed treatment, was to choose childlessness. She didn't have the luxury of a misjudgment. Suddenly she hated the doctor, Matt, all of them, for putting her in this position.

"Kate, what good is my expertise if I can't use it to help you? To help us?" Matt rationalized. He was disgustingly calm.

"You are not my doctor. You are not a fertility specialist."

"Darling—" He gave the word the charm of a mouthful of chalk. "I just don't want to put you through something that will get your hopes up and waste your time. This antibiotic might not have been the right choice, that's all. Scientifically . . ."

She held up her hand. "I refuse to discuss it. Scientifically or otherwise, you were both assholes."

Kate had to drop off Matt's sperm sample at the lab. Matt's previous such activities had occurred in the clinical surroundings of the Sperm Store, but this time there was a special test of sperm motility which Matt joked involved attaching speedometers to the little guys and racing them around a track. Matt had an early appearance on the *Today* show to promote *Why Grow Old,* which had just come out in paperback, and couldn't leave the sample in person. A messenger service seemed ridiculous, so Kate had agreed to handle the errand.

"What do we use?" asked Matt.

"For what?"

"For the sample?"

"Oh, God. I have no idea."

They went to the kitchen. There were four black granite counters, forty linear feet of Poggenpohl cabinetry, a center island, a hanging rack of copper pots and bowls, every spice known to mankind—but no jars appropriate for five cc's of sperm.

Matt opened the refrigerator. "We could empty something out."

Kate pulled out a mayonnaise jar. They stared at it. No discussion was necessary to conclude that a mayonnaise jar was ridiculously oversized for five cc's.

"I have perfume bottles in the dressing room," said Kate.

"Too feminine." Matt started rummaging through the cabinets. "What if we had a son? We'd have to tell him he started life in a perfume bottle."

"Please."

"Caviar jar?"

"We'd have to throw out the caviar. What a waste. Here's an almost-empty wine bottle."

"Too narrow."

"You know what would be the exactly perfect size, except that we don't have one?"

"What?"

"A baby food jar."

By eight-thirty, Kate was on her way to the lab with the sample, which she carried in a cocktail olive jar that she had tucked into a Vuitton tote bag. She decided to walk to the lab and have her car meet her in front of the hospital. There had been a snow, and the trees along Central Park were tipped in white. Fifth Avenue was crowded with morning commuters as she purposefully wedged her way through the oncoming sidewalk traffic, so she barely noticed the man who ran into her full force, knocking her down to the icy pavement. Suddenly she felt a yank on her arm. The man grabbed her bag and raced off into the crowd, leaving Kate in a stunned heap on the ground.

"Lady, are you all right?" asked someone as a small group gathered. A hand reached down to help Kate to her feet.

"He got away," a woman said.

"He had a knife!" yelled a voice.

A uniformed policeman materialized. "Break it up, everybody," he said. "Now, ma'am, are you hurt?" he asked.

"No, I'm fine. Really. Just a run in my stocking," Kate said.

The policeman took out a pen and notebook. "Would you like to file a report? What exactly did the suspect take?"

"He took my bag with . . ." Kate started to laugh.

"Excuse me?"

She shook her head, laughing. "I'm sorry, Officer."

"Was anything of value in the bag?"

"Well, yes and no." She laughed so hard she slipped back onto the sidewalk. When she looked up, a huge, pregnant belly was standing over her.

"So are you going to help this lady up, or what?" shrieked the voice that belonged to the belly, berating the policeman into doing her bidding.

The pregnant woman had bleached-blond, frizzy hair and looked familiar. They stared at each other. "The sonogram waiting room," they said together.

"Angela."

"Kate."

"I'll handle this, Officer," said Angela, shoving him aside with her belly. She took Kate's arm. "Come with me, honey. You were getting hysterical. You need a cup of coffee. You're okay, aren't you?"

"I'm fine. They didn't take—much." *The hell with it,* she thought. "Well, actually, they took my husband's sperm sample."

Angela stared at her. "Was he insured?"

When they reached the hospital cafeteria, the two of them were still laughing.

"Congratulations," said Kate. "You did it."

"Yeah," said Angela. "Finally." She patted her belly.

"What was it—in vitro?"

"No, Club Med. Me and Stan took a vacation. It turned out I was four weeks along when I met you in the waiting room last fall. Wouldn't you know? They plugged me in, and there it was—the heartbeat. A fluke." Angela smiled happily. "How's it going with you?"

Kate shrugged. "Nothing yet. Just tests, and tests, and tests."

"Hey, it can get to you. I know. I've been there."

Kate felt relieved, as she had the first time she'd met Angela, to talk to someone who knew what it was like. "God, I think this can't be happening to me. There's no test I haven't had, no theory they haven't tried. And nothing."

"It gets to you," Angela said. "They get to the baboon one yet?"

"Not yet. What is it?"

"Well, some genius tried an experiment. They crowded all these baboons in one place, and they got all stressed out, and the females turned on each other and they didn't conceive."

"What did that theory prove?"

90

"Everyone should have a country house," snorted Angela. "How the hell should I know? It was just one more of their cockamamie theories. I heard them all, I tell you. Four years' worth. Four years of putting my life on hold. About lost my mind. You gotta forget all this bullshit and get on with your life. That's what this proves." She patted her stomach.

Kate stared enviously at Angela's belly. "Do you have a name?"

"Emily."

"Oh. That's—a name I like, too." She felt tears welling up.

Angela jumped to her side, spilling her coffee. "Jeez, I'm sorry, I'm really sorry. I shouldn't have mentioned the baby."

Kate blew her nose. "Believe me, I would have noticed."

"How's your business? You're a businesswoman, right?" Angela was trying to change the subject.

"I work at a magazine."

"Well, the salon business, it's up. In bad times, people want to look good. I don't know, maybe it's psychological. A frost and tip and a good manicure, and you forget all your problems. I can see it." She stared critically at Kate's hair. "You know, you could use a little lightening up. It would cheer you up, really. No offense, Kate—it is January, after all, and I can see you're the type that sunstreaks—but this color does not do you justice." Angela reached into her bag, pulled out a ring of hair swatches, and held it up to Kate's head. "Ash number twelve. That's what we have right now. Honey number three—now, that's where we should be." She nodded confidently. "Honey number three. I got some time this morning. What do you say you come back to the salon with me? It's just in Chelsea. You got a few hours? You'll feel like a new woman, I swear." She patted Kate's hand. "And while we're at it, we'll get rid of the headband."

Kate stirred her coffee. "Thank you, Angela. That's really very kind of you. I'd love to, but—well, I really have to get back to the office."

"They'll still be there, I promise."

Kate never let anyone but Christophe, who had done the hair of three First Ladies and more *Vogue* covers than anyone could count, touch her hair. For years, she had had the same smooth, pulled-back, coolly classic look. She caught her reflection in the window glass.

She was sick of it. She was sick of a lot of things. Before she could change her mind, Kate jumped up. "Angela, you are absolutely right. The office will still be there when I get back."

"Mrs. Weil, Mrs. Weil," Kate heard Stuart, her driver, call as she and Angela headed for the subway. She didn't turn her head. In a way, she felt like a rich kid on her way to school with a new friend, afraid her money would mark her as different. Right now, she was not Kate Harrison-Weil, publisher, or Kate Harrison-Weil, wife of Dr. Matthew Weil. She was just a woman, and it felt good for a change.

They went down the stairs to the subway, and Angela told Kate about her husband, who owned a grocery store, but had a low sperm count. "And as for me," she chortled, "they told me I had hostile mucus. Hostile mucus!" she yelled over the clatter of the subway. "Can you beat that with a stick?"

Kate laughed in spite of herself. "It's a haul taking all these trains," Angela continued. "The thing is, we got a great deal on the rent. And you get used to it." She shrugged. "New York."

Kate had forgotten what it was like to take the subway. When they got to the turnstile, of course she didn't have a token and she couldn't use her platinum card. She did have six one-hundred-dollar bills in her purse, but she hesitated to pull them out. It seemed pretentious, given Angela's modest raincoat that barely closed around her bulging belly.

Angela shot her a sympathetic look. "No change, huh?" The tone of her voice suggested she thought Kate couldn't afford the fare. She dropped two tokens into the slot. "Be my guest."

It was noisy on the subway platform, but Angela's voice pierced through the din. "You know, honey, I don't know what Stan and me would have done if we weren't in the test program. But, I mean, who can afford it? Five thousand here, eight thousand there . . . I was just plain lucky. I had a customer whose husband was in the construction business, and he was remodeling this doctor's office in midtown, and he was a fertility specialist. This was after Stan and me had been trying to get pregnant for three years. We even tried to adopt, but there was a five-year waiting list just to get on the waiting list!"

The train rolled up to the platform and Kate followed Angela as she elbowed her way on. "You sit," Angela said. "You've had a lousy day. Anyhow," she continued, "I go to see this specialist, Dr. Burkholt, and he takes me on as part of a control group in the hospital experiment. And believe me, it wasn't *voilà*, I'm pregnant. It was a haul. If we'd had to pay full price for that . . ." Angela shook her head. "You in a program?"

Kate didn't know what to answer. She didn't want to make the woman feel inferior. "Sort of," she said.

At Grand Central Station, they changed to the crosstown shuttle to Times Square, where they changed again to the Number One downtown to Twenty-third Street.

"Only six more blocks," huffed Angela as she led the way upstairs to the street.

The Pink Scissors was indeed pink. One ground-floor room of a brownstone done, or overdone, as Kate observed, completely in pink. The walls were pink vinyl, the two basins were pink, the floors pink linoleum with a pink fuzzy bathroom-style rug flanking a fireplace. A turquoise love seat provided the single accent color.

"It's so . . . pink," said Kate.

"Pink is the most feminine color," Angela said, nodding. "My customers love it. It makes them feel like they're in a spa." She struggled out of her coat, refusing Kate's assistance. "Herbal tea?" she offered. "Mineral water? There's a kitchen." Angela pulled open a folding door and flicked on an electric kettle. Then, bending over with difficulty, she lit a small fire, using crumpled beauty magazines as kindling.

It was a strange place, but somehow Kate did not feel uncomfortable. In fact, she felt relaxed. She didn't have to prove anything to Angela. They were just two women who had shared an experience that no outsider could ever understand. It was a relief to sit in front of the little fire with a warm cup of mint tea and listen to another woman say exactly what you thought. For Kate, it was a validation, an exoneration.

Angela flipped through her haircolor swatches. They looked

like scalps on a key ring. "For a long time," she said, "I thought I was losing it. I yelled at Stan every time he turned around. I blew a bridal manicure—had to repolish the whole wedding party. The bride was hysterical; it was awful. I started crying. God, what a day. This went on for like a year. Stan—he hated the whole thing. They made him watch a video, *Your Sperm and You* or some such shit. He almost killed me. We almost killed each other." She nodded emphatically at a hair swatch. "Yes! That's it! *This* is your color."

It had been years since Kate had had her hair restyled. One of the things she liked about Christophe was that he never changed it. "Angela," she said, "I'm not sure I'm ready for this."

"Sure you are, honey." She flipped open a hair magazine with Madonna on the cover and pointed to a short, tousled style with long bangs that almost hid the eyes. "You're ready for this."

Kate had to admit, it was a fabulous style—if this Angela person could pull it off. Angela stood up, pulled off Kate's headband, and piled and rearranged her hair on top of her head. She propelled Kate to the mirror. *I will look like a soufflé,* she thought. But there was something in the moment. Something Kate no longer accepted about herself that she was ready to change.

"Go for it," said Angela.

Kate bit her lip. "Okay," she said. "I will."

Angela took Kate's coat and stroked the navy-blue sheared mink lining. "Almost like real fur," she said admiringly. Kate slipped off her jacket and blouse, and Angela spread a pink smock over her shoulders.

"It really changes things, doesn't it?" Angela said. "The Baby Game."

"Yes it does. It does. I thought it would be such a happy decision. But there has just been one problem after another. I suppose I really have no right to complain, but . . ."

"That's just it. Lean back over the sink here, honey—that's a girl. To their minds, you have no right to anything. I'm one of the lucky ones. Wasn't easy, I tell you. All we did was fight. Blame each other."

"I blame myself." The water was rushing over Kate's head,

swishing across her scalp, and Angela was massaging in the lather. Kate stared at the pink ceiling. It didn't feel like she was in a real place, doing a real thing. She felt like she was in a scene, playing the role of herself, and somehow that made it easier to talk, to let the words run out as the water ran through her hair. "It's my fault."

Angela patted her hair vigorously with a huge pink towel. "Now you stop that! Get up and get into this chair by the mirror. It's nobody's fault, don't you know that?" She mixed a creamy white powder in a little glass bowl. With a brush, she started applying it to Kate's hair, sectioning off a few pieces at a time with a rat-tail comb and wrapping the sections in tinfoil squares. "I thought it was my fault, too, for a long time. Ha!" She bumped the chair with her belly. "Turned out, Stan had a low count, needed a tune-up. But it's not his fault, either. This is a no-fault state." Her laugh was somewhere between a whistle and a snort. "Can you beat it?"

"Well, I feel like I had my chance once and blew it," Kate said, watching but not seeing as more strips of tinfoil accumulated on her head. "I had an abortion." *There.* She had said it. The thing that had been in the shadows. Until recently, Kate had managed to give the abortion the emphasis of, say, a moving violation— a serious problem to be handled at the time, but thereafter worthy of only sporadic memory attention. The fact that she could no longer conceive made it something she preferred to remember even less. But at times she couldn't fend off the bitter irony of having to deal with an unwanted pregnancy, then not being able to conceive a few years later.

It felt good to finally tell someone. No one knew; no one had ever known. Not CeCe. Not Matt. Not Janet. Nobody. She could only tell a stranger.

At the time, it had seemed the best thing to do. She had felt unready. She had wanted to stabilize her relationship with Matt. It was too soon to tell him, because she knew he would have insisted on marrying her right then, on having the baby. But that hadn't been her plan.

Her plan, her stupid plan.

"Well," said Angela. "You had your reasons. A woman does.

95

Stop beating yourself up, honey. If it was meant to be, it'll be. That much I'm sure of."

"I wish I had your confidence, Angela."

"Ten minutes under the dryer."

As the hot air hummed around her, Kate felt drugged by the smell of the bleach. She sat there in a stupor until Angela retrieved her.

"Let's rinse you out."

Kate could hear the tinfoil hitting the porcelain as Angela pulled the little squares off and dropped them into the sink.

"Perfect. Honey blond number three is a real pick-me-up. You'll see."

She guided Kate back to the chair and picked up the scissors and a wide-tooth comb. Big chunks of hair fell to the floor, but Kate did not feel as if they were hers. She felt like the long-haired doll she had given Kim—an object to be experimented on.

"You know," Kate said, "the ironic thing is, I always used birth control."

"Yeah," said Angela. "We all thought we'd get pregnant if we did it just once in the back seat of the car. That was all it took. Everybody knew."

Angela ruffled Kate's hair, or what was left of it, with her hands. "Hey, check it out, ba-by."

Kate looked: blond. Very blond. Thick bangs, layered. No hair over the ears. A long nape to her neck. She looked like an eighteen-year-old who'd just gotten out of the pool.

Angela waved the blow dryer and yelled over its whine. "Just wash and wear, honey. That's the key. You look to die for."

Kate felt the flutter of her new bangs on her forehead. Her hair was dry in three minutes. That was one plus.

Angela whipped off the smock. "*Voilà!* Get on your red dress, baby, 'cause you're goin' out tonight."

Kate found herself face-to-face with Angela's belly as she turned the chair for a back view of the haircut. "Angela, how does it feel?" she asked.

"Truth?"

"Truth."

Angela took a breath. "Like there's just me and the baby. We're in this together. I know, Stan's his dad, but he's mine. My own personal bargain with God." She hugged her belly.

Kate nodded. She would feel the same way. How often in the past long, dragging months had she tried to bargain? *Please, God, if you just give me a baby I will use environmentally biodegradable diapers/call my mother once a week/give up red meat/ real fur/make up for all the bad things I have ever done by being the world's most perfect mother.* The mantra varied, but, as much as Kate told Matt that it was *their* struggle, she felt that it was *hers.* Her hormones. Her ovaries. Her problems. And if it happened, it would be her baby. She understood.

"Call me any time. We can get together, just talk." Angela put her hand on Kate's arm.

"I'd like that," Kate said, and she meant it. "The hair, how much?"

"My treat. On the house."

Kate reached for her purse.

"No. Please. Let me. It's how I can help." Angela's eyes were soft. "I got lucky. I'm paying it back," she said, with a smile.

Kate put on her coat. In the mirror, she caught a glimpse of a blond girl. The shadows were gone from under her eyes.

"Thank you."

"See you soon, Kate. Take care."

"You too, Angela. When are you due?"

"Ten weeks."

"Great. Call me. I'm so excited for you."

"I will, honey. Gotta run." She gave Kate a thumbs-up. "Come back for a bikini wax and a manicure."

On the way down the front steps of the building, Kate felt the wind on the back of her neck for the first time in years.

"Is that a wig?" Matt stared at Kate's hair. His hand was poised in midair over the fish tank. Every night, he fed them a mixture of brine shrimp and pellets of various buoyancies. The heavier foods fell to the bottom, the lighter ones floated, so the fish that patrolled the different levels of the tank each had their special food.

"No. It's not a wig. Would you like it to be?"

He tossed in the pellets and shook his head. "It doesn't look like you."

"Exactly. That's why I like it." Why was she feeling defensive? At the office she'd convinced herself that the new hairstyle would somehow change things, irrational though that may have been. Now, in an instant, she knew that no matter what she changed, Matt would hate it, simply because it was, in fact, change. Did she give Matt too little or too much credit? Kate wasn't sure.

"I met a woman. She cut my hair. She had a shop in Chelsea. I guess I was in the mood. Don't you like it?"

"It's not a matter of liking it or not—it's just so—different."

"I thought a change would be nice." She turned around, showing him the back.

"It's short, too."

Kate circled the room, like the fish swimming in their tank. "She was a woman in the in vitro program who was pregnant. It was really so interesting. We'd been through the same things. This morning—I forgot to tell you—I was mugged. Someone stole my bag. She helped me."

"What! Why didn't you call me at the office?"

"Well, I'm fine, as you can see. They got the sperm, though."

"For God's sake. What would they want with the sperm?"

"I don't know—it was just in my bag. It's not like he pulled a gun and said, 'Your husband's sperm or your life.' "

"He didn't hurt you?"

"No, not at all. I fell down, but I wasn't hurt. The thing is, I found myself talking to this woman . . ."

"Maybe we should call the police."

"The police were there. I didn't fill out a report because I couldn't figure out the value of the sperm. The thing is, this woman, Angela, owns a beauty salon. We got to talking, and one thing led to another, and, well, voilà."

Kate leaned against the smooth, polished surface of the grand piano that no one knew how to play. They'd bought it at auction, thinking they could use a piano player at parties, but it had been so long since they'd had a party. So long since they'd done anything but live their day-to-day lives and Try to Get Pregnant. "Angela understood what we've been going through," she said.

Matt reacted as if Kate had just phoned the *National Enquirer* with an exclusive. "You told a complete stranger about our lives? What's gotten into you, Kate?"

"Actually, Matt, she has no real idea who we even are, but I didn't have to tell her about us. She knew. It took her four years to get pregnant. She had hostile mucus, and her husband had a low sperm count."

"Jesus Christ! I certainly hope you didn't discuss our sex lives with a stranger!" Matt rubbed his forehead.

"I told her about *me*. About how hard it's been, and about the abortion." Kate stopped abruptly. Had she meant for that to slip out? Was this a subconscious mistake, or was she finally ready to stop carrying the burden alone? A little of both, she supposed. She stood absolutely still, waiting.

The room was silent, except for the sounds of the fish tank, which bubbled like a pot simmering on a stove. Kate and Matt looked at each other across the space.

"Kate, what . . . abortion." It was a statement, not a question.

"I had an abortion," she said quietly. "Before we got married. When we first started going out. I—couldn't tell you."

"And why not?" Matt barely moved, only his lips adjusted enough to speak.

"It didn't seem important at the time. I didn't want to pressure you."

"*Pressure* me? *Pressure me?* So instead you lied to me? And told a woman you met on the street?"

"I never lied to you." It had been a mistake to tell him, a horrible mistake, but there was no going back.

"Well, you omitted certain facts. Like the fact that you have been pregnant, by me, that we conceived a child—and here we have both been going through how many months of torture trying now to do just that, and I've been feeling like I failed you, and you let me, and I only knew half of the story! You, of course, knew the whole story, but you didn't care to share it with me. For reasons of your own, which, I am sure, you are about to explain."

"Oh, Matt, there is no explanation. The abortion—well, at the time, it didn't seem like a big decision; it seemed like we had forever to have a child, if we even wanted one, and we didn't know then that we would. We barely knew each other! I couldn't have predicted this. Nobody could have. I never meant to not tell you. It just happened that way. At first, it was so premature. I thought you'd think I was irresponsible, or, at worst, that I tricked you. I knew how important your family was to you. I didn't want you to think I used that in our relationship. Then, as time passed, there never was a right moment." She knew she had been right not to tell him about the abortion at the time. He would have reacted like this. His instinct would have been to reject her, but his sense of responsibility and family would not have permitted it. He would have felt backed into a corner. He would have resented the child and hated her. Yes, she had done the right thing. At the time. But more time and circumstances had destroyed that perspective. Kate knew that there would never have been a "right" decision. She had done what she'd *had* to do. As she was doing now.

"In all these months and years there was never a right moment?" He looked incredulous. "Please, Kate, you're insulting my intelligence. You have to face yourself, Kate, and face me, too. You're incredibly selfish. You don't share—you demand. I thought we had a partnership. Obviously, I was wrong." He knotted his hands in frustration, cracking the knuckles.

Kate raked her nails through her hair. "I don't know—I just can't get through to you anymore. You're unapproachable."

Matt walked over to her quickly and grabbed her arm, his thumbs digging into the flesh. "Listen, damn it, we made a decision—"

"Let go of me!" She wrenched her arm away.

"We made a decision together to have a child. And when you had a problem—"

"*We* had a problem."

"I wonder. Maybe this abortion caused it. We'll never know. Maybe that would have been our only chance."

Kate felt stunned, as if she'd walked into the blunt end of a club. "You think that hasn't crossed my mind a thousand times?" she whispered. "You think I don't agonize about it over and over? But we have to move forward, not look back. What good will it do to live in the past?"

He turned on her, furious. "I'm not saying it's good, bad, or indifferent. I'm saying I didn't get my chance to be part of it. You shut me out. And now, you're making me feel like less of a man—"

"I never!"

"Less of a man because I can't give you a child now! A sperm factory. When all along, of course, I had already given you a child. But I'm apparently the only one who didn't know it."

"I never told anyone. Nobody."

"Except a perfect stranger." He grimaced.

"I'm not saying anything about you being a man or not a man. I'm saying—"

"Oh? Real men have sex with plastic cups and olive jars? Real men do it according to the calendar?"

"This is ridiculous." She turned away. "We can't discuss this now."

He followed her, ranting. "Oh, right. Not now, maybe never. You know, maybe our problem is that we didn't discuss things enough. I thought: she needs to do it this way. It's her decision. It's her body." His voice taunted. "Not that I agreed. It wasn't enough to have Gregory and Kim and our careers and this show-place apartment. It wasn't enough to relax and enjoy what we had. Well, it was enough for one of us, Ms. Hyphenated Weil. But not for you."

"No. No it wasn't. Not quite enough. Almost, but not quite." She was breathing shallowly, in little gasps, hyperventilating.

A bolt of anger singed every nerve ending in Kate's body. *Damn him.* It was somehow always her fault. Her fault she couldn't get pregnant. Her fault she got pregnant and it wasn't the right time. Her fault that she'd had to bear not a child but the weight of a pregnancy that she had chosen to terminate. Her fault for what could have been. "Try to understand my position," she said, grabbing his sleeve. "I refuse to spend the rest of my life crawling on my knees, atoning for something that was a decision I felt I had to make at a certain point in time. I admit, it might not have been, in retrospect, the best decision, or even the right one. I admit, if I'd had a crystal ball, I would have done things differently. All right! I know it was a mistake not to tell you. But it was a decision I felt was right at the time." By now, she was shivering with the knowledge that something horrible was happening.

Matt picked up the fish food and started tossing pellets into the tank.

"Pretty, aren't they, but really stupid. Amazing, isn't it, how even the dumbest creatures can have what we can't. They live, they procreate, they die. So simple. No choices to make, except which part of the tank to float in." He turned to Kate, his face taut. "It's just as well, I suppose," he said bitterly. "I mean, look at how you act with Gregory and Kim. What kind of mother would you be?"

Kate felt faint, as if she might keel over. Well, what if she did? Matt was a doctor. She needed a doctor now, someone who could perform a Life Transplant, a SWAT Team of Fates who could fly into the room with another life in a refrigerated chest, and a specialist who could sever her from the room and hook her up to a different time, place, and circumstance.

"You are a total bastard," she said. Now she was furious. She wanted to hurt him. She grabbed a crystal-and-silver decanter from the desk top and heaved it in Matt's general direction. Usually, Kate could not even hit the wastebasket with the Sunday *New York Times,* but, this time, she watched the scene turn to slow motion as the decanter spiked across the room and smashed a direct hit into the side of the coral reef tank. She stood there as the entire fifteen-foot front of the tank caved in and a miniature tidal wave cascaded onto the floor, coral and anemones and myriads of tiny rainbow-colored fish flopping onto the carpet.

After a stunned moment, both Matt and Kate rushed to rescue the fish, but you couldn't give tropical fish CPR, and Kate knew that it wouldn't matter what they did or how much they tried— they would not survive.

After the broken glass had been soaked up from the ebony-and-brass-inlaid floor with the wet-vac, the salt water had been wrung out of the antique Kilim rugs, and several schools of dead fish had been flushed to their hasty, Sherle Wagner burials, Kate found herself no less angry at Matt. She felt driven to push, to thrust, to stab herself against him, to punish him physically as if to say, *There! Let me hurt you another way, one you cannot deny, one which forces a response.* Her teeth gouged across his shoulders and back until she licked the metallic taste of blood, the angular joints of her knees gouged against his thighs, her fingernails broke the skin. She pummeled at him and against him as he shoved her roughly upright against the wall, and they made love—or its flip side, hate—pounding against the seventeen coats of burnished red lacquer, Kate's head banging against the wall as he crushed her cheekbones into his chest, her spine beating against the plaster as he invaded her body over and over again.

The next morning, in the shower, the pelting water stung Kate's lips, regenerating neon images of the night before. She felt like a survivor of a head-on collision. The fact was that neither of them had the strength to forgive the other—their emotions had been too far depleted, and there was no way to regenerate them now.

At a time in her life when she cried if she didn't like the sound of her shoe size, Kate found she couldn't cry now, when she most needed to. She wanted to mourn the absence of her fertility, the strangulation of her marriage, the disillusionment of her career; but the shower had to be her tears. She rubbed her short, feathery hair. She felt like a hatchling; she felt new.

She walked into the bedroom, wrapped in a robe, her hair wet. "I want a divorce," she said.

It was a separation of resentment. Not over property—neither Kate nor Matt wanted anything but release from the apartment and its baggage. Each of them resented the other's activities too much to compromise or negotiate. The break was complete, but not clean. Too much was left unspoken, but they were both too hurt to bridge the gap.

When they married, Kate had been convinced that nothing could shake her faith in Matt. In the end, she now supposed, it had been the very elements of that faith that had destroyed it.

If she loved Matt because he was strong, dependable, and consistent, could she now leave him because he had acted in character? She knew, had always known, how he would react ... to the abortion, certainly, and to any perceived undermining of his role as a parent, or, in the case of their fertility quest, his inability to be one. Was she surprised? No. And so, in a way, Kate blamed herself, because, she reasoned, if Matt could only react this way, and she had known it, it must have been her fault that the marriage failed. Because she, Kate, was the one who backed him into the corner, with no way out.

Kate debated this with herself, in those evenings when she came home from work late, then ordered out Chinese and picked at it in bed, while Matt slept alone in the guest room. It made her want to get out all the more.

There was nothing about being alone that frightened Kate. "After all," she told CeCe as they waited on the steps of a West Side brownstone to meet one Mrs. Swope, a highly recommended real estate agent, "I've been single about twenty times longer than I've been married."

CeCe eyed her suspiciously. "I'm not sure if I'm buying that," she said. She frowned as she looked down the street, where what looked like an unsavory gang was gathered at the corner.

The real estate agent appeared. She was a small, brown-haired woman in a purple silk raincoat, lugging a notebook stuffed with floor plans. "I have five things we can look at today," she announced. "You said you liked vintage, so this is a good place to start." With a shrug, she dismissed the dreadlocked gang at the corner: "Changing neighborhood. Princess Yasmin Khan bought at the other end of the block." She struggled with the key, wrenched open the wrought-iron door, and they started up the stairs.

The decision to move out of the penthouse had been easy for Kate. Matt had offered to move out—to someplace within finger-snapping distance of Elise and the Kids from Hell, she supposed—but Kate recoiled at coming home every day to a rambling, lonely apartment with the empty nursery and its gaping crib. At this point, they both were interested in numbing the pain of the past few months.

The apartment in the brownstone was up three flights, and by the time they reached the front door, Mrs. Swope was panting. "I know it has no elevator, but there are other advantages, as you will see." She pretended that she was not having difficulty breathing.

A heavy, carved wood door swung open. Inside was a double-height foyer with a huge curved staircase of the same carved wood as the door. A two-tiered brass chandelier hung from the ceiling.

"Now this is city living," said CeCe.

To the left was a large living room with a fireplace and painted tin ceiling. Windows edged in stained glass overlooked a small garden, and Kate could see a tiny, high-ceilinged kitchen with pot racks and a garden view. She wandered down the hall to two sunny bedrooms on opposite sides of the hall. One had a large loft, which was lined in bookshelves. The master bedroom had a tiny dressing room and a fireplace.

"It's fine," she told Mrs. Swope. "How long is the lease?"

"Kate!" said CeCe disapprovingly. "You haven't even looked around. You can't rent the first place you see."

Kate pulled out her checkbook. "How much would they want for a deposit?" The apartment had a warm, welcoming feel, the opposite, she felt, of the huge, imposing co-op. It was like a tiny wedge of a wonderful town-house hotel she'd stayed in once in London, just off Sloane Square. Besides, Kate thought, she did not have the stamina to chase down sixty apartments—a feat not unheard of in New York City. This one was fine. True, it was small, but she could turn the second bedroom into an at-home office and move in her books, computer, and reading couch. The closet space was minuscule, but there was room for her custom armoires in the dressing room. She planned to get rid of most of her lingerie, regardless; it was a throwback to a past life. Wearing lace garter belts now seemed ridiculous. There was nothing remotely comparable to Kate's penthouse terrace, but there was a stairway to a small garden outside the kitchen. Maybe she would grow herbs, get a dog. She envisioned pine furniture, reading in front of the fire. And, actually, she wanted to get as far away from Fifth Avenue as possible in feeling, if not geography.

She would go back to the penthouse and leave word for Matt that she had found a place. She didn't want the furniture, the money, the bad memories. She just wanted to nurse her wounds and readjust to being single and—probably forever, she realized—childless.

"You know," Kate said as she filled out the application for the lease, "it was for the best that I never got pregnant. What if I had a child to worry about? What a scene that would be. I'm going to be working like a slave for at least a year, regardless. This is as good a place to live as any."

"There's no doorman," CeCe warned. "And no elevator."

"Well, I can get groceries delivered, and, besides, when there's just yourself to worry about, life is a lot less complicated. I'll manage fine." Kate was making close to a half-million dollars a year; she could afford almost any apartment in the city, but that wasn't the point. Stripping down symbolized starting over, and she *wanted* to start over, unweighted by life and possessions, erasing the past by surrounding herself with the signs of a future to be filled. She was through with limos and doormen, with live-in housekeepers. It was going to feel good to go back to having everything the way she wanted it, with no one else to account to. If she wanted to eat popcorn in bed at two A.M., viewing old black-and-white movies on the television, there would be no one to tell her to watch in the library. If she wanted to sleep through dinner and leave her stockings on the floor, no one would complain. If she didn't want to come home at all, who would know? That was the up-side of separating, and she wanted to focus on the positive. Kate was determined to handle her divorce better than she had her marriage. This lovely little apartment was the first step. "How much is the security deposit?" she asked.

Seven

Kate's first action after coming on board at *Finance* was to repack her tea set and have it sent home to her new apartment. She had brought the tea set, along with the Biedermeier furniture, from her office at *Childstyle* while she was under the illusion that certain of her rituals had a welcome individuality. That myth was quickly dispelled. The *Finance* offices consciously resembled a set designer's version of a corporate board room. The only feminine touch Kate had been able to detect was the sign for the ladies' room. Even the basket of balloons and candy kisses the staff at *Childstyle* had sent to welcome Kate to her new job seemed out of place, as if color and gaiety were unwelcome intruders. You could have heard a pin drop in the halls, if the carpet had not been so thick. There was no laughter, no music, no air. Since all of her negotiations with Stanton Welch had taken place confidentially off-premises, Kate had never actually seen the offices. The best word to describe them was *brown*. Tobacco-brown walls, carpets, and draperies. Tobacco-brown logo. Tobacco-brown upholstery. All of which blended harmoniously with the pervasive smell of cigar smoke. Cigars and suspenders were a tradition at *Finance,* a standard set by Guardino and perpetuated down the ranks. The place was like a men's club. In fact, Kate saw almost no women, period, except behind word processors.

Tea and sympathy were clearly not the way to make points with this group, Kate could see. Her first lunch meeting with the senior staff had made that clear. The meeting was held in the *Finance* staff dining room, a mahogany-paneled institution notable for its white linen tablecloths and tuxedoed waiters, modeled after the partners' dining room at an investment bank. Guardino had treated Kate not so much like an interloper as a trainee. Taking their cues from Guardino were Al Fitzgerald, a man with a Ben Bradlee complex who had been managing editor for at least a decade, and Phil Moran, a promotion director whose primary asset was his golf handicap.

"Let me explain advertising-to-editorial ratio to you, Kate," Phil had said condescendingly, as if Kate were in the front row of Magazine Publishing 101.

"Thank you, but that won't be necessary. I am familiar with the desirable ratios. The business principles really don't differ from one magazine to the next," she had said. "The key thing is that we bring in some new advertisers, expand our base. I was thinking about the major automotive people—like GM."

"I have a golf game with Tenley from GM next week, matter of fact." He signaled a waiter, who appeared with a polished wooden box brimming with expensive cigars, and pulled out a handful, as did every man at the table. That explained the twenty-thousand-dollar line item for cigars that Kate had noticed on the annual operating expense budget. No wonder they were having financial problems. She made a mental note.

"Wonderful," she said. Mike Tenley was tough to get to, and he was the one person who could green-light her cross-merchandising concept. "I'd like to come along."

Phil stared at her. "Come? Along?"

"We can get together a foursome, can't we? I actually play pretty well, believe it or not. Of course, it's been a while since I played . . ."

The three men looked at her as if she were suggesting a trip to Atlantis.

"Well, Kate, there could be difficulties," said Phil, coughing.

Guardino muffled a snort.

Kate drilled him with her Terminator look. "I have an eight handicap," she said. It wasn't true, but she dared him to challenge her. She hated the shell game of male bonding.

Guardino broke in. "The thing is, Kate, I believe Phil is taking Tenley to Elm Valley." He lit his cigar and puffed heartfully.

Kate knew Elm Valley. It was one of the finest golf clubs in the country—and it did not allow women. There was no getting around this. Archaic as it was, reality was reality. "Oh. Well. I see. Let's try to contact Tenley and relocate the outing to Pebble Beach, then." Of course, no such effort would follow, she knew. Just a pabulum excuse of "too late to change plans." But at least she had made her point.

Guardino and Moran were not going to lay any pipe for her, that much was clear. If she made any headway, Kate was going to have to make it herself. The thing that was the most irritating was how much business was propelled not by real work and opportunity but by male bonding. Kate's previous experience had prepared her to handle every creative and business aspect of her work with total finesse, but she was less prepared to take on the good old boys. Had she been sheltered at *Childstyle* from the realities of the business world? There, recognition was measured by merit of work well done, not by birdies and eagles. Kate could see she had some adjustments to make.

She'd crashed through the glass ceiling and landed smack in the middle of the Old Boy Network. No wonder Guardino had not seemed threatened. The fact that he was now reporting to Kate was simply something on a piece of paper. The man was clearly entrenched, and, as he was well aware, relationships with key existing advertisers made him next to impossible to dislodge. Stanton Welch had given Kate her title, but she knew she'd have to earn the actual power.

This was not an insurmountable problem to Kate, who had never been the type to shy away from breaking new ground. And, after all, her job at *Finance,* she and Stanton agreed, was to open the windows and let out the stale cigar smoke, to perform the Heimlich maneuver on the magazine and give it new life via the younger market.

Once Stanton had given Kate the go-ahead, she had spent the next four weeks formulating her plans and roughing out the creative direction she had in mind, including laying out sample spreads and plotting a year's worth of editorial. After thoroughly reading the bios of everyone on the staff, Kate had realized there would be no immediate allies except Hal Radia, who had come with her to *Finance.* Even the one woman in a staff position could not be counted on. In Kate's experience, senior women who had fought their way to the top were rarely eager to risk their hard-won turf. Kate convinced herself: if she had to be one of the boys to win them over, she could play hardball with the best of them.

At her farewell party, Kate had felt sad and nostalgic. *Childstyle* had been her family for ten years—it was hard to leave. But she still had her stock. And with Margo moving up, she was convinced she had left her creation in good hands. It did feel strange to go from a day-care-center atmosphere to a men's club, but Kate welcomed the escape from the pressure cooker of the Baby Game.

She missed Matt, but she pushed those feelings aside. Those feelings were emotional parasites that sucked her dry, when she needed all her resources to move ahead. The fact was, Kate tried to convince herself, she could barely remember what their relationship had been like before they started trying to have a child. When she closed her eyes to conjure up a memory of her husband, her mind could only dish up a cacophony of calendars, sonograms, petri dishes, and the ubiquitous plastic cups. What a relief not to have to live by the calendar, not to have a hormone injection every day. What a relief not to fight about something that made you feel so intolerably vulnerable; how soothing not to have a scab that was picked open every day.

"How's Matt holding up?" CeCe had asked.

"We don't communicate much."

"That's too bad, if you don't mind my saying so. You'd probably be better off if you did talk, rather than keep it pent up inside."

"I don't think we have anything to discuss," Kate said sadly. "It didn't work out. Raking things over the coals won't help now. You know, in retrospect I think his children were always more important to him than I was. Now those kids can have him all to themselves. They deserve each other."

God, I just want to get on with my life, she thought. But it was harder to do than she had imagined. She pulled herself together and walked to the conference room for the editorial meeting.

Everyone was waiting. Guardino sat at the head of the table, shirtsleeves rolled to the elbow, puffing the cigar that seemed attached to his lip. Flanking him was Phil Moran. Hal Radia was at the center, next to the only other woman in the room— Jean Sherman, from public relations. The men stood when Kate walked in. She had met them before, at the lunch Stanton Welch had held at the Four Seasons to announce her new position.

"Hello, everyone," she said. "I know what many of you must be thinking—what is she doing here, and how is that going to impact on my job. Well, the good news is, we're all here in this room today for the same reason—we want to see *Finance* back at the top where it belongs. Is there anyone in the room who doesn't share this vision? Good. We're going to be a terrific team, I can see that. The opportunity for all of us here is the exciting changes we are about to undertake."

At the word *change,* uncomfortable glances rippled through the room. Kate and Hal exchanged a quick look.

"That's right. Change is never easy. I don't promise any easy business here. But change we will, if that's what it takes to capture this market." Kate held up the current cover. "Let's start with appearances. This cover is all type." She gestured to the framed gallery of past covers, which lined the room like trophies. Every one looked alike—smothered in small print. No color. No splash.

"Our cover is supposed to remind the reader of an annual report, Kate," said Fitzgerald. "That's how annual reports look."

"Yes, I'm aware of how annual reports look, but as of today . . ." She held up a new cover mock-up, which she'd had designed by the German art director she'd used once for *Childstyle.* It was sleek, metallic silver, with a huge reverse supergraphic headline: CASH AND CARRY. There was a strip of four-color photos in

111

montage that featured Edward Carry, the CEO of Omnibank, who was currently making headlines with his new scheme for a global credit card.

"Kate, pardon me," said Guardino, standing. "But you've got to be kidding. This guy Carry, he's a nouveau bozo. Fluff. Not our style at all. This thing just isn't *Finance*."

Kate shook her head. "This is our new style, and I can assure you we will all grow into it. This is a cover that sells. *Finance* can no longer afford to be a textbook full of mouse type on obscure technical issues for a few investment bankers to read. A cover like this will broaden our readership base." She played her trump card. "Stanton Welch has already approved this design. We are targeting for the younger, affluent market, and this is the kind of vehicle that will capture them."

Kate sounded confident, but she knew she was out on a limb. She had showed up at the first meeting with a big stick and had bludgeoned their sacred cow to death with it.

"Now, Kate," said Guardino unctuously, reaching across the conference table for the prototype. "This sure is pretty, no question. Real slick-looking. Nice paper stock. But if we do something this radical, our current readers aren't even gonna recognize us on the newsstands. If we back up and look at this here thing, I have to believe we can accomplish a lot more by cutting some rate deals."

Kate leaned forward and put her palms on the conference table. "I disagree. We shouldn't devalue the product."

"Everybody cuts rates," barked Guardino.

All heads at the conference table pivoted back and forth, from Guardino to Kate, as if a sudden-death tennis match were taking place on the conference table.

"We don't cut rates. Not anymore." Kate stabbed the air with her pen. "It hasn't helped so far. To continue on this rate strategy would be like rearranging deck chairs on the *Titanic*. And once we have a new format, I believe we are going to have to expand our advertising horizons."

Guardino rolled his eyes. Phil smirked.

Kate had anticipated this. Guardino would resist any threat to his power base, the existing advertisers. Of course the magazine couldn't survive without advertisers. Kate had had an inspiration—change the entire advertising structure by converting to individually sponsored issues. The existing advertisers weren't paying the freight, regardless. Kate unveiled her new concept.

"I propose we convert *Finance* to one sponsor per issue. A sponsor would buy out an entire issue, editorially directed toward the sponsor's interests or goals. Each issue would be themed. The credit issue, for instance, is perfect for Edward Carry and Omnibank. We could have a real estate issue sponsored by a major national realtor. An automotive issue sponsored by Mercedes-Benz. It could work beautifully, plus cut the hassle of selling a million quarter-page ads."

"Quarter-pages pay the bills," said Phil. "Besides, sponsoring an entire issue would be a giant stretch for any advertiser. How're we gonna squeeze that kind of weight out of guys who won't even spring for four-color? You gotta be nuts to even try. I mean, they gotta be nuts, not you, Kate. No offense, but it's not gonna fly."

"Kate, *Kate,*" said Guardino, shaking his head mournfully, as if she had just ordered her own execution.

The others simply looked as if she had suggested practicing witchcraft, except for Jean, who stared at the tabletop, and Hal, who nodded enthusiastically. Kate was stunned. She hadn't expected such an across-the-board hostile response. Stanton had been right—this group would have to be dragged kicking and screaming into the nineties.

"We're going to have to make a major effort to create a convincing presence for prospective advertisers." Kate passed out a Xeroxed timetable. "I've broken this down into goals and dates for each of your departments. After everybody's had a chance to digest this, we'll talk again. I don't want to take up too much of your time before you've had a chance to think this through. I'll try to meet individually with each of you in the next weeks so we can go over your plans more specifically. We'll start with editorial. Jim, can we set something up as soon as possible? I'd like your input on the in-depth profile of Edward Carry."

She wondered if Jim Jacobs would quit. He had been with the magazine for fifteen years and was largely responsible for the annual report format. Kate was prepared to lose some dead-wood, but she hoped she could hang on to Jacobs, who was a known name in the field of financial reporting. Jacobs nodded. "I hope we can all be open-minded about this," he said dryly. Then he smiled. "I kind of like it, myself. I'd love a chance to put this guy Carry on the couch." He chuckled. "Just like the old days on the Front Page, kids."

Kate arched her eyebrows in surprise. Guardino may have been hamstringing Jacobs. The man was a bulldog, chomping to get back into the fray.

The cigar smoke in the room was stifling, the odor dense and clinging. Suddenly Kate felt that she had to leave the room to get some fresh air. She nodded to the group and forced herself to walk, not run, out of the room.

In the ladies' room, Kate found herself breaking into a cold sweat. Rivulets were running down her chest, under her blouse. She felt faint and woozy. It was almost lunchtime, and she had skipped breakfast. Her stomach must be rebelling, she decided. But the thought of food made her gag. She sat on a toilet seat with her head in her hands. This was ridiculous! It must be the pressure of the first week on a new job. She willed herself to feel better—this was no time to let this kind of thing slow her down.

The rest of the day was a blur of meetings and appointments. At seven forty-five, Kate took a radio car home. The stairs to her new apartment seemed unusually steep that night, and when she finally reached the third floor, she was exhausted. Maybe CeCe was right when she said the word *walk-up* should exit your vocabulary when you hit thirty. But the charm of the apartment compensated for the steepness of the stairs. There were high, arched windows with the original shutters. The moldings and woodwork were shiny, white enamel. Kate had tossed her collection of antique paisley shawls over tables, couches, and chairs. A group of art bird cages climbed up one wall, an Amish quilt hung in the hall. She sat down with a book on the couch, put her feet up without bothering to take off her shoes, and fell immediately asleep, the book in her hands.

Waking up in the middle of the night, Kate barely managed to undress and stagger into bed. She hoped she wasn't coming down with something. She couldn't afford to be sick. Then, the next morning, as if feeling bloated and lethargic wasn't enough, she threw up. Her head felt hot, so she took her temperature— one hundred. Stomach flu, she decided. Naturally her resistance was down—she'd been under so much pressure, what with the separation, the new job, and the move. Her body was stressed out. She took four vitamin C tablets and a Stresstab, made a container of frozen orange juice, and forced a few sips down. What was it they said—"Starve a fever," or was it "Feed a fever"? Who could remember? She had a fleeting impulse to call Matt and ask him—that was one good thing about being married to a doctor. Squinting into the mirror, Kate could see she looked pale, so she used extra blusher. A positive attitude was half of the battle. So much for being sick; she refused to let it happen.

"This looks personal," said Clair as she handed Kate the pink-and-white envelope, bordered by a line of yellow ducklings. Stanton Welch had allowed Kate to take Clair with her from *Childstyle*. Actually, Kate had pleaded. She couldn't imagine working without Clair. Besides, she knew that Clair, at least, was on her side.

Inside the duckie envelope was an invitation to a baby shower for Angela—to be held at the hair salon. The date was that afternoon. The envelope must have been bouncing around for at least two weeks, Kate figured. Kate's plans for the evening consisted of a squash game with one of the guys from Sales, but, knowing what she'd been through, Kate did want to show her support for Angela. She decided to run out at noon and buy a gift.

Walking through the baby department of Bloomingdale's brought it all back—her fantasies about having her own family, and the longing for a child Kate assumed she'd left behind when her marriage crumbled. Tiny outfits fluttered from miniature hangers like small, pastel ghosts, and when she touched one, actually felt the incredible softness and measured the thumb-length arms and legs, Kate unexpectedly felt the ache again, as if the flat, empty outfits lying on the counter were waiting for her own baby to bring them to life. She cradled a small gown and held it to her cheek. It wasn't rational, she knew. It made no sense. She had made her decision, had moved on in her life. This chapter was closed. Resigned, she watched the saleswoman wrap the little outfit.

Kate was late for the shower. Guardino had appeared in her office at five o'clock to register his "concern" about her decision to change to a heavier, glossier paper stock, and the ensuing dead-end debate had run forty minutes. It was almost seven o'clock when Kate finally arrived at the Pink Scissors.

The salon had been transformed into a baby wonderland: blue-and-white crepe paper bows were tied onto the arms of every chair and on the bonnets of the hair dryers. Booties hung from the chandelier, and the basins were heaped with ice and pink champagne. A sheet cake decorated with an overweight yellow stork was on the table in front of the fireplace, and the ritual opening of gifts was in progress.

"Kate!" yelled Angela, waving a bouquet of ribbon bows over her gigantic belly. "Everybody, this is Kate, from my in vitro clinic. Kate, this is Helen, our nail therapist, Theresa, who does our shampoos, my friend Linda from the neighborhood, Shelly from upstairs, Kiki, who went to beauty school with me, and my sister-in-law, Marie. Everybody, this is Kate. She works at a magazine."

Marie took Kate's gift and brought her a plastic cup of champagne. Angela pushed herself out of her chair and walked over. "Only a while 'til D day," she said, patting her belly. She put her arm around Kate. "Your hair looks good, but you could use a touch-up. Now what's new with you? We didn't hear from you, so we weren't sure you were coming."

"I changed jobs," Kate said, sipping the champagne. "They had to forward the invitation, and I just got it today. You look great." Kate decided not to mention the separation. It would just put a pall on the occasion.

Marie pulled a chair into the circle. "Now you sit here with me," she said. "This is the cheering section." She handed Kate a slice of cake on a paper plate.

To the appropriate oohs and aahs, Angela unwrapped a huge cellophane-wrapped basket, brimming with baby accessories and toys. Kate realized that she didn't even know what some of them

116

were. "That's a changing pad," Theresa pointed out. "And that's a bottle warmer. Comes in very handy late at night."

Kate nodded politely, as Angela unwrapped a giant, talking teddy bear. "I have batteries," one of the women volunteered.

"This kid is going to have so many toys," said Angela. "Kate— I don't see you eating your cake. Everybody's gotta be as fat as me."

Kate licked the frosting off her plastic fork. It was disgustingly sugary, and she immediately wanted more.

"Oh! A—beautiful little— What the hell is this pretty whatsit?" Angela held up a coverlet with teething rings and felt squares attached.

"That's an activity quilt," Theresa called out. "The baby lies on it and plays with the things."

"You must have children," Kate said to Theresa. "You know everything."

"Well, we have a five-year-old, a three-year-old—and another one on the way." She patted her stomach, which was still flat.

"When are you due?" Kate hated this expression, yet here she was at a baby shower not only saying it, but getting tips on warming bottles. She felt totally out of place. To divert the feeling, she turned to Theresa.

"I just found out I'm pregnant, actually," said Theresa. "I took a home test, and my doctor confirmed it. But I knew already—you know how it is. The nausea, the low-grade fever. What else could it be?"

"The flu?" Kate thought of her own symptoms.

"With the flu, you don't get the cravings. I knew the jig was up when I went out and bought a pound of blue cheese and ate it straight from the package with a fork. Didn't even unwrap the sucker."

Kate dismissed the fact that, twice this week, she'd detoured down Madison Avenue to the Godiva chocolate shop and bought a two-pound box, which she'd eaten single-handedly. "Um— what other symptoms were there?" she asked, as casually as possible.

Theresa ticked them off on her fingers. "Constantly in the

bathroom. Have to go all the time. And the breasts—the first thing to go. Blow up like balloons."

Involuntarily, Kate's hands flew to her breasts. They felt tender and strained against her blouse. *No. It couldn't be.* She hadn't even had sex in a month. She hadn't even had a *husband* in a month! She felt the familiar queasiness rise. "Theresa, excuse me, but where is the bathroom?"

Theresa leaned forward and stared at Kate's breasts as if she were evaluating the ripeness of melons at a produce stand. Her eyes narrowed. "I don't know," she said. "Looks like a definite maybe to me."

In the bathroom, Kate managed to get the nausea under control. "It's all the sweets I've been eating," she announced to no one. Her period wasn't even late—she didn't think. Of course, what with the separation and the move she hadn't been keeping track on any calendars—thank God. There'd been no reason to. After all those months of trying to get pregnant, this was one time when she really *didn't* want it to happen. Besides, it was practically a medical impossibility—she'd proven that. And she was fairly certain—no, she was totally certain—she wasn't late.

When she opened Kate's gift, Angela walked over and threw her arms around her. "Now this is what I call cute!" she said. "Thanks, Kate. How are you? You never made it in for that manicure." She grabbed Kate's hand. "These cuticles have got to go!" She shook her head. "You've got to see Helen this week."

"She's four, maybe four and a half weeks along," announced Theresa.

"Kate!" yelped Angela, pushing a bundle of booties into her arms.

"What!" said Kate. She dropped the booties as if they were on fire. "She's joking."

Theresa shrugged. "I see what I see. We're witches in our family. Ask Angie. My mother reads tarot for a living."

"I am not, most definitely not, pregnant," said Kate, rolling her eyes at the ridiculousness of it all.

Theresa reached forward and plucked out one of Kate's hairs. "Give me your wedding ring. We'll tie it to this and suspend it over your stomach. If the ring twirls in circles, you're pregnant.

If it twirls to the right, it's a girl. If it twirls to the left, it's a boy."

All the women at the shower gathered around Kate.

"Here, use my ring," said Kiki.

"I hate to disappoint you," Kate said, trying not to act as irritated as she was, "but, really, let's not jump to any conclusions here. What I have is a touch of the flu— Angela, don't get too close. I probably shouldn't be here. I don't want you to catch this from me."

Theresa patted her arm. "Don't worry, honey. What you got ain't contagious."

On the way home, just to put her mind at ease, Kate stopped at a pharmacy and bought a pregnancy test kit. Just to be safe, she bought three.

The instructions said you had to wait till first thing in the morning to get the best results. Kate set her alarm for seven A.M., but she woke up with a start at five-thirty.

The instructions were complicated, but, with all her experience with the ovulation kits, Kate felt as if she had a Ph.D. in chemistry. She followed the instructions, then went to the kitchen for an English muffin. When the alarm went off, she padded back into the bathroom.

Blue. The stick was blue.

Kate ripped open the second kit and repeated the test. While she waited, she ate another English muffin, but this time more nervously.

Blue.

She opened the third kit. This time she didn't go to the kitchen. She sat there and watched the kit, which was not unlike watching ink dry.

Blue. Blue. Blue. The three blue sticks lined up on the bathroom counter.

There was, of course, the possibility that the kits were defective. God knew how long these things had sat on the pharmacy shelves.

Kate sat absolutely still until seven-thirty, when she called

Clair at home to say she'd be running late this morning because of a breakfast meeting.

She had a meeting, all right. With a pregnancy test.

When the stores opened, Kate raced back to the pharmacy and bought ten more pregnancy kits, all different brands. The heavy-lidded cashier blinked at her from behind thick glasses. "Buying in bulk?" she said.

"None of your business," Kate snapped, scooping up the kits in a shopping bag.

Conducting ten pregnancy tests at once, each with different instructions, required Olympic-level coordination, but Kate was determined. Assembled on the countertop were: twenty little plastic cups; ten eyedroppers; seventeen miniature test tubes (three kits were tubeless); a flurry of leaflets, pamphlets, and brochures; five alarm clocks, including Kate's travel alarm, international clock, and the egg timer; and various kinds of plastic sticks. As each alarm went off, Kate rushed to the appropriate test site to complete the next step.

Finally, exhausted, she lined all thirteen sticks up on the edge of the sink.

Blue.
Blue.
Blue.
Blue.
Blue.
Blue.
Blue.
Blue.
Blue.
Blue.
Blue.
Blue.
Pink.

"Five and a half weeks, I'd say, judging from the fact that the cervix is starting to soften up very nicely," said Dr. Warneke, who had squeezed her in at lunchtime. "Of course, we'll need a blood test to confirm it, but I'd say you and Matt will be doing some celebrating tonight."

Kate sat bolt upright on the examining table. "It can't be," she said. "It's impossible."

The nurse swabbed her arm with alcohol and snapped on a tourniquet for a blood test. "I know," she said, smiling. "It really blows you away."

"That's not what I mean. I mean— Oh my God." Kate sat stunned. Why now, when she was on her own and immersed in the new job? Now, when she had finally begun to adjust to this new life? There was no way she was going back to Matt, that much was certain. She didn't really want to tell him, although she didn't want to mishandle this the way she had the abortion. It was his right to know. Besides, a baby had to have a father. She wouldn't want any child of hers to grow up as she had after her own father had died, wondering why it was singled out among its friends to receive a half portion of love. Yes, she was going to have this baby. There was no question this time. There was no need to wonder when she had actually conceived. After all those months and months of torturous tests and calendar-watching, it had to have been that last night, that time of raw and elemental sex, more a collision of bodies than lovemaking.

"We'll just watch the hormone level with a few blood tests," said Dr. Warneke. "It should double and triple in the next few days, and that'll tell us that things are progressing nicely." He readied a syringe. "Now there are no special instructions—but no flying, that's out for a while, and no aspirin, caffeine, or diet products. And you can keep up with your normal activities, but nothing too strenuous. Rest with your feet up a couple of times a day if you get a chance. After all, we have to consider this a high-risk pregnancy, given your age."

"Great," she said bleakly, thinking about the media tour she had planned to seven key markets. And resting with her feet up was about as realistic as being carried to work on a sedan chair. Kate didn't even feel the sting of the needle for the blood test. She felt nothing except a hammer blow of confusion. As she struggled to pull one thought out of the mess in her head, something like a tiny pinpoint of light surfaced and grew until, as

121

Kate sat there on the edge of the examining table, still draped in the white sheet, it glowed immediately and blindingly inside her, and she knew what it was, and that everything would work out, that she could handle anything, because it was love.

Walking down Madison Avenue after the examination, Kate cradled her hands over her belly. It was so hard to imagine that there was another being in there, but she wanted to protect it, in case they were jostled by the crowd on the sidewalk. She passed Praetesi, the linen boutique where she and Matt had once spent three thousand dollars on one set of sheets. In the window was a natural wicker bassinet, lined with cloudlike linens and a tiny lace pillow. Kate was drawn by the bassinet. She imagined it at the foot of her bed, a soft, tiny infant asleep on the coverlet, its chest moving up and down like a feather in the wind. She went into the store and bought the entire setup.

She wondered when she should call Matt. She would—she knew she would—but not just yet. Kate wanted to savor the warmth she was feeling and keep it to herself, if only for a little while. Angela had once told Kate that if women could have babies without men, they probably would. Now Kate knew what she meant. She did not fear having the baby alone, or even raising it alone. She felt strong and capable and in control. She knew she could deal with Matt. After all, he was an expert on split families. And, for the duration of the pregnancy, there wasn't much he could do at any rate. They'd negotiate a plan for after the baby was born, but that was many months away. The office was a tougher issue. The men were unreceptive enough to a nonpregnant woman. Her condition was not going to help her case at all. But she felt sure she could handle it—even if she had to lumber in there in a Laura Ashley maternity smock and kick ass.

Kate hadn't been back to the penthouse since she'd moved out. It seemed like a different life—so cool and still. She was glad she'd left it to Matt. There was none of the warmth and coziness of her brownstone, where you could reach out an arm and touch a wall at any time. There was a new doorman, who didn't recognize Kate and seemed surprised that she had a key. She supposed he thought she was a girlfriend of Matt's.

She hadn't told him why she wanted to meet. Her plan was to keep it mature and businesslike—two adults with something important they had to deal with. She had come directly from work, in her business suit, to reinforce that impression.

The first thing she noticed was that Matt looked great. Well, good for him. The breakup was clearly doing them both good. He gave her a polite kiss on the cheek and they went into the library.

"You didn't get a new fish tank," she said.

"No—just one more thing to take care of. How's your new place? Do you need any of this stuff?"

"It's too small. The piano would take up the entire living room."

"You know, you could have this apartment. I'm not tied to it. It's half yours."

She shook her head. "I'm not into real estate." She remembered how offensive she'd thought it was that Elise had demanded that Matt transfer ownership of their triplex to her.

Matt picked up a folder from the coffee table. "I've had everything inventoried, room by room. You can go over this when you want. Check off anything you'd like. If you don't want it now, we can always send it to storage."

"The decorator picked most of these things anyhow," she said. She wondered how she could have gotten so excited about pieces of furniture and accessories. The delivery of each piece had been an occasion for celebration, and Kate had loved just standing in the rooms, admiring them, as if she had lived in a decorator show house. Looking back on it, she felt that she had never really *lived* in this apartment at all. She and Matt had kept their clothes here, spent time here, entertained here. But their life together had been more a matter of two parallel lines that occasionally intersected.

"You wanted to talk, Kate?" He touched her arm, and she jumped to her feet. "Would you like a glass of wine?"

"No."

"But you always have a glass of wine."

"Not anymore. Not for a while." She looked directly at him and spoke as evenly as possible. "Matt, the thing is—I'm pregnant."

The color drained from his face; he opened his mouth, but no words came out. A muscle in his cheek twitched. Then he smiled and started to reach out for her. "No kidding. That's great news. Just great." His hand hung in the air, as if waiting for her to take it.

"The baby is due in October. I thought you'd like to know." She moved briskly away and paced along the side of the room, her high heels bayoneting the parquet.

"Well," Matt said quietly. "That's interesting news. I'm very pleased, of course—about the baby. But what about us?"

"We're the baby's parents."

He poured himself a scotch at the bar. "And that's all? This doesn't make us rethink things?" He watched her intently. "Aren't things different now, with the baby?"

"It doesn't change things between you and me. We have to get on with our lives. You and Elise have worked out a good custody arrangement; I assume we'll do the same." She tried to sound businesslike, but it was difficult.

Was that her voice shaking? What would happen, Kate wondered, if right now, this minute, they stopped talking and touched? Would Matt reach out for her? Would she want him to? Yes? The moment hung poised on a fulcrum, and Kate knew that if either of them opened toward the other, they could change things now. Maybe it should be her. But she hesitated. Pride, anger, stubbornness—something—immobilized her, as if she had taken a drug that numbed everything except the question: *What if?*

Matt tossed down the scotch. The moment was gone. "Fine, Kate. Whatever you say," he replied, his voice suddenly chilled. "But I am this baby's father, and I intend to be an active partner in his upbringing, just like I've been for Gregory and Kim."

"How are the kids?"

"Very upset about our separation. They love you, Kate."

Kate laughed. "Oh, that was obvious."

"They were just confused. They're kids. Listen, Kate . . ." he began.

She didn't want to hear the apologies she sensed were coming. She'd known the baby would do this—trigger Matt's indefatigable sense of commitment. Somewhere inside him, Ward Cleaver lived. A man who felt a father belonged with his family, no matter what. But you should be with your family because you wanted to be, Kate thought, not out of obligation. She refused to be an obligation. She was not an alimony payment to be made, cleaning to be picked up. "Listen, I have to go," she said quietly. "I just wanted to tell you myself."

"What about the next seven and a half months?"

"What about it?"

They stood facing each other. For a minute, Kate was torn between mentioning the letter her lawyer was going to be sending, and turning back into Matt's arms.

"You know," Matt said, "any medical bills, anything you need for the baby—" He hesitated, as if he expected her to say more.

"Thanks. We're fine. I'll let you know if I need your help. We have some time to work things out." She started toward the hall, then stopped. Part of her wanted to be independent and strong, but there was another part that wanted to share the closeness and excitement of the news of her child with the baby's father. But that was an emotional luxury, Kate decided. It wouldn't do either of them any good. She swallowed hard and kept walking.

"I'll let myself out," she called over her shoulder.

Eight

On Saturday morning, Kate took a train up to CeCe's. Even though it was bitterly cold, CeCe was outside gathering up firewood.

"Do you think I should stack it by the door, or at the end of the driveway?" asked CeCe.

"I'm pregnant," Kate said, skipping over the preliminaries.

"Oh my God. I mean, oh my God! No kidding! Kate, what are you going to do? I mean, congratulations!" CeCe dropped an armful of wood and raced over to Kate, hugging her.

"This is great, just great. When?"

"Around mid-October, I think."

"Will you take time off? Maternity leave?"

"I can't. We'll be in the middle of the relaunch. I'll be lucky if I get the delivery day off. I'll probably have the baby at my desk."

"What about those male chauvinist throwbacks at that place? Didn't you tell me they won't even let you in their golf club?"

"I'll make them all uncles. But I'm going to keep this pregnancy quiet as long as I can."

"It's pathetic in this day and age. But, listen, scarves are very concealing. And after the kid is born, you can hide him in your briefcase. No one will be the wiser."

"Well, you know the situation isn't without its complications."
Kate picked up a twig and tore off the bark. "They'd use this
against me if they could—all very nicely and politely, of course,
but it wouldn't be pleasant."

"And—well, I hate to use the M word, but what about Matt?"
CeCe asked.

"He's happy about it. I think. Telling him was torture, though.
He seemed . . . wounded, hurt."

"Are you surprised? And?"

"And nothing."

CeCe took off her gloves. "That's too bad, if you ask me."

"He's a nice guy. A wonderful guy. But it just didn't work."

CeCe tapped Kate on the shoulder. "Forget it for now. Get
up; let's go into the house. I have a bunch of maternity clothes
to give you."

"It's way too soon, CeCe. I only just found out."

"That's obvious. Only a novice would turn down free maternity clothes. But I'm giving the shower. Just remember that."

Kate sat on the ladies' room floor, her head pressed against
the tile wall in hopes that its coolness might bring some relief.

No such luck. She'd woken up nauseous and it wasn't letting
up, in spite of the crackers and teaspoons of mild herbal tea. She
tried to will the nausea away, to convince herself that she felt
fine, but every time she stood up, it swept over her again in a
rush. Now she was drenched in cold, clammy sweat, the back
of her hair soaked through. From time to time, she could hear
women chatting outside the stall—mostly young secretaries and
assistants gossiping about their boyfriends. Where would her
credibility be if they knew their boss was prostrate on the bathroom floor? She wondered what kind of role model she was
providing. She was supposed to be the woman who could handle
pressure with grace, but here she was, retching, crushing her suit
on the tile.

Something must be wrong. Morning sickness was supposed to
last only a few weeks, but hers had dragged on for the past three
months. And whoever had invented the term *morning sickness*
had it wrong, too. Kate was sick morning, noon, and night. Dr.

Warneke said there was nothing to worry about, that this happened sometimes in the first trimester, that it would probably calm down by the end of the fourth month. But as of now, there was no telling what might set it off—smoke, odors, food, or nothing at all. Kate groaned.

"Kate, is that you?" She heard Clair's anxious voice outside the stall door. "Kate? Are you all right?"

"I'm fine, Clair. No problem." She tried to sound normal.

"Can I do anything?"

"No thanks. Probably something I ate at breakfast. Bad croissants." Kate was still trying to keep her pregnancy a secret until absolutely necessary. She had told no one, and she was still in normal clothes, although almost everything had to be let out, and she'd bought several new suits, size twelve, as compared to her usual eight. With a long jacket, you really couldn't tell, although under the jacket, the waist was usually unbuttoned and the zipper open at least an inch. The fabric of the suit she was wearing was stretched to the limit, and Kate worried that sitting on the floor might burst the seams. She knew she was going to have to break down and get some maternity things, but she hated the idea. She wondered if Chanel had a maternity line.

"Kate," said Clair, "Mr. Welch is in the office, and he's looking for you. What do you want me to tell him?"

Kate struggled upright. The waistband of her wrinkled skirt felt like it was cutting her in half. She had to pull herself together. "Tell him to wait in the conference room. I'll be right there." She flushed the toilet and smoothed her hair. She knew she looked a mess. As soon as Clair left and the ladies' room was empty, she forced herself to go to the mirror and rinse out her mouth. Sure enough, she looked like a train wreck. Where in hell was the fabled glow of pregnancy? Kate's skin was sallow, and dark circles smudged her eyes; the result, she was sure, of getting up four times last night to go to the bathroom. She couldn't remember the last time she'd slept through the night uninterrupted. She even had a pimple, the first she'd had since she was a teenager. *God! Wrinkles and pimples at once!* Her hair looked like straw. Maybe she'd call Angela for an emergency touch-up and a facial. She couldn't go through five more months of this.

Coming out into the hall, Kate almost collided with Stanton Welch. "Kate," he said excitedly. "There you are. I've been looking for you. Now. Listen to this. I can get a third-party introduction to Akio Akito—Japanese electronics, Hiro Computers. My brother-in-law went to Harvard with him. He's kind of the *enfant terrible* of Japanese electronics. He's interested in possibly sponsoring an issue of *Finance*. It's a whole new angle for them—they've never done anything like this, but, hell, we'll convince them. God knows, they can afford it."

Kate was thrilled. "Perfect! This is wonderful. We'll get them—I'm sure of it. We can base an entire three-part series on consumer electronics, industrial electronics, and communications electronics."

"Now, we need to get to Tokyo by the eighteenth with a breakdown of the materials, and I told them we'd be there. When can you leave?"

"Tokyo?" She stopped in her tracks.

"That's where Hiro is based."

"Can't they come here?" she asked, scrambling.

Welch frowned, his eyebrows meeting in a straight line across his forehead. "I think we should go there, as a good-faith measure."

Tokyo! Kate knew Dr. Warneke would have problems with letting her fly to Japan. What if she had a complication in the air? Or in Tokyo? But the opportunity was tremendous. And how could she say no to Stanton Welch?

"I don't know, Stanton. It's just such a hard time to leave, right now."

"Guardino can hold the fort for a week or ten days. Now, when can you leave?"

Trapped. There was no way out of this, Kate knew. "Stanton, could you come into my office? Hold my calls, Clair."

He followed her inside. "What's the problem, Kate? This would be a historical association. Don't you see the potential?"

"Yes, of course, you're right. The thing is, there is a personal issue here, and I'd like to tell you in confidence."

Welch's eyes narrowed. "Guardino?"

"No, no, not the office."

129

Welch patted her shoulder. "Kate, I heard about you and Matt. I'm sorry to hear it. But I know you won't let it affect your work. I was divorced myself, you know. But the trip'll do you good. Take your mind off it. Trust me." He pulled out an itinerary. "Now, we depart Sunday and fly to Hawaii—"

"Stanton, it's not that. It's— I'm . . ."

"You're not afraid to fly, are you? You always fly."

"Well, the thing is, Stanton . . ." She couldn't tell him. Not like this. It would be the worst possible blow to her career, to what she wanted to do for *Finance*. Guardino would step in, and she'd lose everything she'd accomplished. Kate quickly calculated how much longer she could keep her pregnancy secret. So far, she'd gained about fifteen pounds, but next month she'd really start to show.

"The thing is, I have a thought. Maybe we should have the meeting here. The Japanese might like to go up the Empire State Building, see the Rockettes. The wives can go on a shopping tour. They can go to plays, Broadway. We'll show them the time of their lives. They'd be our guests; we'd be on home turf, a much better bargaining position. Like—the Mets. We all play better at home."

Welch banged the table. "Great idea! Why didn't I think of that? After Tokyo, we'll invite Akito here."

She smiled weakly.

"I like the part about the upper hand at the bargaining table. Goddamn brilliant. You know, I was just saying to Guardino the other day, 'Guardino, you listen to that lady. You know what I like about her? She thinks like a man.' "

What the hell—he was going to find out soon anyway.

"Well, Stanton, not in every single case."

"Well, figuratively speaking, of course."

"Figuratively speaking, I'm pregnant."

He stared at her. "How the hell did that happen?"

"How do you think?"

His ears turned red. "Well, fancy that. Congratulations. That's wonderful news. Wait till I tell Linda."

"Thank you, Stanton, but I want you to know that my work is top priority."

"Don't you worry about work, honey. That baby is the most important thing right now. You take care of yourself. Now. When can you leave for Tokyo?"

Kate sat sullenly in Dr. Warneke's office.

"Absolutely not," he said firmly. "And that's final. No overseas flights—and to Tokyo? That would be foolhardy, Kate. You're in a high-risk pregnancy, I'm afraid."

"I could lie down the whole way, keep my feet up."

"No. Who knows about their medical care, if you had a problem? You could end up in a Japanese hospital for weeks if there was a complication. But the real problem is on a long flight. There's no medical care available for hours, even if you're just flying to California. We can't risk it."

"Somehow I knew you'd say that." Kate sighed. "I must be psychic."

Dr. Warneke smiled. "It's not the end of the world, Kate. It's just a few months, after all. You'll adjust. You're doing quite well."

"Doctor, could you do a favor for me?"

"If I can. What is it?"

"My boss—well, he's insisting that I go to Tokyo."

"Well, tell him you can't," Warneke snapped.

"I think you have to tell him. Can he call you?" Kate felt like a sixth-grader asking her father to write an excuse to miss study hall.

The doctor sighed. "I've seen this happen before. Here's how we handle it." He scribbled a note on a prescription pad. "I write a note that says 'To whom it may concern; my patient is under advisement to restrict all travel to a one-hour radius from her hospital.' File it with your personnel department. They won't want to risk a lawsuit, if you go against my orders."

"I feel ridiculous."

He ripped off the note and handed it to her. "Well, I guarantee the pressure will be off. It never fails."

Walking down Park Avenue, looking for a cab, Kate knew what this meant: Guardino would go to Japan. The thought was infuriating, but she couldn't do anything about it. Or maybe she could. First, she'd stall for time—call Stanton and tell him she was working up an in-depth presentation, maybe call in an international consultant to help her come up with an angle. If she couldn't use her body, she'd use her ingenuity. She'd always imagined a flawless, Earth Mother pregnancy, smoothly fitting into her routine, and now things weren't working out that way. Then again, the Earth Mothers didn't usually play golf, fire people, or negotiate with the Japanese. Kate supposed she'd have to revise her imagery and figure out another kind of role model. Elizabeth Dole? Forget it. She didn't have kids. Barbara Bush? A grandmother. Mother Teresa? Admirable, but totally unrealistic. That was the problem, Kate thought. You were flying blind these days.

She hated the idea that something as basic as this was out of her control. After all, as she had often told Matt, it was her body! She, the one to whom the pregnancy was happening, seemed to have the least to say about it. Kate was used to making things happen; to achieving her objectives; to picking up the phone and fixing it, whatever it was; to paying a premium and getting it faster; to working harder and getting results sooner. Now her hands were tied. She was stuck, stalemated.

At another time in her life, Kate knew, she might have taken the chance. Her job, her own life, would have come first. But that had been then, before this baby.

In a way, Kate was angry with herself. Her resolve was crumbling, her independence unraveling. But she could not, would not, risk this child.

How had the baby become so important, usurping every other priority? When had it seeped into every corner of her emotions? By what osmosis had it entered the fiber of every decision? It had not happened consciously, Kate knew, but it was a fact.

Wasn't it amazing, she thought, how she, who specialized in agendas and goals, had not planned this course of events at all. And yet this pregnancy which had defied her planning and organizing from before conception managed to rule her every move. The prenatal management skills of this child would put Lee Iacocca to shame.

It was time to admit it: the baby had the upper hand, and it wasn't even born yet.

Kate pulled the dress over her head and let it fall onto the floor, where it looked like what it was: a sack. A pastel-pink sack with two floppy, rabbit-eared bows.

"How was it?" called CeCe through the dressing room curtain.

"Wonderful, if your name is Goodyear. I look like a blimp. A big, strawberry blimp."

It was a disgruntling experience. After weeks of straining size-fourteen seams, Kate had begun to look forward to shopping for maternity clothes. In the sitcom of her imagination, this was one of the more pleasant episodes of her pregnancy, the one in which she was suddenly, magically transformed from bloated to Madonna, in which fat and bloblike became pregnant and glowing.

Ever since Kate had been six years old and worn a white tutu for Halloween, clothes had been the magic carpet to a new image. When real life shorted out, there was always Donna Karan to transform her psyche from frazzled to forcefully feminine. When she was feeling athletic, tennis whites could conjure up Chris Evert at Wimbledon. And a vintage satin negligee evoked sultry images of Colette's boudoir. Kate had never been a fashion victim, but she did love the feel of fine materials, the warm caress of cashmere, the heathered nubbiness of tweed, the crisp smoothness of starched cotton. And she loved how the fabrics fell along her body, at once pampering and defining.

Now, that feeling eluded her—worse, it taunted her. She had accepted the fact that Chanel was out for a few months, but she had hoped for at least some semblance of style.

"CeCe, don't they have anything that's not pastel?"

"Like what?"

"Black. Basic black. Go look, okay?" Kate stared in the mirror. She didn't look pregnant—just fat. Her belly bulged, but not enough to suggest a baby. Her breasts ballooned, but so did her thighs. She looked like she'd had a few dozen too many éclairs, subcutaneously applied.

What she was looking for was a maternity business suit—if

such a thing existed. What she was finding was a froth of ruffles and flourishes that would have looked girlish on Princess Di at nineteen. On the dressing room floor were:

The powder-blue shift with the gathered drop waist that made Kate look like an overaged Valley Girl.

The yellow-and-white polka dot overblouse and yellow pleated skirt that turned her into a refugee from *Pirates of Penzance*.

The plaid sailor suit with the big white collar that would have suited Queen Victoria at her christening.

And the strawberry blimp.

Surely, Kate thought, she wasn't the only pregnant executive in the business community. Fifty-two percent of all women over age eighteen worked outside the home these days. Some of them *must* be having babies. What did they wear? Where did they buy it? Kate tried to remember if she'd ever even seen a pregnant senior executive before. She must have, but she hadn't paid attention. There certainly weren't any at *Finance*. She didn't want her pregnancy to divert attention from the business issues, so it was important that her maternity clothes ease the transition. Kate wondered if there were any pregnant CEOs anywhere. Or five-star generals. She envied the generals, if they existed. At least they could wear uniforms.

"How's this?" CeCe's arm thrust in through the curtains. From it dangled a bright red blazer, white Peter Pan blouse, and red print bow tie. Maternity dress-for-success. "This is the best I could do."

Kate frowned. This outfit would look dated on a junior-level trainee, but at least it wasn't pink or ruffled.

She stepped out of the dressing room and cringed at her reflection. She looked like a melted candle. They said the Mona Lisa was pregnant, and that accounted for her secret smile. Kate now knew otherwise: the Mona Lisa was smiling because she had found a black, bowless maternity dress.

"How are we doing?" A short, round saleswoman in a ruffled blouse materialized.

"This isn't . . . great," said Kate. Her voice sagged. She was exhausted from shopping, but then, it didn't take much these days to tire her out. At four months, she was moving into her second trimester. According to the books, she was supposed to be feeling an energy surge. The books were wrong.

"Now," proclaimed the saleswoman. "You need *this*." She produced a strange-looking pillow with strings dangling from the four corners. "Tie this on *under* the dress," she said. "But *over* your underwear. The pillow will add a good three months." She patted Kate's belly. "Then you'll have a better idea of the fit, for when you need the extra room. See the extra buttons in the waistband? The skirt is expandable. You can even wear it postpregnancy."

That'll be the day, thought Kate as the saleswoman strapped the gruesome stomach-padder around her.

"There! You look like seven months!"

"I look like a mushroom cap. A red one."

"No you don't," said CeCe. "You look pregnant."

"CeCe, it's *polyester*. It's shiny." Kate recoiled as if a vampire had dropped into the dressing room.

CeCe shrugged. "They don't make maternity clothes in real materials. That's just the way it is."

Kate tugged the pillow off. "This is the dumbest thing I've ever seen."

"Wait till you see your figure in nine weeks."

"Can I show you some lingerie?" asked the saleswoman. "Some panty hose?"

"Panty hose? Where will my stomach go?" The thought of maternity panty hose reminded Kate of washed-ashore giant squids.

"*Maternity* panty hose."

"They come up to your armpits," added CeCe helpfully, "so your stockings won't sag."

"Great." Kate thought of her drawersful of imported lace underwear, her French satin garter belts and real silk stockings. But they were already part of a dim past.

"Will you be nursing?" The saleswoman dangled a handful of bras at Kate. They were huge, at least six inches wide, and reinforced. There was enough elastic to cover a trampoline.

"I—haven't decided." Kate had never worn anything but tiny silk bras. Now she would be strapping the U.S.S. *Enterprise* to her chest. It wasn't fair that this happened to your body. It didn't even seem like *her* body anymore. It was the baby's body. She was the host. The baby was her sleep-over guest, and there was no end in sight to the visit.

"Now maybe you're starting to get it," said CeCe later, as they walked up Madison Avenue in a brisk early spring wind.

"Get what?"

"The idea. Of being a mother. You have to give in to it. You can't fight it. It takes you over."

"I refuse to believe that, CeCe. Whose pregnancy is this anyway? Mine, I believe."

"Uh-huh. Tell that to junior, here. Just because you can't see that kid doesn't mean she isn't running things."

"It's a he."

"How do you know?"

"I feel it."

"Okay. He. He's in charge now. You'll see."

Kate remembered visiting CeCe in the editorial offices during her publishing days, where she was the staff wunderkind, precocious, smart, and in charge. What had happened to CeCe? Before she was married, before she quit her job, before the kids, she'd been the most rational of Kate's friends, the one Kate could always count on. Now, instead of offering encouragement and support, she was trying to convince Kate that in five months she would lose herself, as if her personality and priorities were about to be jettisoned over the Bermuda Triangle.

"What are you, the unbiased panel of judges?"

CeCe shrugged. "Okay, I'll lay off. I'm sorry, Kate. Sometimes I get carried away. I have my priorities, I guess, and you have yours." She laughed. "I guess I figure if your priorities are like mine, mine are more acceptable. I mean, the day after your kid is born, when you join the club and preenroll her—him—in nursery school, I'll feel I'm not as nuts as I sometimes think I am for doing stuff like that. I hate to admit this, but I actually found myself getting a little crazy if Ashley wasn't enjoying Gymboree. I'd ask myself, what did this mean? A left brain misfunction? A learning disability? I thought about getting her a tutor. The kid was only a year old! There's just so much you have to do for these kids, things you never suspected, and it gets out of hand sometimes, but you learn. You go with the flow. Eventually."

"I know what you're saying," admitted Kate. "Already things are out of my control. So many things. My own body is a stranger, for God's sake. It's not like I imagined."

"Scarves," said CeCe.

"What?"

"Scarves! If I told you once, I told you a thousand times. Now, let's go!" She yanked Kate off the sidewalk and into a boutique.

"We want to see scarves," announced CeCe.

The saleswoman laid ten large silk squares in jewel colors on the glass countertop, and CeCe grabbed two and twined them together around Kate's shoulders, trailing the corners down her chest.

"Turn sideways. There! You'd never know you were pregnant. You look great!"

Kate turned in front of the mirror and smiled. The colors picked up her complexion, the flowing silk camouflaged the bulge. "I'll take these five," she said, feeling optimistic. "CeCe, you should go back into the fashion business."

CeCe shook her head. "I've been out of practice too long. But it's coming back to me now. Let's pay for this and move on to knit separates. Those will work, even if they're not maternity, if the waists are elastic and the tops are long."

"What happens when I really get huge?"

"Buy the pink thing, get a seamstress to copy it in black gabardine, and throw it out."

"Perfect."

"Feeling better?"

"Much. Now. Where can we get ice cream?"

"You're having a craving?"

"No! No cravings! I'm having a . . ."

"Serious relationship with dairy products?"

"A perfectly normal desire for mint chocolate chip."

"Of course, Kate. I myself was just thinking, it's twenty-seven degrees outside. Wouldn't ice cream hit the spot?"

"Okay. So it's an irrational desire."

"But not a craving."

"Not a craving."

"Whatever you say."

On Monday, Kate wore a maternity dress to the office for the first time. It wasn't something she was looking forward to. Kate suspected that the more she differentiated herself from the status quo, the more the old guard would shut her out. She chose a navy-blue dress with a Chanel scarf and chains, her least "maternity" outfit.

Kate had not officially announced her pregnancy, but she knew the word was out. Still, when she ran into Jim Jacobs in the hall, his eyes never left her stomach, as if the situation was now sinking in and he was trying to gauge the exact month of her pregnancy. When she walked into a meeting, Guardino jumped up and pulled over a chair. And the dirty jokes stopped. Suddenly she was Mom.

Kate wasn't sure if this was a good or bad thing. It was just strange. And just one more thing to keep her from being a team member.

Jean stopped by her office to officially congratulate her. "I've been here ten years," she said. "Don't ask me how I survived. And you know, Kate, it won't be the new design that will wake these guys up, it'll be this baby."

"Why do you say that?" Kate asked.

"Well, you'll have to admit one thing, they did all have mothers."

So did the Alien, thought Kate.

Nine

"Do you know a Theresa Sabatini?" asked Clair. "She says it's important."

The only Theresa Kate knew was the woman who did Angela's shampoos, from the shower. Angela must have had the baby.

"It's a girl," Theresa announced happily. "Emily Camille. Eight pounds, six ounces, born last week. Angie's already home from the hospital. She's been pretty busy breast-feeding and all, so she asked me to call you."

"I'm glad you did. That's great. Stan must be thrilled."

"To pieces. But enough about us. How're you doing? Was I right or what?"

"More right than imaginable. I am definitely pregnant, according to thirteen pregnancy tests and a doctor."

"Hey, don't mess with The Force. I guess we'll have two reasons to celebrate. Here's the deal: Thursday night. The girls and I are taking Angie out for a little break. It's kind of a tradition in our family—girls' night out after the baby. Gives Dad his turn at the wheel. We'll go to a play, have dinner after, nothing fancy, something easy for everybody on the West Side, near Lincoln Center. It's fun. I know you're busy with work, but Angie will be real upset if you can't make it."

"The play might be a little tough—I never can predict when

I'll get out of here. But dinner would be nice, if I can catch up with you. Where will we meet?"

"There's a restaurant on Columbus Avenue and Sixty-ninth. Very trendy place. Baryshnikov is one of the owners. My cousin Stevie is a bartender, so we'll get a table. Ten o'clock?"

"You're on."

By Thursday afternoon, Kate regretted making any plans. She was exhausted, really dragging. There were constant personnel issues to deal with, editorial questions to answer, and the pressure of finding potential sponsors was endless. Nothing would have felt better than going straight home and crawling into bed, but she was too tired to cook, and, because of the baby, she had to eat, so she decided to make a quick appearance, maybe have a little vegetable plate, and leave without lingering.

Five or six limousines were stacked up in front of the restaurant when Kate arrived, and inside it was packed. It was a bare-wood-café kind of place. Kate picked several celebrities out of the crowd. She wedged her way through a small mob at the front door to the maître d'. "Sabatini?" she asked. "A large party?"

"You're the first to arrive, and I'm afraid I can't seat you till you're all here," he said. "Why don't you have a drink at the bar for a few minutes."

Miraculously, a seat opened up at the bar. Kate ordered a tomato juice and occupied herself making mental notes about tomorrow's schedule. She was going to have to spend more personal time on the Carry issue.

Suddenly someone lurched into Kate, and her tomato juice bounced onto her chest. "Hey!" she said. "Watch it!"

"The lady's right. Watch it. And while you're at it, apologize." On the stool next to Kate, an extremely large man was mopping up his own drink while staring intimidatingly at a red-haired stockbroker type. The big man dabbed at his sleeve. "Good aim. You got me, too."

"Sorry, Larry. Miss—it was an accident."

Kate waved him off. All she wanted was a napkin.

The large man next to her had one of those, too. He started dabbing at her chest.

Kate grabbed the napkin. "I can do that, thank you."

"Just trying to help. Things can get hazardous sitting at these bars."

"I am not sitting at the bar."

"Could have fooled me."

"I'm just waiting here for my friends." She scanned the doorway for Angela or Theresa.

"Whatever you say, miss, but club soda works great. I learned that from a stewardess. I fly a lot."

"Good for you."

He signaled the bartender. "Stevie, some club soda please. And a bar towel."

"Sure thing, Lar."

The guy was a regular, obviously—everybody knew him—one of those types who had nothing better to do than hang out at a bar. He looked too old for it. He was pathetic, Kate decided. Probably harmless, but pathetic all the same. She hated men who hung out at bars. This guy looked like a construction worker. He had huge hands and shoulders—the type who'd been a star athlete in high school, and never grew up.

"Just let me get this off your skirt." He reached toward her lap, and Kate jumped off the stool.

"Don't touch me!"

"Calm down. Lady, you're a nervous wreck. It's just a little tomato juice."

It wasn't the juice that bothered her. "Keep your hands off me," she said. "You are not my dry cleaner."

Suddenly, someone in the crowd lurched into both of them, and the entire bottle of club soda poured onto Kate's sweater, drenching her chest.

"I told you, stay away from me!"

He looked concerned. "God, I apologize. It's just so crowded in here."

She mopped at the front of her sweater. "I can't believe this. I'm supposed to meet some people any minute. And I'm soaking wet." She stood up.

"You can't sit here like that," said the man. He took off his navy-blue jacket and handed it to her. She could tell from the feel that it was cashmere. "Take this. Just go in the ladies' room and take off the sweater and wear this. Button it up, roll the sleeves. I'll get them to wave your sweater in front of one of the hand dryers. By the time you leave, it'll be dry."

Kate looked at him suspiciously.

"You'll get sick if you wear a wet sweater all night." He shrugged. "Just trying to help."

Kate saw Theresa, Angela, and their friends come in. A blast of cold air seemed to blow from the ceiling. She shivered. She couldn't afford to be sick. "Thanks," she said. "I'll return it when I leave." She dashed to the ladies' room, pulled her wet sweater off, wrapped the soft coat around herself, rolled the sleeves, and tied the waist with her scarf. It was the best she could do for now.

"Where'd you get the coat?" squealed Angela as soon as Kate got to the table. "From him?" She pointed to the man at the bar. "I saw him give it to you. Now that's fast work."

Kate leaned over and kissed Angela. "You look great. But there was no work involved there. I don't even know the guy. He spilled club soda on me, that's all."

Theresa leaned over. "Don't you watch channel seven?"

"No. Why?"

"Even I recognize that guy, and I'm blind. He's Larry Sedlacek, the guy from 'Sports Afar.' He does the play-by-play and the color commentary for all the big sports. He's in my living room every single weekend. Stan watches all that stuff."

All the women turned to look. "I saw him on the Olympics," said Theresa, jumping up. "I'll get details from my cousin—he's at the bar."

"Really," said Kate, "I don't care about the details." She handed Angela the tiny silver rattle that she had wrapped in pink ribbon. "This was in my purse, so it didn't get wet. For the baby. Do you have pictures?"

Angela passed around a small color shot of a blanket-swaddled infant. Kate looked at it, unable to imagine that she would have similar pictures in a few months.

"You know, Theresa's a witch," she said. "She knew I was pregnant before I did."

"How are you feeling—like shit, like I did?" Angela asked Kate.

"Let's put it this way—I don't throw up too often, just whenever I breathe."

Angela nodded soberly. "Take my advice, avoid any food that looks like you need to blot it."

Theresa reappeared. "Yep, that's him. Larry Sedlacek. Stevie says sometimes he comes by after work—the studio's just down by Lincoln Center." She laughed. "Don't tell your husband you were wearing this guy's coat—he'll get real jealous."

"Well, we're separated, unfortunately."

Angela winced. "Is this good news or bad news? What's the prognosis?"

"Zero, I'm afraid. But not a tragedy. I'm coping."

Angela smiled sympathetically. "But that means you're in the right place."

"For what?"

"Meeting men."

"Men? Angela, men are the last thing on my mind. I'm not looking to replace a man, I'm looking to eliminate men from my life for the time being, so I can concentrate on this pregnancy and on my work. All of which is a full-time job. I have no intention of dating. Pregnant dating—it's a ridiculous concept."

"Who knows? You might need somebody to throw a cloak down so you can walk over it. Besides, didn't your mother tell you you should always try something before you say you don't like it?"

"Yes, but she was talking about string beans." Kate wished she had never taken the jacket. "Tell me about the baby," she said, trying to change the subject. "How much did she weigh?"

"Eight-six," said Angela. "Five hours of labor. Nothing to it." She snapped her fingers. "I made Stan rub my feet with almond oil the entire time. He was worse off than me."

Angela introduced Kate to the three other women—Carmel, who had been one of her bridesmaids, Allie, a neighbor, and Cindy, a cousin. They ordered dinner, and Kate gulped her salad as fast as she could, keeping her head down. She didn't want to risk eye contact with the sportscaster, or whoever he was. When she finally looked up, he was gone—without his coat, which she was still wearing. She excused herself and went up to the bartender. The crowd had thinned out.

"Excuse me," Kate said. "Are you Steve?"

He nodded.

"Can you help me? This jacket belongs to a gentleman who lent it to me because my sweater got wet. He's supposedly a sportscaster . . ."

"Oh, Larry Sedlacek. The Sed. Busy guy." Steve nodded. "I think he left about ten minutes ago. Someone said he had to catch a plane for Italy or something."

"What planes go to Italy at this hour?"

"Maybe it was a private plane."

"Oh. Well. Did he leave my sweater?"

"I didn't see it. I'll check."

Kate went back to her table. "Angela, I'll see you later. I've got to leave."

"Bend down." Angela ruffled Kate's hair. "I see some regrowth. You'd better call me next week or your roots are gonna show."

"You won't be back at work by then!"

"Sure. I'll bring the baby in with me. She's portable."

Steve appeared. "I'm sorry—no sign of a sweater. But I know he works at ABC."

"I guess I'll get his jacket cleaned and messenger it over to the network," Kate said. She waved to the table and left.

"Let's see if I've got this down," Kate said to Stanton Welch as they went into the flag-lined marble-and-brass entryway to the Omnibank Tower. Hal Radia trotted behind like a bodyguard. *Finance* had not yet been able to secure an interview with Edward Carry. Jim Jacobs couldn't even get his phone calls returned. But this was better than an interview, and besides, if things worked out, the interview would be no problem. "Edward Carry. His father started out as an entrepreneur during the Depression. Bought land cheap, Carry sold high thirty-five years later. He's number one hundred of the *Fortune* Five Hundred in his own right. Founded a bank as a stabilizer for his other investments—the airline, the hotels. Committed to the concept

144

of global credit. Loves Winston Churchill. Has a world-class collection of Churchill memorabilia. The man is conservative, hates small talk—"

"And women," Welch supplied helpfully. "Unless they're on his arm. Then he loves them."

Kate walked purposefully forward, careful not to trip on the slick terrazzo floor. Even though she was wearing flats, her six-month belly had thrown her balance off. It didn't make it any easier that she couldn't see her feet any longer.

"For God's sake, Stanton," she snapped. "Get a grip. The man's in business."

"Well, you're right. He couldn't hate all women. His mother was one."

Kate pounded the elevator button. She smoothed her hair back behind her ears. The new short haircut fell into place. Actually, she felt naked without her headband, but she reminded herself that a one-hundred-sixty-five-pound woman in a headband looked ridiculous.

In spite of Welch's pronouncement, Kate felt that a lot of things were falling into place. As she stepped onto the elevator, she felt confident about her presentation. She had it nailed. Every *i* was dotted, every *t* was crossed. She had worked ten days—and nights—straight on the charts, and every detail of Carry's life history had been completely dissected and reassembled. Whatever question Edward Carry might ask, she was prepared.

These last weeks, Kate had felt a sudden surge of energy. She felt unstoppable, capable of anything, on top of the situation for the first time in weeks. She'd called every nanny service in the city to get a head start on interviewing, she'd bought some books on breast-feeding, and she'd put all the long-term forecasting for the magazine on paper. She felt competent and complete. *Bring on the dragons,* she thought. Even if Edward Carry breathed fire, she could handle him.

Carry's Winston Churchill memorabilia dominated the elaborate suite of rooms that was his office. His secretary led Kate and her group into the library.

"Mr. Carry collects Churchillian antiquities," she whispered. "The Prime Minister used this cigarette lighter in the War

Room," she said, pointing to a very ordinary looking lighter under a glass dome, marked by an engraved brass plaque. "These maps and books were from his Blenheim collection. And, of course, this brass planter was a personal gift from Clementine— he kept it in his study at Chartwell, the Churchill family home. It's our prized possession." She paused reverentially for a moment.

If you wanted to make points with Carry, word had it, all you had to do was ask about Churchill, whose blustery demeanor Carry could imitate at any given moment. A discussion of, say, interest rates somehow would lapse into a performance: "Interest rates!" Carry would exhort. "We will fight them in home mortgages! We will fight them in private banking! We shall never, never, retreat!" This was Carry's idea of wit.

Setting up took no time at all. In spite of her large belly, Kate hefted the slide projector and pulled the table into position.

"Kate! What are you doing!" Hal pushed her away.

"Please, Hal. I'm pregnant, not sick."

He frowned, picking at his tie. "You shouldn't lift something this heavy. *I* shouldn't lift something this heavy."

"Plug this in," Kate said, thrusting the projector cord at him.

"The cord won't reach the outlet."

"I have an extension cord in my bag." She pulled one out and rigged the projector.

"You're going to impress the hell out of Carry," said Hal. "Here, have a croissant."

Kate was suddenly starving. She took a flaky pastry from the tray on the sideboard and ate it in two fast bites.

Edward Carry walked into the room, and she swallowed quickly. He wore a loose navy suit, striped shirt, and a black tie. He looked bored, his mouth pursed in a tiny smile, his eyes narrow.

"Kate Harrison-Weil." Kate extended her hand.

"Carry. Let's begin, gentlemen," he said, ignoring Kate's presence as he sank into an oxblood leather armchair. "I don't believe in fluff. Get right to it, if you don't mind." He looked at his watch. "I have another appointment in twenty minutes."

Kate stepped to the front of the room. *I can do this,* she

thought. *Piece of cake.* She flipped on the slide projector, cleared her throat, and said, "Let's begin by mapping out an overview of some of the exciting changes that are happening at *Finance*. Our new format . . ." She coughed. "Our new format . . ." Something felt wrong. She started to gag. Thrusting the remote control at a wide-eyed Stanton Welch, she ran out of the room.

Behind her, she heard Hal Radia make an excuse: "She probably forgot the batteries for the remote."

"Excuse me," Kate choked out to Carry's secretary. "Where's the ladies' room?"

"Two floors down. I have a key." The woman eyed Kate closely. "On second thought, you might want to use Mr. Carry's executive rest room, right there." She pointed to an adjacent door, and Kate ran for it.

Leaning against the marble wall of the bathroom stall of Edward Carry's private washroom, Kate did her best to steady herself. Her stomach heaved, and she choked, trying not to vomit. *Morning sickness! You can handle this,* she told herself. *Relax! Relax! Re—*

She gagged into the toilet, leaning over to avoid her silk blouse, the only silk maternity blouse that still fit. Her breasts were so big, they were unmissable targets.

She castigated herself for eating the greasy croissant. She should have known better—but oh my God, she was always starving. No wonder she weighed a hundred and sixty-five pounds. The thought made her throw up again.

She had to pull herself together. Everyone was waiting for her back in the conference room. Mr. Carry was a man with a notoriously short fuse. He hated to be kept waiting. And she'd kept him waiting fifteen minutes while she barfed in his bathroom.

Kate flushed the toilet, wobbled out of the stall, readjusted her clothes, checked her stockings for runs, dabbed water on her face, and rinsed out her mouth. She felt slightly better. Gathering her composure, she pulled back her shoulders and strode into the conference room, smiling confidently. She stood at the front of the room with a veneer of bravado that was not oblivious of the uneasy glances the men exchanged. They probably thought she was going to give birth right then and there, forcing one of them to cut the cord with his cigar clippers.

Kate readjusted her slide projector. "Sorry for the interruption," she said. "Now. Back to the overview. As you know, *Finance* has always been the gold standard in financial publishing. We are actively expanding that position with a major new initiative to the younger, affluent market. *Your* market, Mr. Carry. I have a leave-behind piece that has our new prototype, plus all the details. But what's key here is that we also propose a unique merchandising opportunity for Omnibank."

"I can see anyone benefiting from an Omnibank association," said Edward Carry. "But what do we get from this tea party?"

"Well, Mr. Carry, your consumer banking business could use the influx of young money. This thirtysomething generation is looking for more ways to utilize credit—say, putting mortgages on credit cards. We see a mesh here with the goals of Omnibank." She flipped the charts. "Here you see the demographics of our newly expanded readership target. This group is your target as well, in the credit arena. We propose a launch-issue editorial devoted to credit. An issue totally sponsored by Omnibank. We see this as an exclusive opportunity. You are the first sponsor we've approached."

Kate felt a feathery little bump, like the brush of a butterfly wing, in her stomach. "Oh!" she exclaimed. *Bump! Bump!* Someone was playing bumper cars in her stomach. *BUMP!* Her entire belly heaved to the left, like a tipsy bowl of Jell-O.

Edward Carry stared.

Kate cleared her throat. *The baby was moving!* Actually moving! She wanted to savor the moment, communicate with the little person inside, tap her belly and send it a return message in code, strip off her clothes and press her hand to her stomach. Instead, she pulled her jacket around her, as if to give the baby some privacy.

She struggled to get back on track, but couldn't recall what point she was making. Suddenly Stanton Welch was at her elbow, deftly stepping in.

"What Kate is saying is that we are offering a chance here,

Mr. Carry, to be first with a breakthrough concept. We thought Omnibank would want to be part of that."

Kate tried to step out of the way, but her protruding stomach cast a bowl-shaped shadow on the screen, covering half of the charts. The other half was projected onto her body. She retreated, pressing her back into the wall.

She could feel Carry's eyes burrowing into her. It was infuriating.

There was only one thing to do: walk back up there and take command again. Regain the floor. Run the meeting, like she'd set out to do. As Kate took one step forward, her insides rebelled with a wave of nausea. As unobtrusively as possible, she sidled to the back of the room. *Crackers!* There were crackers in her briefcase! As she unwrapped the crackers, the cellophane wrapper crinkled loudly. She took a bite of the Saltine. The crunch seemed to reverberate through the room. If only she could have a sip of water.

The meeting seemed to zoom out of focus, the voices tinier and tinier, as Kate's head whirled. She felt wrung out, limp. Sweat trickled down the back of her neck. She was wondering if she should leave the room when everything in her stomach seemed to pole-vault upward into her throat, and she knew she wasn't going to make it.

As unobtrusively as possible, Kate stepped to the back of the bookcase and threw up into Winston Churchill's planter.

Back at *Finance,* Kate closed herself in her own office. *God, what a horror show!* She'd totally blown her first big presentation to a prospective sponsor. Hal Radia had stepped in and completed the presentation, but it had been humiliating to sit on the sidelines, perspiring, while someone else did her job. Stanton Welch had whispered to her to "take a Midol" and stay off her feet for the rest of the day. And Edward Carry, she was sure, just thought she was a major nonprofessional.

Her body had betrayed her. Her baby had sabotaged her. Maybe this was its way of telling her to quit work, stay home, and bake brownies. Kate didn't even know how to bake. The kid couldn't live on her one dish—spaghetti—forever. And now she didn't seem to know how to do her job, either. She felt as if she were on a roller coaster, out of control. She was wondering if anything could be salvaged from the meeting when Clair buzzed.

"There's a man at the reception desk," she said.

"That's not unusual," said Kate.

"He says he has to see you."

"Who is he? He doesn't have an appointment."

"I don't know. He's saying it's personal. I saw him; he looks normal."

"I'll check it out." Kate sighed.

She walked down the hall into the reception area, where Larry Sedlacek sat sprawled on the couch, reading *Sports Illustrated*.

"You!" he boomed when he saw Kate. "You stole my jacket."

Hal Radia, who was passing by, looked startled.

"Please, Mr. Sedlacek. I did not steal your jacket."

"Oh, right. It walked out on your back of its own free will." He was shouting and waving his arms.

Hal inched over. "Kate," he said. "Excuse us a minute." He pulled her aside. "What's going on? Don't get into it with that guy. I recognize him. He's an animal!"

"Oh, he's harmless." She had to smile at Hal's concern. He was acting like a big brother.

"Do you know who he is?" Radia was incredulous. "Larry Sedlacek? Ex-marine, Heisman trophy winner, first draft pick for the Raiders. A major heavy until he racked up his leg. They used to call him the Crusher. Do you know why? Because he crushed things. Especially people. Once, he crushed a Volkswagen with his bare hands on national television. I saw it. The man does not deserve your sympathy. He deserves your fear. Whatever he's got to say, agree with him and get him out. Should I call Security?" He glanced warily at Larry, who was pacing back and forth.

Kate patted Hal's arm. "It's okay. Thanks for your concern, but I can handle it."

Hal looked at her with, she thought, new respect.

"If you say so," he mumbled.

Kate went back over to Larry.

"Now, Mr. Sedlacek," she said. "I'm sure it's all been a simple misunderstanding. You left without your jacket . . ."

"I was in the men's room for five minutes, and you sneaked out with it."

"Well, they told me you left. If you'll calm down, I have your jacket here, and I was planning to send it to you. As you can see," she opened her suit coat, revealing her belly, "I have no use for it."

"Luckily the bartender knew your girlfriend. Otherwise I'd never have seen my jacket again. Except on a milk carton."

She had to get him out of the lobby. People were staring. "Come with me."

In Kate's office, she took the jacket out of the closet and handed it to him. He took it and inspected it.

"You didn't even have it cleaned," he said.

She snatched it back. "Fine. I was planning to have it cleaned. The cleaners will deliver it to you. Prepaid."

"I'm only joking," he said, suddenly smiling. "I didn't want to upset you. I really came by to ask you to lunch." He pointed at her stomach. "Now I see, maybe I'm a little off base here. Is this what I think it is?"

"It's a stomach with a baby in it. All right?"

"Well, congratulations. Your husband must be very proud."

"We're separated."

"God. I'm sorry." He slapped his forehead. "I'm a jerk. You wouldn't want to have lunch with a jerk."

"True."

"Would you?"

She stacked a pile of papers.

"It's nothing personal, but I never eat lunch."

"Well, you have to. Now."

"I don't have time."

"You have five minutes?"

"Well, five minutes . . ."

He grabbed her arm and started steering her out the door. "Get your coat. I know a little place where we can be in and out in five minutes."

*   *   *

151

"One hot dog with mustard, three with everything, hold the onions. One orange soda. One Coke. Two chips." Larry handed Kate her hot dog, wrapped in foil. "Sorry about that. I guess New York hot dog vendors don't have milk." They sat on a bench in an outdoor plaza, enjoying the warm sunshine.

"At least I know you're getting a hot lunch," he said. "And we can have ice cream for dessert."

The hot dog tasted delicious, although Kate wondered if she would pay later. "This reminds me of football games," she said. "So you were a big football honcho?"

"Well, I played for a while." He crunched on a potato chip. "It was fun while it lasted."

"Why'd you quit?"

"Spiral fracture of the knee. After that, forget it. Now I'm just another talking head on TV."

"That's not the way I hear it," Kate said, her mouth full. "And that's not what your card said, either."

He smiled. "Yeah, I get paid to talk about sports. Can't believe my luck sometimes."

Kate nodded. "I know what you mean—that's how I feel about publishing. Sometimes I feel like I should be paying them for my job."

He crushed a bag of potato chips in his hand, tilted back his head and shook the crumbs into his mouth. "You know, I really didn't believe you were pregnant." He crunched for a moment. "You look great—I mean, normal. On the surface, that is. But then, I'm no expert. I'm not even married."

"No kids then?"

"Not even a dog. I had a girlfriend until last week, but that didn't work out either." He winced. "So where's your guy, if you don't mind my asking?"

"We're getting divorced."

"Sorry."

"It's no problem."

"Oops. No napkins." He dabbed fruitlessly at a glob of mustard on his tie.

Kate reached into her tote bag and pulled out a tiny bib, embroidered with pink and blue lambs, that someone at the office had given her as a joke when she'd announced her pregnancy. She handed it to him. "Here, use this."

"So who looks after you?"

"I do."

"Pardon me, but I don't think you're doing a very good job."

"How can you say that? You don't even know me!"

He pointed to the remnants of the hot dog. "You eat junk. They put snouts and ears in these things. Now, I don't know a thing about having a baby, but I know all there is to know about training, and you should not be eating snouts and ears."

"It was your idea!" The man was crazy.

"And, I saw you in a bar."

"It was a restaurant! I ate a salad!"

"Whatever."

Kate stood up and brushed off the crumbs. "I really have to go now. Thanks for the hot dog."

"You're welcome," said Larry. He waved the little bib. "I'll have this cleaned and get it back to you." He ticked an oversized finger under her nose. "But from now on, you're on a health kick. Remember, you're in training, and I'll be checking up on you."

The guy had nerve, Kate thought. She'd give him that much.

Kate lay on her back, rigid, so nervous that she didn't even think about the fact that she was missing a full day of work. Just being on an examining table, helpless, draped in sheets, brought back a horror show of memories of the Fertility Odyssey. She had to remind herself that this was different. This was positive; this was about the future baby. Still, it was amniocentesis. It was a needle in her uterus, extracting fluid to find out things about the fetus. It was pain. It was invasive. It was risky. She hated it.

Janet sat at her side, blinking rapidly, more nervous than she. Kate had asked Mother along because Dr. Warneke had said she shouldn't come alone. Matt had volunteered when Kate had called and told him about the test, but she didn't want him there. The test was going to be traumatic enough; Kate didn't want any emotional upset. Dr. Warneke had told her that there would be a two percent chance of miscarriage after the procedure, but that the figure was near the normal miscarriage rate, so it was actually not as risky as it sounded. Still, Kate had reason to be concerned. Matt had not been happy about being excluded, but he had gone along with her wishes. She knew he'd be on the phone with Dr. Warneke the minute she was off the table, anyway.

Kate wasn't sure why she'd decided to ask Janet to accompany her. Janet had never exactly been a pillar of support. She was just Janet, inundated with her own life of superficialities. But when Kate told her about the appointment for the test, Janet had said firmly, "I'd like to come with you. In case you need me." *Need* her? Kate couldn't remember the last time she'd actually needed her mother. In fact, she saw herself as valiantly independent, powering through the test invincibly on her own. Yet, when it came right down to it, she didn't feel all that invincible. And the doctor had been adamant that, for medical reasons, just-in-case reasons, she should not go alone. And so Janet was there, holding her hand, as she had when Kate was five years old and learning to cross the street.

After all these years, Kate was again holding her mother's hand, as the child soon to be disclosed would one day hold hers. Lying on the table, she felt like part of a circle. What did it take, she wondered, to be a real family? Could you be a family without a husband, and with a child not yet here? Could women be a family of their own? What would her own child, one future day, feel about her? It seemed impossible to Kate that she had once been a tiny, quickening force in the belly of the woman now sitting beside her.

"So I decided on the robin's egg blue for the new bedspread," Janet rattled on. For once her patter didn't irritate Kate; it was an amiable distraction.

It had always seemed to Kate that her mother had filled her life with meaningless words, but now she could see that those words were an effort to fill empty spaces that went beyond pauses in conversation. What Kate had seen as chattering was often—how often, she now wondered—an effort to bridge a gap, in the only way she knew.

"I know it's not an 'in' color this year, but blue is always so soothing, don't you think?" Janet said as the technician squirted ice-blue jelly onto Kate's abdomen in a spiral pattern, then attached wires and suction cups to it. To the right of the table was a little television monitor, where the baby's picture would appear in black and white. Kate knew this was the way they would track the fetal position, so that when the needle was inserted, it would be sure to miss the baby. Then a sample of the amniotic fluid would be drawn out and analyzed for chromosome patterns, so that, if there were a problem, she would know in time to make an informed decision.

Of course, Kate had already made her decision. It didn't matter—even if something was wrong with the baby, she didn't see how she could do anything but keep it. She loved it too fiercely already. She could feel it. She knew it. It was her little companion, her only real companion. They had already seen too much together. This was her child.

The amnio specialist appeared. Kate had never seen her before. Turning her head to focus on the screen, Kate caught a glimpse of the longest needle she had ever seen. "Can't I have novocaine?" she asked, panic rising.

"Then we'd have to stick you twice," said the doctor. "It won't be so bad, you'll see."

Onto the screen came a little head and hands. The head was turning, the hands were waving. "Is that the baby?" asked Kate, suddenly forgetting about the needle.

"Oh, my gosh, look," gasped Janet. "Little fingers!"

It was truly astonishing. The camera panned along the baby's body, and the little image looked like a tiny X ray, transparent, but alive. Kate could see the bones. A miniature foot looked perfect, and, my God, she could actually see a small protrusion that looked like genitals. A boy! She knew it!

"Can you tell the sex?" she asked excitedly.

"If you want to know, it's possible, but we can't be absolutely sure till the test results come back in three weeks. Pictures at this stage can be deceiving. A lot of things look like other things. Do you want to know the sex in advance?"

"No. I'd rather be surprised." But it was fun to speculate—and Kate usually trusted her instincts.

Kate felt it—the pungent prick of the needle. *Not too bad.* And she was too excited to care.

"Don't move now," said the doctor.

Janet gripped Kate's hand tightly. "My grandchild," she whispered. Kate squeezed her hand back. *My child,* she thought. It was funny. Now, at age thirty-nine, almost forty, for the first time she felt like a mother; and, for the first time she could recall, she also felt like a daughter.

Lying on her living room couch, sipping the cup of herbal tea that Janet had left with her, Kate cringed when the phone rang. She had anticipated this. So that she would not have to get up, she had surrounded the couch with her mobile phone and fax, bottles of Evian, magazines, the TV remote, and the entire contents of her briefcase.

She knew it was Matt. He'd left two messages on her machine.

"How do you feel?" he asked anxiously. "I wish you'd let me come with you."

"I kept the Polaroids for you. I'm fine. The baby looks perfect. I think it's a boy. I told them I wanted to be surprised, but I really thought I could tell it was a boy."

"A boy." Matt's voice glowed. "A brother for Gregory."

Why did he always put everything in terms of Gregory and Kim? "I'll get the results in three weeks. It seems so long."

"I'll phone the lab and ask them to rush it, but the cultures take a certain time."

"I hope that everything's okay, but please don't do that. For once, can we do this my way, where *I'm* the first to know? He looks so terrific, though. He even moved!"

"That's wonderful. Kate?"

"Yes."

"Maybe we should rethink things."

Kate was startled. Rethink. Was it possible? Should she hope for—what?

"Why? What's changed?"

"Well, I think we should at least put off the divorce proceed-

156

ings until the baby is born. I don't like the idea of him being surrounded by negative activity."

How academic of him, Kate thought. She should have known. After all, he was totally detached from her and was putting things in terms of the baby. Which was fine. And he was right; she'd been reading about how science has shown that fetuses are more sensitive than anyone suspected, how they respond in the womb to voices and music. "Well, we could do that, I suppose. A few months won't hurt. I want him to get the best head start."

"So do I."

They were both silent for a minute. Kate felt relieved that at least she didn't have to face the divorce just yet. Some part of her was still not yet willing to let go of Matt completely, the same part that was now feeling the comfort of his voice, the voice that had once soothed her so well in the middle of the night. Well, divorce was never clear-cut, she realized. Did people love each other after divorce? At another point in her life, she would have discussed this with Matt. Her confusion exhausted her.

"I have to hang up," she said. "If I need anything, I'll call."

"I'll check up on you later. Remember to keep quiet today. Kate? I . . ."

"Yes?" Her voice was abrupt.

He sighed—she thought. "Take care of yourself."

Ten

"**I** have your conference call to Mr. Welch and Mr. Nagamichi set up," Clair announced. Kate nodded and picked up the phone. She'd spent the past weeks intensively researching how she should approach the upcoming meeting with Mr. Akito, with the help of Rick Nagamichi, an international business consultant who specialized in Japanese business practices.

"Stanton," she said after the introductory pleasantries, "Rick tells me that it would be a mistake for you and I to show up on Hiro's doorstep in Tokyo."

"Why's that?"

"I'll let Rick tell you. Rick?"

"Well, Mr. Welch, a better approach would be to establish lines of communication by having your third party set up preliminary meetings with their advertising and promotion people. Rank is important to the Japanese. You and Kate are too senior for this, in the eyes of appropriate protocol. Having gone through this first-step procedure, you and Kate may then become involved. Also, I would suggest sending ahead a written proposal with all the details. The Japanese will evaluate it. The actual meeting between your top management and theirs will then serve to develop the rapport you will need to conduct business with the Japanese. It is a multi-tiered process."

"I see," said Welch. "Yes, that's probably accurate."

"We would lose face if we went ourselves," said Kate. "At this point, at least. I suggest we send Guardino to Tokyo."

"Good call, Kate. I hadn't considered the protocol issue, but you're absolutely right. When can they leave?"

Kate was relieved. She was not only doing the right thing for her pregnancy, but also for business. She'd read everything she could on Japanese business and come to this conclusion herself, but Rick Nagamichi had confirmed it and had given her recommendation credibility. The next step would be to set up a meeting in New York with the Hiro negotiating team, which, she knew, routinely came to the United States on business. She would be sure to be part of that meeting, and she had personally prepared the briefing package that would now be sent ahead to Tokyo, as she had learned that the Japanese respected factual detail and tended to be turned off by the traditional American sales pitch.

Kate had just booted up her computer when Clair opened her office door.

"Just a minute, Clair, I'm trying to get to these projections. Can I get back to you?"

Clair smiled knowingly. "Sure, any time. But I don't think *they* want to wait."

"They who? I don't have anyone coming in."

"Oh, I wouldn't bet on that." She disappeared down the hall. Three minutes later, there was a perfunctory knock, Kate's office door swung open again, and in marched Gregory and Kim.

"Gregory! Kim! What a surprise!" Kate pulled herself up—there was no longer such a thing as jumping to her feet. She wondered if Matt was in the lobby. "Kids! It's so nice of you to drop by. Were you in the neighborhood? Are you alone? Is your mother or father with you?"

Gregory, in his blue school blazer and pants, shook his head solemnly, and was mimicked by Kim, in her little gray skirt and white blouse. "We're alone. We took the limo. Can you keep a secret?" Gregory said. "We won't take up much of your time."

"You're not taking up time," Kate said. "You're family. Do you guys want anything? Cokes? Cookies? Fruit? Secrets are so much fun." She wondered if Matt had sent the kids down on a peace mission.

Gregory closed the door. "The secret is that we were never here. We'll deny it if you say we were, and it'll be two against one."

"What about Clair? She let you in."

Gregory shrugged. "Secretaries can be bought."

Kate sat back down and folded her hands in her lap. "I see. And to what do I owe this top-secret occasion?"

Gregory took a thick envelope out of his backpack. "Business," he said. "I understand you are expecting a child."

Kate nodded and smiled. "Yes. Isn't that nice?" She couldn't believe it. The kids were actually here to congratulate her on the baby.

"Maybe for you. And it. But Kim and I have spoken to our therapist about this, and we feel we have to get certain things settled."

"I understand," said Kate. "Like feelings."

Gregory frowned. "No, this isn't personal. Like I said, it's business." He took a binder from the envelope. "As the firstborn son of Matthew Weil, it is my duty to speak up. Kim has given me her power of attorney."

Kim nodded adorably. Her mouth was a perfect Cupid's bow.

"We're here to discuss this contract with you." He handed a binder to Kate. There were about fifty pages, perfectly typed, complete with color graphs and bar charts.

"What's this?"

"A prenatal agreement. I did it on the Mac."

"What?"

Gregory stared at her, suddenly bearing an unsettling resemblance to the twisted progeny in *Village of the Damned.*

"We figure, once the kid is born, it's after the fact. It's better that we clear everything up now, cut and dried. And get it in writing."

"Of course." Kate wondered what he was leading up to. She never underestimated Gregory.

"What we're talking about here is our rights as the original children. We don't want anyone forgetting that fact later."

Kim shook her head energetically.

"I've taken the liberty of drawing up a fifty-point agreement that just verifies the facts. All you have to do is sign it."

"Well, that sounds simple enough." Kate offered them some miniature Tootsie Rolls, which Kim started to reach for, until her brother stopped her with a look.

Gregory paced the room, like Darrow addressing the jury. "You know, Kate, in the olden times, the firstborn son automatically inherited everything." A gratuitous glance toward Kim. "Of course, he took care of his sisters, but the other brothers, well, you might say, they were toast. And half brothers, well, forget it. Then along comes Thomas Jefferson with some proclamation, and he busts that up. But actually, I was checking up on the right of primogeniture, and I'd say Jefferson left some major loopholes. That whole thing's gonna blow some day. Of course, me, I could care less."

"Of course."

"But there are certain unalienable rights we're dealing with here. And provisions." He wiped his nose with his sleeve. "I won't bore you with all fifty, but here's a few key points, and, I might add, they are deal-breakers."

Kim handed Kate a Xeroxed sheaf of papers.

"We need to see a few things in writing. First, point one, there at the top of page one, is that we need our own credit cards, preferably Optima and platinum or, at minimum, signing privileges. If our dad's tied up, say, changing diapers, we want to be able to move on major purchases, like books and school supplies."

Kate knew for a fact that these children had never had to purchase so much as a pencil for themselves. Elise bought whatever they needed and charged it to Matt. Still, she nodded seriously. "Yes, that would come in handy," she said.

"Moving right along to point five, custody. The calendar chart in illustration A roughs out the weekends and holidays. But then there's Action Park and Disney World. We require two trips each per year. And point seven, communications. Subclause B, the beeper. We want our father on beeper, so all we have to do is beep him if there's something we need to talk to him about."

Kim swung her legs, kicking the polished finish of the Biedermeier chair.

"And a fax machine. We'll need one each for communication purposes. And subclause F, education, a Nintendo Power Glove—that's educational."

Kim kicked her brother.

"Okay, okay. And on page forty you'll find a pony for Kim."

"Uh-huh," said Kim. "A Lippizan stallion."

"Second choice," said Gregory. "A palomino."

"Why do you kids need a horse in the middle of New York City? I realize this is a minor point in the scheme of things here, but . . ."

Gregory oozed disdain. "Who said anything about New York City? If you read this document carefully, Kate, you'll come to point thirty-six, subclause ii, which points out that we require a weekend house at the beach. Preferably Southampton, on the same block as Jimmy Clefton's. You can't expect Kim and me to grow up getting mugged in Central Park and breathing fumes all summer. We'll get lung cancer and probably die. You'd benefit from this, too. Once he's old enough to drive, the kid could come out once in a while and visit."

"How generous of you," Kate said. "But you know, none of this is up to me. Your upbringing is between your mother and father. I'm sure they'll want to hear how concerned you are."

Gregory leaned closer. "Kate, get real. The kid gives you leverage. Whatever you say is gonna go. If you think this is a good idea, so will Dad." He made a face.

"What's that supposed to mean?"

"Daddy talks about you all the time," whispered Kim. Her big eyes looked pleadingly at Kate, as if she wanted to say more.

"Shut up, Kim," snapped Gregory. "She makes things up."

"I do not!"

"Oh yeah? How about the time you said you had a mermaid from Atlantis in the bathtub?"

"I did!"

"That was a goldfish."

"It was not!"

"Was too!"

162

"Was not!"

"Whatever. Anyhow, Kate, if you'll just read this through, I'm sure you'll agree, it's in everybody's best interest that you sign."

"I'll read it."

He pulled out a pen. "Is anybody in this place a notary?"

"Gregory, let's get one thing straight. I promised to read it, not sign it."

He rummaged through the backpack, took out an electronic calendar, turned it on, and scrutinized the little screen. "Well, I'll be home tonight. You can messenger it over."

Kate lay back in the claw-footed bathtub and watched for signs of life. Her white, pearly stomach poked through the faint bubbles floating on the surface, reminding her of the underbelly of a fish, neither specifically beautiful nor notably unattractive, but undeniably fascinating. She noticed that her navel protruded now, a small, curled shell washed ashore on what had once been a flat landscape. A faint brown line had appeared, bisecting her roundness like a fruit marked for cutting. Occasionally when Kate was still, deep inside she felt a flutter or a kick, and sometimes she swore she saw a sudden protrusion from what had to be a tiny elbow, knee, or hand.

At times like this, she felt the reality of the baby. She wanted to talk to him, to explain why they were alone, and that she was sorry, but that she loved him enough for any two parents. That he still had a father who would love him, too. She envisioned the baby, attached by his little spiral cord, and she imagined calling him on the phone as he rested in his warm, dark cocoon. She wondered if the sound of her voice would comfort him, if he would know it when he was born.

In the end, she did not speak to the baby. Instead, she decided he could read her thoughts. And why not, since he and she were one? She decided to send him some thought-pictures. Closing her eyes, Kate pictured herself cradling a beautiful, doll-like infant in her arms. She had a white satin ribbon in her hair, and the baby cooed softly. In the theater of her imagination, this was motherhood. She conjured up another image: the baby in its carriage, and herself pushing it. She was stopping to point out flowers, leaves, and shadows to him. It amused Kate to think how different this image was from her carriage nightmare, before she got pregnant, in which the baby buggy ran her down. Things were different now. She and the baby had a relationship. He was her little buddy, her pal. With every tiny kick and movement, he reminded her of his presence, even in her sleep. In a way, she dreaded giving birth, not because she feared labor or pain, but because it would separate them forever.

When her guard was down like this, Kate thought of Matt. It would have been nice to be able to call him into the room, to have him sit on the edge of the tub and share this time with her. Did he think of this, too? Kim had hinted that he missed her, but then, Kim would say almost anything for the impact of saying it. Kate had not yet responded to the contract the children had given her. It was ridiculous, but she didn't want to ignore or dismiss it. She wanted Gregory and Kim to know she took them seriously and cared about them. She decided she would write them each a letter, telling them just that. She wondered how Matt would handle it. Should she call him to discuss it? No. She tried to block Matt from her mind. He was right—hashing over things only led to negative thoughts, and she didn't want to impose those on the baby. Thinking of Matt inevitably disturbed her, and she knew that if she started a litany of what-ifs now, it would be impossible to sleep, and she would spend yet another uncomfortable night tossing in bed between the beautiful, wrinkled sheets that were too fine to send to the laundry.

She remembered the ritual of caring for the sheets. When she lived with Matt, the sheets had been changed every time they used the bed, even for a nap. It was a routine supervised by a full-time housekeeper and a three-day-a-week laundress. First, the sheets—which had to be the purest white, highest thread count Egyptian cotton, with filigreed Madeira embroidery—were washed in cold water. Then they were spun damp and placed overnight in plastic bags in a refrigerator which existed for that sole purpose to let the fabric "rest." The next day, they were ironed by hand, upside down, protected by a thick terry towel to keep the relief of the embroidery from flattening out. Finally, they were folded, with sheets of verbena-scented tissue between them, and stacked on fresh, piqué-lined wicker trays in the linen closets, which took up an entire wall.

It was amazing to Kate that she had once set such store by sheets, which were, after all, just pieces of cloth. It was as if the sheets had been her babies, as if she had to have something on which to focus her nurturing instincts. Now she saw it—Matt had his fish, and she had her sheets. And now those things were gone and over, surrogate stand-ins with their purpose spent and past.

Would she fixate on the child like this? Kate wondered. She hoped not—it would be too smothering for him. She hoped that in satisfying her emotional emptiness, the baby would eliminate her neediness.

Kate climbed out of the tub and wrapped herself in a silk robe. It was a lovely June day, but she had no desire to go outside. She sat on her iron bed and opened a book called *The First Nine Months*. There was a picture of the five-month fetus. It would be ten inches long by now, the book said, with teeth and hair. In the pictures, the baby looked like it was praying, its head was transparent, and you could see the meticulous network of veins webbed beneath the skin. It was hard to relate this image to the child inside her, although she knew it was a fact.

She padded into the study, which would soon become the nursery, and surveyed her progress. Rolls of yellow duckie wallpaper were stacked on the floor, ready for hanging. A mobile of pastel elephants was packed in its box on her desk, on top of the computer. Swatches of yellow polka-dot and navy-blue striped fabric were taped to the wall by the window, but Kate hadn't gotten around to ordering curtains yet. There was the wicker bassinet she'd bought. That was it. She knew she needed a crib and some other furniture, but she just hadn't gotten around to it yet. It seemed like all her organizational skills were being funneled into the magazine, and there were none left over for her and the baby.

There was still the question of the nanny. When she'd lived with Matt, she'd been committed to the idea of a British nanny, someone like Mary Poppins, ideally the product of a London nanny service. She'd actually had someone on hold, but of course her body had not cooperated, and now she had to wonder if she'd find a nanny at all. Last week, Kate had phoned all the nanny services she'd registered with, only to learn that she was still at the bottom of their waiting lists. In desperation, she decided to run an ad. Sitting at her desk, she wrote:

> Experienced nanny, live-in position. Nursing/education degree preferable. CPR trained. Non-smoker, non-drinker. Creative approach. Light housekeeping and cooking. Infant experience. References necessary.

Perfect! She'd have Clair call the *Times* and run the ad for a week. In this economy, Kate was certain there would be lots of takers.

The problem would be finding the time to interview them. Between redesigning *Finance*, trying to drum up potential sponsors, tiptoeing around the office politics, and pulling together the proposal for the Japanese, Kate had no free time. She'd given up on trying to make the prenatal exercise class and dropped out after one session, and she wondered when she'd be able to squeeze in Lamaze. There was still the nursery to finish and the layette to buy. It was easier to launch a magazine than a baby, Kate concluded. At least you could delegate.

Still, there was no denying she'd have to get moving. She got out her pen and a pad and made a list:

diapers
bottles
blankets
crib
crib sheets
nightgowns
T-shirts
changing table
rattles and toys
booties
hats
sweaters
overalls
rocker

one dress-up outfit
baby bath

It seemed easy enough. Babies were small. They didn't take up much room, and they didn't need a lot. When she had finished her list, Kate felt wonderful, as if she and the baby had accomplished something together. Maybe the fabled maternal instinct had finally kicked in.

Taking a personal day off was something Kate rarely did, but, after all, she hadn't so much as had a weekend vacation for almost a year. She would use the morning to pull things together, beginning with the baby's room. In the afternoon, she would interview nannies. Thirty women had responded to her ad, and, on the phone, she'd narrowed it down to four.

Her plan was to sleep in till nine, luxuriate with a cup of herbal tea and the papers, then be at the stores, list in hand, by ten. Now, she realized she had no idea where to start. She was sitting on the bed in her robe, staring blankly at the list, when the phone rang.

"Hello."

"Hello. This is Larry Sedlacek. Are you all right?" He sounded concerned.

Kate was irritated. Why was he calling her at home, and how had he gotten her number?

"When your secretary said you were at home for personal reasons, I got worried. I bribed your home number out of her with a pair of Knicks tickets."

"I'm not sick. I'm just home."

"Thank God. I was worried that something had happened with the baby."

"Well, that's considerate of you, but, really, you don't need to be concerned." Kate wanted to hang up and get dressed. She tucked the phone under her chin, walked over to her armoire, and pulled out a pair of maternity support panty hose. The things seemed like headless boa constrictors, springing free with a life of their own. She wriggled the panty hose up one ankle and over the knee, where they stuck like glue. She yanked at the demon elastic, hopping on one foot like a lopsided stork. The phone dropped to the floor.

"Hello? Hello?" came the voice from the floor.

"Damn!" She lunged for the phone, lost her balance, and crashed loudly against the bed, tangled hopelessly in the panty hose.

"Kate, are you all right? Kate? Kate! Jesus, she fainted!"

Finally, she grabbed the phone. "Larry? Larry?" He had hung up. Just as well.

Ten minutes later, as Kate was combing her hair, her buzzer rang.

"Open up! Police!"

"Oh my God!" She raced into the hall. She could hear sirens in the street. The building must be burning down!

Up the stairs charged Larry Sedlacek, leading a phalanx of police, an ax-wielding fireman, and white-coated paramedics with a stretcher. He barged right past Kate, oblivious.

"2-F, that's it. Spread out! Move! Move! Move!" Larry barked, as the group fanned through her apartment.

Kate stormed back in, running after him into her bedroom. "Just one minute, you!"

"Kate!" He stopped cold.

"Would you please explain what in God's name is going on here?" The heavy boots of the fireman tromped through her living room.

"You're all right? You came to?" He strode over. "Get off your feet. Sit down, put your head between your legs, and let these guys take your pulse." He yelled over his shoulder, "Paramedics!"

"Get your hands off me! You're always *touching* me! I am not a—a—contact sport! What are you doing here? What are they doing here? You owe me a big explanation."

The police, fireman, and paramedics stood gathered in the doorway.

"You fainted on the phone. I heard you."

"I did not faint."

"You dropped like a stone. I heard the thud when you hit."

"I dropped the phone. And this is a ridiculous conversation."

She turned to the group in the doorway. "I'm sorry, gentlemen, there seems to be some misunderstanding. As you can see, I'm perfectly fine."

"Just let them listen to your heart for—"

"I said, I am perfectly fine." She glared at him. "*You* are the problem."

"Okay, fellas, you heard the lady. She's *fine!* Can't you see that? Now clear the premises!" He pointed to the stretcher. "Get that thing out of here! Let's go!"

One of the policeman came over and shook Larry's hand. "Pleasure working with you, Sed."

"Thanks, Neil. See you Sunday at the game. Just give my name to the gate guard."

The group filed out.

"You know, lady," said Larry, mopping his forehead, "you almost gave me heart failure. I thought I'd find you lying here . . . well, we don't even want to go into what was going through my head. And I was blaming myself the whole way over here. I figured you were home recovering and you had some sort of delayed reaction or something. Actually, I don't know what I figured, I'm just so damn glad to see you standing here telling me you're fine."

He looked too sincere and too relieved for Kate to be angry.

"Admit it. You did overreact just a little bit," she said.

"As Patton said, better to overreact than not react."

"He said that?"

"Well, he would have if he'd thought of it."

"I appreciate your vigilance, but I have some shopping to do."

"Let me drop you. I have a car."

"A little something with a siren?"

"Maybe I can help you. Carry your packages."

"I'm going to be buying diapers."

"I love diapers," Larry said, following Kate out the door. "Wore them for years. Besides, what are you having, boy or girl?"

"Boy. I think. I asked them not to tell me, but it looked like a boy on the amnio screen. And it feels like a boy."

He grimaced. "No offense, but you're gonna need my help for sure."

"Why is that?"

"I saw that lambykins bib. Come on. Let's start this kid off right."

Kate figured that Larry Sedlacek would take off the minute he saw where she was headed: a fancy, Upper West Side baby store called Bambini. But instead of dropping her off, he followed her inside and grabbed the list from her hand. "Let's see, what have we got here. Leave it to me. I've got eight nieces and nephews." He picked up a tiny rattle and shook it, his hand knocking over a display of stuffed animals. "Take this. Good for the grip."

"May I help you?" a saleswoman said, materializing by Larry's side.

"I'm due in three and a half months, and I need a few things, starting with diapers."

"Of course. Cloth, disposable, or ecologically biodegradable?"

"Which is better?"

"It's a value judgment. Disposable, of course, comes in his and hers, and it's convenient, but who knows the long-range environmental consequences. The biodegradables are morally commendable, but between you and me, they tend to leak. Cloth, well, there's quilted and plain thirty-six-inch squares, but you need a diaper service."

Kate hadn't considered the global consequences of diaper choice. She decided to put off that decision.

"Cribs. I'll need a crib."

Larry was already on his hands and knees, inspecting the construction of an eyelet-trimmed white one. "He'll have a hard time breaking out of this one," he said, shaking the bars. A woman with a stroller shoved her way through the aisle, rolling over Larry's hand. "Ouch!" he yelled, leaping to his feet.

"Mister, you're blocking the aisles," said the woman, pushing on.

"This converts into a junior bed later," the saleswoman enthused, ignoring the commotion. "You just remove the side rail. It's got European craftsmanship—made in Italy." She looked

170

sorrowful. "Unfortunately, it won't work for you, if you need something this year."

"Why not?" asked Kate.

"You have to order all our Italian lines eight months in advance of delivery."

"Eight months! I didn't even know I was pregnant then!"

She shrugged. "These days our mommies seem to plan so far in advance. Well, what about this one?"

She motioned to a high-tech model, sleek and red.

"That's more like it," said Larry.

"We call this the Mercedes. It's one thousand dollars, not including bumpers and coverlet."

"A thousand bucks?" said Larry. "For a thousand bucks they should throw in air bags and cruise control."

Kate opened her notebook. "The Mercedes," she wrote. "Now I'll need a changing table."

The saleswoman nodded. "May I suggest this? We call it the Baby Mondo Condo." She led them over to a network of white laminate pieces. "Crib converts to flip-down changing table, with attached drawers at both ends. A real space-saver."

"Isn't this incredible?" Kate asked Larry. "Larry?" He was down the aisle, penned in by two nine-month bellies and a double stroller, sweating profusely.

"Larry, are you all right?" she called out.

He inched his way clear. "I've never seen so many pregnant women under one roof," he panted. "I didn't know so many existed." He shook his head. "I'm getting claustrophobic. They're using up all the air in here." His eyes darted around the room.

Kate pulled out her charge card.

"I gotta get out of here," Larry mumbled. He looked pale.

"See you," Kate said merrily. That would be the end of him, as she had suspected.

"Just do me one favor," he yelled from the door on his way out. "Hold off on the crib. That thing's not for kids. It's for cave dwellers."

By two o'clock Kate was back in her apartment, waiting for the first prospective nanny to arrive. She flipped through her notes on the twenty-some women she had ruled out. Most of them were baby-sitters, not nannies, and several had no experience or references. The four she would speak with today had seemed the only plausible possibilities.

The buzzer rang, right on time, and Kate opened the door to see two nicely dressed, middle-aged women.

"Hello," she said, extending her hand. "I'm Kate Harrison-Weil."

The two women stepped in, and Kate took their coats and ushered them to the round table in the living room.

"I am Mrs. Avias and this is my sister-in-law, Mrs. Ochera," said the first woman.

Mrs. Ochera nodded pleasantly. *"Obrigada,"* she said.

"Yes," Kate said to Mrs. Avias. "We spoke on the phone. Now, what is your experience with newborns?"

Mrs. Avias shook her head. "Oh, I have no experience. My sister-in-law, she is the one. She is very experienced. She has raised four children and she has worked for wonderful people in Porto."

"Where is Porto?"

"Portugal. She has just come from Portugal."

"Mrs. Ochera," Kate said, "tell me, what were the ages of the children you worked with?"

"Oh, they were very young," said Mrs. Avias. "Babies."

Mrs. Ochera smiled, but said nothing.

"Mrs. Ochera, tell me what equipment you like to have in the nursery. I'm a new mother, you see. I'll need lots of advice."

Mrs. Avias turned to her sister-in-law, and they engaged in a short, rapid-fire conversation in a language Kate did not know but assumed to be Portuguese.

"She says, whatever you have is fine, she will make do. But a rocking chair is good."

Kate nodded slowly. "Does—does your sister-in-law speak English?"

Mrs. Avias looked surprised. "No, not yet. She has only been in America one month. But she will learn."

"But she knows some English, doesn't she? I thought I spoke to her on the phone."

"No, you spoke with me."

"Oh."

"Do you speak Portuguese?"

The next candidate was due at two-thirty. By three-thirty, when the third appointment buzzed, she still had not arrived, and Kate crossed her off the list.

Candidate number three was an attractive young black woman in her early twenties.

"Hi," she said energetically. "I'm Shelly Marie. I know it sounds like two first names, but it's not; Marie's my real last name." She laughed pleasantly and looked around. "Nice place."

"Hello, Shelly. I'm Kate Harrison-Weil. Tell me about your experience with babies."

Shelly handed out two letters of reference. "I worked with two families in Maine. One had a three-year-old, and one had a two-month-old. Little Kevin. He was adorable. My degree is in early childhood education."

So far, so good. "Can you use that in infant care?"

"Of course. I believe in an integrated approach—creativity combined with structure. For instance, I like to put the child on a schedule right away, but even with a newborn, we can experiment with textures by, say, putting them on a lambskin, a piece of velvet, and a quilt."

Kate was almost embarrassed to take out the mundane list of questions that CeCe had told her to ask.

"What formulas do you like to use?"

"Well, Enfamil if the baby's not allergic to milk, or, if he's milk-sensitive, one of the soys."

Kate nodded. Shelly Marie knew her stuff. She went down CeCe's list, and Shelly had all the right answers, from how to take care of the umbilical cord to how to administer vitamins. The interview was promising.

"You'll be living in, is that all right?" Kate asked. "You don't have to go home to a husband or a child?"

"No," said Shelly. "But I like to make it clear up front that I have my own life."

"Of course."

"That's why I left Maine. There was nothing to do."

"I see."

173

"After five-thirty, I consider it my personal time. And weekends."

Kate knew there was no way she'd be home by five-thirty.

"And," said Shelly, "if you have a car, we'd work out access to that occasionally, I'd assume."

"Really."

"And I'm a vegetarian. But I do eat macrobiotic."

"Thank you, Shelly. I'll call you."

The fourth appointment was a large woman wearing a scarf who stood at the bottom of the stairs and refused to come up to the apartment.

"I don't do stairs," she announced, peering up at Kate. She turned and left, shaking her head. "I don't do stairs," she repeated, muttering on her way out, as Kate stood dazed in the doorway, staring after her.

Eleven

Roy Guardino shrugged off his jacket, pushed up his shirt-sleeves, and slapped a videocassette into the player that had been rolled into the *Finance* dining room for the occasion. "Japan," he said intensely. "Land of Sushi, Egg Foo Yung, and opportunity." He waggled his wrist, calling his audience's attention to a huge, gleaming watch. "They sure can make a timepiece." He held it to his ear. "Still ticking." He bowed from the waist. "People-san," he said. "Allow me to give you a guided tour through the Land of the Rising Sun." He punched a button and as the tape rolled, his image burst onto the screen, standing in front of Hiro headquarters in Tokyo.

Kate leaned back in her chair. It was unbelievable how much play Guardino had managed to squeeze out of five days of fact-finding in the Orient; suddenly the man was the Marco Polo of publishing. Stanton Welch's go-between had set up meetings with the marketing managers of the consumer electronics and office products divisions, but it was a known fact that this was just protocol—all decisions were made by Akio Akito, the company president and founder, and his senior team of advisors. Kate just hoped that Guardino's Egg Foo Yung–isms hadn't turned off anyone in the hierarchy, but, then, she also wondered in all honesty if she would have done any better herself. Japanese businessmen were notoriously anti-female; worse than even the most archaic of their American counterparts. Even Rick Nagamici had not minced words when he pointed this out to Kate during his crash-course phone briefing.

"To be frank, you're really walking into the lion's mouth," he had cautioned. "You're a woman. You're not Japanese; you don't even speak Japanese. And you're a *pregnant* woman. In Japan, working women are called *jimsho no hana*—'office flowers.' Trying to negotiate with Akito! I can't even think of any precedent. If you pull it off, I'm going to personally write it up as a Harvard Case Study."

"Isn't there anything I can do?" Kate had pleaded.

"Well, you could go out drinking with them," Rick had suggested helpfully.

Would it never end, this shell game of being a woman in business? Since she was almost two decades into her career, she supposed it wouldn't. First, a woman had to outperform men in school, just to be eligible for the best entry-level jobs. Then, if she didn't have an MBA, she'd damn well better be brilliant, which was a good idea even if she did have an MBA. But even that was no insurance, because if she had an MBA, *and* she was brilliant, the shells got shuffled, the rules changed, and she required either: (a) international experience, (b) a law degree, or (c) a CEO mentor; all the while appearing unaggressive on the surface so as not to threaten the system, while unobtrusively maintaining the inner drive of a nuclear warhead. The thing was, the so-called glass ceiling wasn't glass at all. It was just always under construction—and constantly being raised.

And now, here was Guardino, bulging with the glory of it all like a blister that was ready to pop.

Guardino paused the tape at an image of himself with his arms around two costumed geishas. "This," he announced, "is the key to Japanese commerce: these guys love a good time. They're goddamned party animals—a couple hundred million of 'em squeezed vertical on a bunch of islands. Okoto took me to the Ginza— then there's the Whatchamacallit District—an entire borough, I swear to God, of red-light hotels. That'll give you some insight."

Phil Moran and the five or six others in the room gaped at

Guardino with a mixture of horror and fascination. "When Akio and the boys hit town next week," said Guardino, "I know precisely how to handle them. I've lined up an authentic Japanese evening so we can share some culture and get to know each other." He looked at Kate. "Anybody who can't keep up better stay at home."

Kate sagged back into her chair, deflated. Guardino was right. She'd read enough to know that the Japanese would indeed expect to be entertained—vigorously, for lack of a better word—and she wasn't sure how she would handle this. It was critical that she be taken seriously, but she knew she couldn't reverse thousands of years of cultural attitudes. It wasn't looking good.

Guardino started the tape again, pointing to a picture of himself cheering at a Japanese baseball game. "The Japanese were perfect hosts," he said. "They're *nuts* about sports, especially baseball." He restarted the tape. "Say, Phil," he said. "Let's get some cigars in here."

Phil's eyes swung to Kate.

"Sorry, Roy," she said. "We had to stop the cigar thing. Budget reasons."

The room was dim, but she could make out Guardino's expression—as if his tie had suddenly become too tight, and all the blood vessels in his face had rushed to the surface, expecting a lynching, preferably hers.

"Mr. Akito," Kate said, at the end of their initial meeting one week later, "now that we've shared this thorough review of our plans for the new *Finance,* I hope you'll agree that we have the ideal forum to communicate the Hiro message to your consumers, and that by sponsoring an entire issue, you'll make that message synergistically more impactful." She flicked off the overhead projector and sat down, trying not to show that she was out of breath. These days, Kate was finding it harder and harder to stand on her feet and give three-hour presentations. Still, it seemed to have gone well; at least she'd made all her points. But there was no telling how the six members of the Hiro entourage were going to react.

Kate had presented to all kinds of groups in her career, but never to an entourage. There were six of them. According to Stanton Welch's brother-in-law, although Akio Akito was a financial genius who had built a billion-dollar electronics empire, he was nonetheless the "black sheep" of his family. In his youth, Akito's expulsion from school had resulted in his being sent to America to be educated, and his openly rebellious ways had early-on isolated him from his old-line, traditionally minded family. As Stanton's brother-in-law put it, "Aki grew up outside the system, so he likes renegades and dropouts."

To Kate, Akito looked like anything but a nonconformist. Elegant, urbane, attired in Armani, he seemed the epitome of the multinational businessman. Flanking him at the conference table, however, were his marketing director, an unreadable, older man whom Guardino had met in Japan; a right-hand man, whose title no one seemed to understand, but whose function seemed to be court jester; a consultant with a Wayne Newton pompadour, who understood everything about electronics and nothing about American magazines; and a young woman—Akito's secretary?—who never took off her sable coat and never opened her mouth.

The minute the lights were up, Guardino jumped to his feet. Skirting the table, he stood behind the marketing director's chair. "Mr. Matsushita and I have already discussed all this in detail," he said, patting the man on the shoulder, receiving an icy stare in response. "And, as we discussed in Tokyo, if you feel sponsoring an entire issue is too big a commitment, we have a page rate plan." He signaled Phil, who passed out some Xeroxed sheets.

Kate seethed. Guardino was actually selling against her idea! She knew he didn't support it, but he was openly rebelling. God only knew exactly what he had promised in Tokyo.

As soon as Akito and his group had left to go back to their hotel to freshen up for dinner, Kate confronted Guardino.

"You must be confused, Roy," she said. "The plan is to sell an entire issue to one sponsor. That's how the editorial is structured in the prototype we showed them. Nothing else makes any sense."

Guardino slapped his forehead and spun sideways. "Of course! Forgive me! How could I forget! We want to back these guys into a corner so there's no way out, and when they don't spring for the whole nut—which, in my experience, is an impossible sale—we lose them, and along with them, our shirt. Kate, let me tell you the first rule of sales, which is give the man a choice."

"I believe we are giving him a unique *product*. That's what he's buying."

"Or not."

"That's right. And I'll take that risk."

Guardino's cheek twitched. "You walk in here and take an American institution like *Finance* and rearrange it like it's your living room furniture, then you come up with this scheme for advertising which has no relation to what's going on in the marketplace, and you absolutely refuse to listen to reason, is that it? Because I'll tell you, missy, you're not going to make this sale."

Roy's head moved in a combination nod-shake.

"I'm no sexist—hell, I've got a wife. But the Japanese are not going to listen to a woman. Period, point-blank. So we'd better understand each other here and now." He poured a glass of water and sipped it. "I'm willing to say, okay, handle your editorial however. But the advertising, that's my territory, and if I'm accountable, I've got to handle it the way it can work. I'm not some goddamned junior numbers cruncher. And I'm not going to force this plan of yours on them at gunpoint, because it won't work." He cracked his thumbs.

"This is not the time for this discussion," said Kate. Summoning her most authoritative tone, she thrust one of her handouts at Guardino. "In fact, there *is* no discussion. *This* is the plan. I suggest you study it."

On her way out the door, she heard his muttered response: "Don't hold your breath, babycakes."

The worst part was, Kate knew Guardino was right. The Japanese weren't going to listen to her. She had to give herself some credibility, but how?

For the first time in her career, Kate wished she were a man. Someone who could toss shots and trade sports stats with the boys. Someone like Larry Sedlacek.

Suddenly, she smiled. *Yes. Someone like Larry Sedlacek.*

"This place has the freshest sashimi in New York," said Roy Guardino as he tapped on the glass of the huge aquarium. "You

179

choose your fish, the girl nets it, and in thirty seconds it's on your plate. The specialty is, we choose one fish as a group, and they bring us that very fish, served four different ways, in four courses. Mr. Akito, would you care to do the honors?" He bowed in Akito's direction.

Kate averted her eyes; she didn't care to get too friendly with her dinner. Besides, the fish might recognize her for what she was—the mass murderer of their tropical cousins. She was over her nauseous period, but she still preferred to eat cautiously. And of course, drinking was out of the question. She focused on the rice-paper screens.

Two hostesses in full geisha costume escorted the group through the restaurant, which was decorated like a turn-of-the-century Japanese mansion, to their private room. Their faces were masks, their hair frozen, their platform shoes so high they hobbled. The low wooden table was almost level with the floor, and Kate had to angle her way on to her tatami mat, doing her best to minimize her pregnancy. It was a difficult task, considering the fact that her belly hung over the edge of the table.

"Sorry I'm late." Larry Sedlacek appeared as the beer and drinks were being served. "Hi, everybody."

"Who's this?" snapped Guardino. Clearly he did not recognize Larry. That didn't exactly surprise Kate, since he often boasted that he never watched television.

"My guest, Larry Sedlacek," said Kate, as Guardino gave her a look signaling that guests were not welcome.

Guardino motioned Larry over to his side. "We'll be talking business here tonight," he said. "I don't know if Kate told you. You might not enjoy it."

Larry smiled. "Oh, she did and I will."

Kate introduced the people at the table. "This is Mr. Akito, president and chief operating officer of Hiro. And this is Mr. Matsushita, the marketing director, Mr. Ikuta, division director, George Haneda, their consultant, and—miss, excuse me, I don't think I got your name."

The girl, still wearing the sable coat, said nothing.

"Miko," said Akito. "Her name is Miko."

"Hiya, Miko," said Larry. "Hello, everybody. Don't get up."

He curled up his long legs and painstakingly wedged himself up to the table.

The geishas gracefully carried in a variety of small dishes on a lacquered tray, beautifully served and garnished, an edible artwork consisting of covered bowls of rice and soup, the sashimi slices of the fish Akito had chosen, and a small pile of grated green horseradish and seaweed.

"Look at that," marveled Guardino. "Live bait! The sucker moved!" He stabbed the sashimi with the chopsticks and popped a piece into his mouth.

Kate's appetite vanished.

Akito nodded. "The very best," he agreed. "A delicacy anywhere in the world."

Dropping her chopsticks, Kate decided to try to make Miko feel at home. She knew all too well how it felt to be a token woman. "Miko," she said. "What exactly do you do?"

There was a silence. Miko smiled a sidelong smile.

"She is with Mr. Akito," said George.

"Oh."

The Wayne Newton impersonator–consultant leaned over to Kate. "Mr. Akito bought her contract from the geisha house when she was fourteen," he confided.

Kate stared at Larry in astonishment, but even he looked shocked.

Guardino leaned across the table, motioning suddenly to Kate. He whispered to Phil, who in turn whispered to her. "Move your chopsticks, Katie. Roy says if you put your chopsticks straight up and down in your rice bowl, it's imitating the way they make offerings to the dead!"

Kate plucked up her chopsticks.

Guardino caressed his beer glass. "You know, Mr. Akito," he said thoughtfully, "it's interesting to compare and contrast the role of women in our two societies."

"Yes," Akito answered, nodding. "I find it fascinating that more than a quarter of Japan's college graduates are women."

"In America, there are actually more women in graduate business schools than men," Kate pointed out.

Guardino poked a chopstick in Kate's direction. "Well, that

181

trend is starting to reverse, isn't it? My own daughter, for instance. She wants to be a mom. And why not?"

"How old is your daughter?" asked Mr. Akito, politely.

"Five."

"It's good that she plans ahead," observed Kate. "You can't start that hope chest too soon."

"I say, men, women, *vive la différence,*" toasted Phil.

"That raises an interesting point," said Kate. Why not go for it? She had nothing to lose. "You know, a few years back, they did a major study of business behavior in men and women, and you know what they found?"

"People took too many coffee breaks?" Patronism seeped into Guardino's voice.

"No, Roy. They found an interesting correlation with the Japanese. Correct me if I'm wrong, Mr. Akito, but the Japanese managerial style is based on a group orientation and long-term decision making, which the researchers called Beta style."

Akito nodded. "Basically, that is true. The group is very important. And Japan is an island. The long term is important historically because we do not have boundless resources from which to recoup errors."

"Well," said Kate, "in America, they found the predominant managerial style to be individual-oriented and short-term in nature. They called this the Alpha style. This was true in every facet of American society except one, which is the family. The family is run for the benefit of the group, with decisions that benefit the long term. And most American women in business were found to be Beta-style managers. So, in other words, if more American women were in management, American business would be more like Japanese."

"Fascinating," commented Akito. "But then, who would run the family?" He smiled politely, unwilling to debate the point.

"Here, here," said Guardino, loudly patting the table.

"What will you be doing over the weekend, Mr. Akito?" Kate asked, switching tacks. "We've arranged for a box for the opening Mets game."

"The Mets!" Akito snapped to attention. "Darryl Strawberry. A man who hit home runs but was lazy in the field. I suspected he wanted to be traded. I have a Japanese friend who owns a baseball team who would gladly have paid him a lot of money."

Guardino seized the moment. "Baseball, what a great game. I used to be a catcher in college, myself. People said I reminded them of Yogi Berra."

"What'd you do, smash four home runs in four consecutive openers?" asked Larry.

"Huh?"

"Oh, just a little trivia." Larry chuckled.

"Trivia!" beamed Mr. Akito. "A hobby of mine. Yogi Berra was one of only two players from the same major league club to catch in the All-Star Game." He smiled at Roy Guardino. All six sets of eyes were on Roy now. "Who was his teammate?"

Quickly Larry whispered behind his menu to Kate, "Elston Howard, 1961."

"Elston Howard, 1961?" she said tentatively.

Mr. Akito turned to her in surprise. "Yes! And Berra was replaced when in the game?"

Larry drummed nine fingers on the table.

"Ninth inning," Kate announced.

George nodded happily. "Mr. Akito—baseball is his life."

"Since when did you learn about baseball, Kate?" asked Guardino, his eyebrows sloping incredulously.

"Oh, it's been a pastime of mine for a while," Kate replied.

Akito was off and running. "A contest!" he proclaimed. "I will pitch the questions. Losers must drink."

"Accepted." Mr. Ikuta spoke for the first time.

Mr. Matsushita filled his beer glass and raised it in challenge. A childlike grin crossed his face. Even Miko looked interested.

"How many home runs did Mickey Mantle score for the Yankees in 1956?" Akito asked.

Guardino threw up his hands. "Talk about obscure!"

Surreptitiously Larry drew a five and a two on the table with his finger.

"Fifty-two," supplied Kate.

"Amazing," said Akito. "A woman who knows baseball." He lifted his glass, and everybody drank. Kate sipped her mineral water.

"A fluke," said Guardino, his smile conveying a joint death wish

183

for Larry and Kate. Guardino excused himself, motioning Phil to follow. Obviously, they were going to the men's room to regroup.

Kate was relieved that her pregnancy had not become an issue. The Japanese completely ignored the fact. Maybe they just thought she had a terrible weight problem or water retention. She cleared her throat and decided to try again with Miko.

"Miko, what do you enjoy doing in New York?"

George translated Kate's question and Miko's answer: "Shop."

"She likes designer brands," George added. "Gucci, Tiffany, Versaci."

"Oh, of course. So do I. I mean, so did I."

Miko said something in Japanese.

"She asks the designer of your lovely suit," George translated.

Kate laughed. "No designer. It's just a maternity dress."

George nodded slowly, then spoke to Miko, who stared, albeit politely, at Kate. None of the Japanese men seemed to register the information, but Kate noticed that they seemed decidedly awkward. The energy of the trivia game seemed to dissipate.

"I think I need a miracle," she whispered to Larry, as Guardino and Phil returned to the table.

"Coming up," said Larry. He clanged his chopsticks on his beer bottle for attention. "Attention everybody! I have an announcement to make! How long will you be our guests in town, Mr. Akito?"

"Three more days, then we leave and return again next month."

"Just enough time, then, to meet Mr. October."

"Mr. October!" Akito fairly gasped. "Really? That would be wonderful. You know him?" Akito was beside himself, all Oriental restraint out the window. He was giggling like a teenager. "Mr. October!"

"Who the hell is Mr. October?" steamed Guardino to Phil. "A playmate of the month?"

"Uh—I'm not sure myself," said Phil. "But I think he's a talking horse."

"Reggie Jackson, Mr. October," explained Akito impatiently. "He always came through at playoff time. To actually meet him!

You could arrange it?" He looked at Larry with undisguised admiration.

"He's in town. So are Joe DiMaggio, Ernie Banks, Brooks Robinson, Mickey Mantle, Henry Aaron—for an old-timers' charity dinner I'm hosting. You'll be my guests, of course, at Reggie's table."

"Now just one minute," interrupted Guardino. "Mr. Akito and his party are guests of *Finance*. We have plays, Broadway, a private tour of Bergdorf's men's store. . . . There won't be time, sorry."

"Of course they are *Finance* guests." Kate cut him off. "At the dinner."

"Unfortunately, seats at the table of honor are limited," said Larry. "So, for *Finance,* only Kate and Mr. Akito will be seated there. But she'll be a gracious hostess, I'm sure."

"Of course!" exclaimed Mr. Ikuta. "Most gracious!"

"To Mr. October," toasted Akito. "And to Kate-san, who wins the trivia contest."

It was only polite to ask him up, Kate assured herself. After all, the evening had been such a success, and without Larry, it could have . . . would have gone the other way completely. There was no question that he had pulled her out of the fire. The least she could do was ask him up for a drink.

It wasn't as if she was *asking him up for a drink,* she told herself, as in—*I am your date and I am being provocative.* As in all the time-honored maneuvers and ploys of the courtship dance. No, asking him up for a drink meant just that: asking him up. For a drink. Take it at face value.

As they climbed past the third landing, Kate pulling her leaden legs after her, she amazed herself at her rationalizations. She was basically forty. Pregnant. Married. Hardly a teenager fluttering a wrist corsage on a first date. Yet, she still had to justify inviting a man to her apartment simply because he was a man. It was ridiculous. Inviting someone up for a drink was nothing more and nothing less than a basic social gesture, the liquid version of the handshake.

"What would you like to drink?" she asked, winded, when

they got to her apartment. God, she felt like she'd just lugged a caribou up the north face of Mount Everest.

"No thanks."

No drink! If she didn't have a drink, and he didn't have a drink, what were they doing here? That was one of the amazing things about pregnancy, Kate thought. It unfailingly forced you to confront all the things you'd automatically done in life for so long, like eat, drink, and sleep. Even the simplest activity—like, say, eating a donut—became a philosophical joust: Why am I eating this donut? What will its impact be? What are the ingredients? Will the powdered sugar inhibit my future child's college potential? Kate usually found that she was so exhausted by all the internal discourse, she took a pass.

"Well," she finally said, clearing her throat, "I'd like a glass of water."

"Sounds good to me," said Larry.

She started toward the kitchen.

"Sit." He patted a cushion. "I can find the faucet." He rummaged in the kitchen, she heard the water pour, and then they sat there with two glasses of ice water.

"I'm glad I never really had to deal with the corporate types too much," Larry said. "They make me nervous."

"You didn't show it. You creamed them."

"Well, what if they'd asked me about Theory Z?"

"They wouldn't have. Not after they realized you knew Reggie Jackson. Mission accomplished, and thank you very much."

"You know, Kate"—he laughed gently—"I have to tell you something. I never imagined a pregnant woman could be so cutthroat."

"I am not cutthroat. I'm a realist. There's a difference."

"Right. One doesn't carry a knife. He just beats you to death with the facts." Larry crunched his ice cubes.

"You aren't one of those people who believes in hormones, are you? Like, she's got all this surplus estrogen so now she's going to paint her apartment pink and dress in marabou, and never beat up anything but a boneless chicken cutlet?"

"No. But I believe in motherhood. And you. You just went in there like the Lawrence Taylor Blitz."

"Who?"

"He demolishes people, too." Larry was frowning, but there was an unmistakable element of pride in his voice. "He just does it on the field."

He leaned over and patted Kate lightly on the belly. "You're gonna have a feisty kid there."

"I don't know. Who can predict? The sonograms don't tell you what a baby will be like. But maybe he'll take after me and throw his weight around. In fact, he already is."

"What are you going to name him?"

"I'm not sure yet."

He touched her hair. "I like his mom. I just wish I knew where I stood with her." He addressed her stomach. "Kid, you there? Do me a favor, will you? Could you talk to your mom for me? See, I'm a friend of hers and you know, I'd like to be a better friend. I need a little support from the team."

Kate wondered if she should ask him to leave now. She hadn't planned on this kind of segue. But, in a way, she was intrigued.

"You see, little buddy, I kind of like you both, you and your mom," said Larry, now looking at Kate. "But I'm not good with this kind of thing because, well, let's face it, she and I are never going to be alone. And that's usually what it takes, if you're going to be more than friends."

"Larry," Kate said. "We can't go on dates, if that's what you mean. I'm fond of you, I really am, you know that. But there is no such thing as pregnant dating."

"Okay. So we won't date." He took her hand, very gently, and held it, palm open, in his. "We'll just hold hands."

They sat like that for a long time, maybe half an hour, saying nothing, until it felt right. And then there was a kiss, the kiss of a friend that, in the kissing, became more, as kissing has a tendency to do. It became a kiss that lasted too long and too late, until the sky was gray, and Larry led Kate into her bedroom, where he took off her clothes, piece by piece, and replaced them with a long, soft gown, and tenderly tucked her into bed. Then he got on the bed beside her. Not in it, on it.

"I'm just going to watch you sleep," he said.

And he did.

Twelve

*L*arry helped Kate gingerly pick her way down the steps to level E of the Klingenstein Pavilion of Mount Sinai Hospital.

"How considerate of them," she said as they dodged a pipe. "They timed their renovations to coordinate with my Lamaze classes." Kate still couldn't get over the fact that Larry had volunteered to be her Lamaze coach. More than volunteered—insisted, really.

What would I have done without Larry? Kate wondered now, in her seventh month, with the end of her turbulent pregnancy in sight. He seemed to have fallen in love with her as much because she was pregnant as in spite of it. He openly adored her roundness, the ripeness of her body. To him, the pendulousness of her breasts gave her the seductiveness of a Madonna.

"This is the way women were meant to be," he liked to announce, loudly and often, especially when she was naked.

"You embarrass me when you say that," Kate would say.

"Why? It's natural. Like a ripe fruit that feels just so when you touch it."

Kate was always surprised by Larry's frequently poetic language. He was such a big man—over six three, with muscled forearms and huge hands—that, although she'd known him for two months now, she still sometimes slipped into stereotyping him. Considering the fact that Larry Sedlacek was a former pro football player, who had lost his chance for a career on the field when he shattered his kneecap in his rookie season, most people automatically assumed he was a bruiser who got a break as a television sportscaster because he looked good and knew everybody in the locker room. But Kate knew Larry was more of a writer than a sports newsreader. He kept a journal, and was working on a collection of sports stories. He idolized Red Barber. He read. The one thing he did not do was play football, of which Kate was glad, because she found it difficult enough just accompanying him to the endless matches, bouts, and games. The problem was, Kate hated sports.

"I'm in a competitive business," she told Larry when they met. "People fight to the death every day—the gladiators of Madison Avenue. I don't need to see it every weekend and night. There's enough blood in the office." Considering her own uncooperative attitude, Kate thought, it was amazing that Larry was so anxious to attend the Lamaze class. Maybe he saw it as a sort of primitive tag team event.

"Are you sure this isn't some kind of maternity fetish?" Kate would ask as she noticed that her protruding navel was now showing through her T-shirt.

"It is. It's a Kate fetish. Probably illegal. I'll have one of the researchers at the station check on it."

"God, Larry, you don't have to do Lamaze with me. It's so—unromantic. You'll lose your virginal image of me forever."

"I lost that when I met you. A six-months-pregnant woman is on the far side of virginal."

"But you don't realize—there's nothing fun about Lamaze classes. It's not exactly up there with, say, celebrity bowling."

"Kate," said Larry. "Coaching is something I understand. The Power Sweep. The T-Formation. The Flea-Flicker. Name the play."

"A woman in labor is a little different, Larry."

"How?"

"For one thing, there's no instant replay."

"I'll survive."

Kate hoped Larry wouldn't back out, because realistically, she

189

needed him; there was no one else she could ask. True, Matt would no doubt show up for the birth, but she planned to leave strict orders that he was not to be admitted to the labor room. She didn't even want to be notified of his presence. She wanted to have her baby as naturally and supportively as possible. No bad thoughts, no accusations, no stress—this would be the time for all the love and wonder she imagined the birth experience to be. Matt's time with the baby—and confrontations with her—would come later. For now, she was determined not to let their problems intrude. Besides, if all went well, they'd be divorced by the time the baby was born.

When she'd discovered she had to have a coach for Lamaze, Kate was unpleasantly surprised. "You mean I can't do it alone?" she'd complained to the woman who registered her for the classes.

"Well, I suppose that in theory you can. But we recommend having a coach. Your coach doesn't have to be a man, though. You can have a friend, or a relative."

"This Lamaze thing is the worst example of bad management. You'd think that in the nineties we'd have a better system," Kate had railed to Larry. "What friend or relative can I possibly subject to eight weeks of three-hour classes, and God knows how many hours of labor, not to mention the birth itself?" She'd briefly considered calling CeCe, but that wouldn't work—CeCe lived almost two hours away from the city.

"I'd really like to do it with you," Larry had said. He was quiet, firm, and definitive.

"Why? You feel sorry for me? Don't feel sorry for me!"

"That's not it at all. Why are you always so defensive?"

"What, then?"

"I've always wanted to be a gynecologist, okay? I'm thinking maybe they'll show that groovy sixteen-millimeter movie of a woman giving birth. Give me a break!"

"Larry, how are you going to do this? It's every week, seven to ten. You don't even leave the station till midnight after the sports news. For that matter, sometimes neither do I. I should just forget the whole thing."

"We'll go to an early class. Before the news. It'll be a good excuse for you to leave the office at a reasonable hour. Believe me, I'll be there, Kate. And so will you. If I have to handcuff you to my wrist, we'll be there together."

He was as good as his word.

Kate pushed through the stairwell door and followed handwritten signs with arrows into a small, beige, windowless room with exposed ductwork and hard blue plastic chairs. Several pregnant women and their partners were already in the room, and most of the chairs were taken, so Kate and Larry squeezed into seats at the back, behind a slide projector. A few of the men turned to stare at Larry.

"Hey," said one. "It's the guy from Sunday-night sports."

None of the women seemed to care.

"I'm the oldest person in this room," Kate whispered to Larry, as he helped her off with her coat. Every other woman looked one step removed from a teenager, Kate thought. She was the oldest woman in Lamaze, as she would one day be the oldest den mother and the oldest woman in the PTA.

"Hi, I'm Terry," said the olive-skinned woman in the next seat. Kate noticed she'd brought her own pillow, and concluded she must be a Lamaze veteran.

"Kate," she said.

"When are you due?"

"October tenth."

"October thirtieth."

"Boy."

"Girl."

It was amazing, Kate thought, how expectant mothers could shorthand an entire conversation down to a few basic words. As if pregnancy stripped away the pleasantries, reducing all communication to what went on inside their bellies.

Terry's husband leaned past her and waved amiably at Larry. "Knicks game on tonight," he said.

"Well," said Larry, "I'm sure this will be just as entertaining."

The conversational rumbles died down as a short, sturdy-looking woman in a white lab coat strode into the room. She had a ring of keys dangling from diaper pins clipped onto one pocket, and a beeper on the other.

"Hello, I'm Coral Gaskar, R.N.," she said in a foghorn voice, as she handed out a stack of papers. "This is a vocabulary sheet—and a blueprint for your breathing technique."

"I'm not going to do any of these," muttered a young blond woman in front of Kate. "My breathing technique is going to be inhaling the anesthetic."

Coral Gaskar arched an eyebrow in the blond woman's direction. She walked purposefully to the front of the room, unzipped a gym bag, and pulled a life-sized cloth infant doll onto a Formica table, where it lay looking strangely forlorn. Kate had a crazy urge to lend the doll her coat.

"I want you to go around the room and introduce yourselves and tell when you're due, and a little bit about yourself."

"I'm Julio," volunteered a Hispanic man. "My mother had fourteen children." Every woman in the room winced.

"Nature," said Julio, throwing his hands wide. "It's a beautiful thing."

"I'm Maria," said his wife. "We're due November one. I got gestational diabetes and we're having sort of a hard time. We have three other children."

Kate was next. "I'm Kate. I work." She didn't know why she had to say that—as if having a career somehow justified being the oldest woman in the room.

Coral nodded. "We have working women all the time. Here they're running Citicorp and they're nervous about wiping the baby's eye. 'When I wipe the baby's eye, how much water will be in the cotton?' "

Everybody laughed, and Kate thought she heard a familiar laugh in the chorus. *Too familiar.* She looked up and saw Matt in the doorway. No, actually he was not in the doorway, he was coming into the room. He was sitting down behind her.

Kate felt dizzy and confused. "Why are you here?" she hissed, throwing a helpless glance at Larry.

"I'm the baby's father, if I'm not mistaken. You told me you'd be at this class. You told me you needed a coach. So I'm here."

"Thank you very much for your concern, but I *have* a coach. You really don't need to be here."

The entire class was dead silent, staring, except for Larry, who tapped his pencil loudly on the metal arm of his chair.

"Larry, this is Matt. Matt, Larry. Larry is my coach. See? You can go. Now."

Matt patted Larry's huge shoulder, which dwarfed his hand. "Wonderful of you to volunteer," he whispered. "But I'm here. I'll take over now."

Kate turned, ignoring the class, and attacked Matt with fierce whispers. "Matt, you have been no help for seven months and you are upsetting me now. Please leave! This is harassment. This is—"

"May I help you, sir?" called out Coral, her voice impatient.

"Oh," said Matt, pulling his chair closer to Kate's, "I'm this little guy's dad." He pointed to her stomach. "I'll be her coach."

"He will *not*," said Kate, emphatically.

"*I* am Kate's coach," said Larry evenly.

"Okay, I'll coach the *baby*," Matt replied.

"Look, lady," interrupted Julio. "I don't care if your coach is Knute Rockne. We have a three-hour class here and everybody's had a long day, so mellow out, will you?"

"You really should not have two coaches," said Coral, suspiciously eyeing Matt.

Matt waved her off. "I'm a doctor, affiliated with this hospital. I'm entitled to observe."

"Jesus Christ," muttered Larry, rolling his eyes.

Coral jerked to attention. "Well, that's different—Doctor."

Kate wanted to scream, *He's just a dermatologist!* But hadn't she made enough of a scene already? These pregnant women had not dragged themselves here tonight to hear about her problems. She'd have to handle this later.

Matt settled into his chair, all seriousness.

"Now," announced Coral, "back to business. Remember, a first-time mother will usually be in labor twelve hours, and most will be overdue. So think in terms of a longer delivery. But, remember, you won't be in labor forever, and you won't be pregnant forever, so there is a light at the end of the tunnel. Now. Let's look at the three parts of Lamaze: conditioning, concentration, and discipline. You need to concentrate on the pattern of labor, not the pain."

Kate shifted in her seat. Out of the corner of her eye, she saw Matt nodding attentively.

Larry dug his pencil into his pad, snapping the lead.

"Let's go over the role of the coach," said Coral. "The first role is to be a support person. At the beginning, your jokes are cute and funny; at the end, it's all your fault, I'm divorcing you."

"Sounds about right," said Matt, just loudly enough so that only Kate, and not even Larry, could hear him. Was he going to sit here and embarrass her all night?

"You coaches need to have a real role, not just running to the store and back because you can't sit there and watch her in pain." Coral held up a large picture of the uterus. "Imagine the cervix as a donut." She handed out a plastic card with circles indicating various dimensions of dilation for the class to study. Then she held up a large red-and-white-striped knitted sock.

"This," said Coral, "is a knitted uterus." She picked up the rag doll, which Kate noticed had a snap-on umbilical cord dangling from its navel, and stuffed the doll into the sock.

"Ouch," whispered Matt.

Kate inched her chair closer to Larry, who put his arm protectively around her. She made an effort not to look at Matt.

"When you're in labor and not effaced," said Coral, "the cervix is closed. Now, as a warm-up, I'd like everyone to stand up and try the pelvic tilt." She demonstrated, waggling her pelvis in an exaggerated motion, like a striptease dancer doing a bump and grind. "Dads and coaches, too," she said, waving the entire class to their feet.

"Just like Flipper the dolphin," Kate heard Matt say as he tilted his pelvis back and forth. On her other side, Larry glared as he tilted. Kate felt like she was stuck in the middle of a pelvic tilt sandwich.

"Okay, enough of that warm-up," said Coral. "Now, everyone, close your eyes, take a deep breath, and concentrate on my voice."

Kate welcomed the chance to shut out Matt; she squeezed her eyes shut.

"Concentrate on the muscles of your scalp, all the tension of the day coming out . . ."

How could he do this? Kate seethed, as Coral droned on in a singsong voice. The divorce was going along so smoothly. It was all so civilized. She felt confused. She hated Matt for his insensitivity, for just showing up with no regard for her. One part of her wanted to grab him by the collar and butt him into a wall with her pregnant belly, but on the other hand she had resolved to be fair to her unborn baby, to not deprive him of his father. Wasn't it the baby's right to have his father partici-pate—didn't a woman owe it to her child to put aside her per-sonal feelings so he could begin to bond with his father even now, before birth? Whichever psychologist invented the concept of paternal bonding suddenly became Kate's unknown adversary. Before male bonding was an issue, a mother was one hundred percent in charge of the birth. They pulled a curtain around the bed and sent the father out for cigars. Now, you had to do all the work and let somebody else share the joy of the birth, even if you selfishly wanted, that one time, that only time in your life, to have your baby all to yourself.

"Feel the tension slipping out of the thighs," said Coral, as Kate felt rigid, with the realization that this short nine months the baby was inside her, untouchable, was the only time he would ever be truly and only *hers*. From the minute of his birth, she would share him with others for the rest of their lives. Never again would they belong to each other. Already, she had to share him with Matt. She sighed in exasperation.

"*Very good*, Kate," called out Coral. "I hear that tension releasing. Now, everybody, I want you to squeeze your fist until I tell you to stop."

Kate felt like squeezing her fist right into Matt's face, but she didn't. Seconds ticked by as she wondered how she and Larry should leave. Should they ignore Matt? Should she acknowledge him? Should she threaten him? Should she kill him? Here they all stood, three in a line, squeezing their fists in unison like the Three Stooges, and there wasn't one thing she could do about it.

"Okay, open your hand and eyes and take a seat," said Coral.

"That was a sixty-second contraction. Your hand represents your uterus, and, by the end of labor, you're going to have these contractions every two and a half minutes." Coral moved to the back of the room and flicked on the slide projector. It whirred in Kate's ear, as slides detailing the stages of labor flashed onto the screen. For the baby's sake, Kate forced herself to concentrate on Coral's description of the amniotic sac. Then, even though she didn't want to, she glanced at Matt. He was taking notes. She looked at Larry. He was watching her. *What a melodrama,* Kate thought; *I am a soap opera.* By the time the slide presentation was over, she felt as wrung-out as if she'd gone through labor and delivery already.

The lights flicked on, and Kate stretched in her seat. Her back ached, as it always did these days when she had to sit in a hard chair. She checked her watch: five to nine. She couldn't postpone it anymore; the class was over.

She leaned over, cupped her hand to Larry's ear, and whispered, "What do you think, Larry?"

"Ignore him," Larry said loudly.

They stood in unison, walked purposefully past Matt to the front of the room, then continued out the door and up the stairs.

"I am so sorry, Larry. I had no idea he'd show up here tonight."

"You know, I could always get involved here. We have a few options. First, I can just tell him to get lost. And if he keeps pestering you, we can file for a court order to keep him at a distance. Or I could get in touch with Lewie the Loop."

"Who's Lewie the Loop?"

"The middleweight contender. A buddy."

"Great. What about his rights as the baby's father?" Kate asked as they looked for a cab on Fifth Avenue. In her mind, she tried but failed to imagine Matt taking on Lewie the Loop.

"Your right to a peaceful and healthy pregnancy comes first. If we can get a doctor to say your condition is being affected . . ."

"The effect on the baby will be that his *father* is concerned," a voice behind them said. Kate spun around and saw Matt. "Listen, this is not your concern, my friend," he said to Larry.

196

"I'm not your friend. I'm Kate's friend."

"Fine. I happen to be her husband. Go ahead and be her—whatever. But until this baby is born, Kate's welfare is my concern. I'm sure you can understand that."

"Taxi," yelled Kate, as it started to rain.

"I have a car," said Matt, pointing to the Mercedes limousine hovering down the block. "In light of the weather, I suggest we share it."

Larry bristled.

"Let's be reasonable, Larry," said Matt, shaking out an umbrella and holding it over Kate. "You too, Kate. If you get a cold, or pneumonia, what's that going to prove?" He motioned to the driver, who cruised to the curb beside them.

Damn him, Kate thought, moving from under the umbrella. *He's always so well prepared.* Like she used to be herself. These days, she was never ready for anything. When the baby was born, she'd probably be wheeled down the hall yelling, "Wait! I'm not *ready!*" Why hadn't she thought to call a car herself? The rain was soaking her hair and collar, her ankles were spattered with mud, her shoes were soaked, and there were no cabs in sight. She felt like a galleon, awash and waterlogged. She looked at Larry, they shrugged at each other, and got into the car, Kate in the middle.

"Now, where can I drop you?" asked Matt. His shoes weren't even wet.

Kate looked across him and out the window. The city was a dark, watercolor blur. "My place," she mumbled. "West Seventy-third Street." She tried to make herself as small as possible. Larry hunched silently against the window. After all these months apart, it felt strange to be in a car with Matt, and, at the same time, strange not to be going home to Fifth Avenue with him. He'd never even seen her little walk-up in the brownstone.

"Scotch?" Matt held out a cut-crystal glass and decanter from the car's well-stocked bar and poured a drink first for Larry and then himself as the two appraised each other. "You know, it's senseless and unnecessary to be hostile about this," Matt said. "We all have one good cause in common—the baby. Larry, I'm glad you and Kate are together. It makes it healthier for the baby. He'll know who his father is; I'm not concerned about that. Why can't we approach this as a team?"

"Just who is the captain of this team?" Kate said testily.

"Kate, you are in charge of your own pregnancy. Naturally. But there's room for others. I can't give birth to the baby, and you and I are not together, so I'm asking you to be generous and share this birth. Please." Matt spoke quietly, but Kate could tell this was important to him. More important than she would have thought.

Kate wondered when Matt had become so involvement-oriented. She knew for a fact, because Elise had told her, that when Kim was born he'd been in the doctors' lounge, playing cards. She didn't feel like being victimized by his recent psychological retread, but she also felt she couldn't say outright, "No, Matt, I will *not* share the birth of your son with you." She couldn't discount the fact that he had been to hell and back with her for their marathon attempts to conceive. And Larry seemed to be capable of understanding that she could draw the line between romance and compassion; he probably wouldn't be threatened. Even now, as he sat sipping his drink, he seemed calm and unruffled, managing far better than she was so far. For a moment, they rode along in silence.

"Nobody's disputing that you have something at stake here," Larry finally said. "That much is fact. What's in question is the scenario you seem to be proposing here."

"It's not a scenario, it's a suggestion. A solution, I think. For all of us. Otherwise, it's going to be a tough couple of months." He turned to Kate. "Kate, you want your privacy, and I respect that. You have a relationship with Larry, and I respect that, too. We all have our own lives. But what I propose is that all of us attend Lamaze. Larry and I can both coach you, Kate. Then I can be a part of my child's birth." Matt's eyes were pleading, but she didn't reply.

"Come on, Kate," he said, sounding unequivocally reasonable. "I don't want to make the same mistakes I made with Kim and Gregory. God gave me another chance, and I'm not going to blow it. Please help me out. It's a compromise, really, if you think about it. And a fair one. Counselor"—he lifted his chin in Larry's direction—"you be the arbitrator here."

"If she agrees—well, it's her decision."

Kate wondered if she would ever see Larry again after tonight. She knew that if *she* had been in his shoes, she'd have jumped out of the car at the nearest corner and run for it. There was certainly no etiquette that covered Lamaze dates with an estranged husband in tow. It gave the phrase *ménage à trois* new meaning.

"Kate?" Larry touched her shoulder.

Suddenly, she started laughing. She laughed as they drove through Central Park, and as they turned onto Central Park West, and her laugh was infectious. Larry's small, tight smile transformed into a laugh, and Matt doubled over and roared as if he were watching the funniest movie he had ever seen. When they drove up in front of her brownstone, Larry, Kate, and Matt were all leaning on each other, heads thrown back, lost in laughter. Kate felt as if the bittersweet tears streaking down her cheeks would cancel out, in advance, the jealousies and resentments she knew they were not, for all their good intentions, about to avoid.

Thirteen

The following week, Kate surprised herself by setting up a lunch with Angie and CeCe. CeCe, of course, was her oldest friend; Angie was her newest. Angie and CeCe couldn't have been more different, but perhaps that was why Kate thought it might be fun to introduce them. As she sat waiting in the Oyster Bar of Grand Central Station, Kate decided that this was either the best idea of her life, or the worst. She hoped it wouldn't turn out like it always did when you decided to introduce a current man to an ex-man, as in the case of Larry and Matt. With men, there was always the drive to one-up; and, in Matt's case, he had the permanent, once-and-for-all one-up, which was currently moving around her belly as if doing the crawl. It was just, Kate thought, munching an oyster cracker, that CeCe and Angie had absolutely nothing in common, except her; she hoped she wasn't being either selfish or insane by supposing that was enough.

"Hi, sweetie," CeCe said, sliding into the booth. She was lugging two huge shopping bags, stuffed to the brim. "I brought along some things for the baby. My kids donated them. It was a good excuse to clear out some of the clutter before we move."

"Move? Where? Did somebody get a new job?"

"No, somebody didn't. I did. Ex-wife."

"What! You're leaving Steve?" But Steve was wonderful! He

shared. He burped babies at midnight. Baked banana bread from scratch. Bragged about his wife. He'd even been pictured in a Gap ad, holding the baby. If Steve didn't make it as the perfect husband, hope for mere mortal men was rock bottom.

CeCe blinked, and Kate noticed that her jaw was tight and there were shadows under her eyes. "Actually, I think he left me. I mean, he did. Leave me."

"And of course you said nothing to me! For God's sake, why not?"

"I didn't want to upset you. You were under enough pressure. Anyway, it happened rather suddenly." She choked on a non-laugh.

"Yo, Kate!" Angie waved wildly as she bounded up to the table, breathless, the fringe on her red leather jacket swinging in crazy eights. "Geez, I thought I'd never get here. I had three double processes going at once. It was wild."

Timing was everything in life.

"Um, Angie, this is CeCe MacGraw. CeCe, Angie Belladone."

"Hello."

"Surely."

"Angie's a cosmetologist," Kate pointed out, trying to ease CeCe's awkwardness. "Like I told you, she brilliantly turned me into this gorgeous blond bombshell you see today. The hair of a bombshell, the figure of a band shell. That's me."

CeCe smiled, but Kate could see she was still far from happy, and why not.

"Honey," said Angie, "if you don't mind my saying so, you look a little under the weather."

This was not as rude a statement as it might have been, since CeCe was now crying.

"CeCe." Kate reached out for her.

She could barely make out her reply in the din of the Oyster Bar: "He left me."

Angie rallied immediately. "The fucking scumbag!"

"It's probably male menopause," said Kate, hating this limp excuse even as she said it. Menopause for women meant drying up like a prune and getting the sweats. For men, it was ten years' worth of free excuses to fuck around and act like assholes.

Angie pulled a black lace handkerchief out of her purse and handed it to CeCe.

"I'm sorry." CeCe sniffed. "I'm making a spectacle of myself."

"No you're not. Your mascara isn't even running. What brand is that? I want to stock it."

CeCe twirled a damp strand of hair nervously. "The kids and I are moving out. I got a two-bedroom with a loft in Chelsea."

"Why? Okay, so you left him, or he left you, but why would you leave that gorgeous house?" Kate asked, genuinely shocked, recalling the thousands of hours CeCe had spent renovating it. An image of CeCe on her hands and knees in goggles, working a power tile cutter, flashed through her mind. It wasn't like the penthouse, which had little of Kate and a lot of decorator. CeCe had thrown herself into that house.

"Waiter! Gin and tonic." She lifted her chin. "I won't go back there. It's tainted. He had *her* up there. In our room! I found her earrings—oh, God, it's so sordid." She rubbed her forehead as if she were rubbing off a scar.

"Jesus."

Angie closed her eyes heavily. "This slug deserves that you should rip off his head and shit down his throat."

It all went to prove, Kate thought in the silence that followed, that nothing was certain. There were no guarantees. Was it any surprise the divorce rate was one in two? Was it any surprise she and Matt had split up? No, it was more like inevitable. Men that looked good and felt right turned out to be optical illusions, like those oversized perfect peaches you paid too much for at specialty stores, only to find they tasted like sawdust. It was better to have a bruised peach, a smaller peach, an ugly one, even, if it tasted sweet. Which was true about Larry; he tasted sweet. Not that she was about to bring that up.

"So did you see that guy Larry, from the restaurant?" Angie asked. She was only trying to change the subject and ease CeCe's discomfort, but Kate squirmed regardless.

"Yes," she said.

"Who is Larry?" asked CeCe, relieved at the diversion.

"Larry is a sportscaster whose jacket I had cleaned."

"He likes Kate," said Angie. "The plot thickened."

"He helped me out on a business matter. Stop it, you two!"

CeCe straightened up. "If you let him near you in this condition, it must be love." She blew her nose.

"Please. It was convenience, nothing more." Why was she denying it? Something *was* going on with Larry Sedlacek, there was no question about that. Why was denial always Kate's automatic front-line emotional response? Not because there was no emotion, but, she would have admitted if pressed, because it was less disruptive to the flow of her life. She preferred the Swiss Bank Account Theory of Emotions—you deposited them, then sealed the vault door. Nobody knew what was in there, but *you* always knew you could go back for a withdrawal undetected and at your convenience. Or could you? Kate had to admit, you could also walk away and forget it for so long that you yourself didn't even remember what was on the other side of that door.

"Well," Kate finally said. "Actually, I guess you could say I'm seeing him."

Angie smiled knowingly. CeCe stared, astonished. "Seeing?" she said. "As in how?"

"Well. Hmm. He came over after dinner, and we've been talking a lot. He's such a nice person. He saved me with the Japanese. I think."

There was an awkward silence. Nobody wanted to shovel more dirt on the grave of CeCe's dead marriage, but neither was Kate particularly a conversational motherlode. There was so much to talk about, Kate was aware, and an equivalent unwillingness to speak.

"You know, one thing about being a cosmetologist," said Angie, finally. "You work up close and personal with people's bodies—their hair, their nails, their pores. People open up to you real fast. The things I've heard! Last week a customer told me about her breast implants, every detail. Well at any rate, people always say to me, 'Angie, you should be a psychiatrist, you know so much about people.' And I do have a knack. Husbands and men friends in general are my specialty. But, you know, I always give the same advice: If it feels good, do it. If it doesn't, lose it." She folded her hands in front of her on the table and nodded philosophically. "That applies across the board. Usually."

"I think my husband followed that advice," said CeCe wryly.

"It's hard to believe about Steve," Kate said carefully. "He always seemed so committed."

"Committed!" said CeCe. "He should *be* committed. Sentenced for sex with totally inappropriate partners. This woman was our *au pair,* for God's sake. She was barely past puberty." CeCe laughed bitterly. "She still used Clearasil." She paused and unclipped her earrings. "Shit."

"CeCe, come stay with me. Just for a few days till you feel better," Kate said.

"I can't. I'd love to, but I can't right now. Maybe later. In fact, I have to go pick up Cindy from school," CeCe said, and quickly hurried off.

"Waiter!" called Angie. "Another couple of tomato juices, please."

Kate felt dazed, as she tended to feel when her role models crumbled in front of her. She remembered feeling vaguely this way when she first read that JFK had had affairs in the White House. Maybe, she thought, the point wasn't so much that she and Matt hadn't succeeded because she hadn't measured up/conceived in time/communicated. Maybe all that didn't matter, because no matter what you did, it worked against you. Kate's imperfections, CeCe's perfection—in the end, what was the difference? Kate felt like her brain was going to burst, and she couldn't even take an aspirin.

She knew what she wanted, though. As soon as lunch was over, she wanted to lay down on a soft comforter and have Larry rub her head.

And she knew that could be arranged.

"So what do you hear from the Japanese?" asked Larry.

It was a hot, muggy day, the kind of day that made Kate long for real fall weather. She draped herself over the bridge above the Central Park boat pond and watched the mini-regatta of toy boats. Most of the "toys" were radar-controlled, and some of them seemed fit for an ocean crossing.

"Not much, but that's their way, I hear. The Japanese like to examine things from every angle, take time to develop a relationship, that sort of thing. They did call with a new list of questions, which we answered on paper. But since then . . ." She shrugged helplessly. "I'm not counting on it." She sighed. Losing the Japanese as sponsors would lacerate her business plan. There was no other strong prospect in the wings. In fact, Kate had spent an exhaustive week compiling a new list of potential sponsorship targets. But time was running out, and there was also a recession, and of course her maternity leave was coming up.

"I'd like to get on a plane to Tokyo," she said, leaning forward to take the weight off her ankles. "But it's out of the question. It's just so frustrating."

"You'll figure out something."

Kate stood up and stretched. She was feeling really comfortable with Larry now. If she weren't pregnant, maybe they'd be having a real relationship. Although, she had to admit, how much more real could you get than discussing your cervix with a man you were seeing, which they had done at length after last night's Lamaze. Larry, who had technically never made love to her, knew more about her female organs than any man on earth except her obstetrician.

As they walked down the red cement steps to the boat pond, people smiled benignly; Kate knew they assumed she and Larry were married, a happy couple expecting a child. Suddenly there was the whir of a camera motor. A bearded man ran backward ahead of them, snapping pictures.

"Paparazzi," muttered Larry. In two strides, he caught the man, jerked the camera from his hand, and held him dangling six inches off the ground.

"I'd appreciate it if you'd give me your film. I'll pay for it," Larry said.

The man refused. "It's a free country, Mr. Sedlacek. I'd appreciate it if you unhand me. Now."

"But these pictures aren't free, right? Who's paying you? The tabloids?"

The man yanked his camera back. "You have your job, and I have mine," he said, brushing himself off.

"Great," said Larry to Kate as the cameraman jogged away.

"Tomorrow we'll be headlines in your local supermarket. Or maybe they'll strip your head onto someone else's body."

"More likely, they'll strip someone else's head on my body. Maybe Marilyn Monroe's. That would be a real story. *Marilyn lives and she's pregnant.*"

Larry unwrapped five pieces of gum and wadded them into his mouth. "Well," he said between chews, "it's amazing nobody's picked up on us yet."

"This could be bad for your image," said Kate. "A soap opera star would be better. Preferably somebody single who's had breast implants."

Larry swung his arm across her shoulders. "But then she'd only be half as interesting. And pregnant women don't need silicone."

"That's a truism," said Kate. "Along the lines of 'Real men don't eat quiche.'"

They sat down on a bench at the edge of the pond. Kate noticed a three-foot scale model of a sleek white sailboat dominating the pond, circling like a predator, frequently ramming the other boats. Looking across the pond, searching for its remote-control owner, she spotted Gregory behind mirrored wire-rimmed sunglasses. Beside him was Matt. And beside Matt was a woman. A very pretty redhead with long, Botticelli hair. Heads bent together, absorbed in discussion, they didn't notice Kate, and Larry noticed none of the above.

Well, thought Kate, drawing a breath. And Matt, as she squinted into the sun, got smaller and smaller, as if the boat pond had suddenly expanded, making it even farther to the other side of the shore.

Down the hall from her office, Kate could hear Stanton Welch's voice as he stopped at every office in turn, saying a few encouraging words to the staff. Stanton was masterful at this; even the most junior clerk in the mailroom always felt like part of Stanton's business family, because he never failed to remember details like the names of kids, wives, and favorite sports. The man had the memory of a mainframe computer. The question was, what was he doing here? Welch's days, Kate knew, were mapped out with clockwork precision. Not a minute was wasted. He never made an unscheduled visit to any of his offices without a reason.

"Kate," Welch called out as he finally got to her office door. "I was in the neighborhood; thought I'd stop by."

Something was definitely up. For a second, Kate panicked, wondering if he was going to say he was tired of waiting for her to close on this Japanese deal, and to move on with Plan B. She had no Plan B. Plan B would mean reverting to the Ray Guardino status quo, which was doomed to fail.

Welch closed the door and settled himself into a comfortable chair.

"Coffee? Can I get you anything?" Kate asked.

"No, no. I'm off caffeine. Watching that and the triglycerides. So, how's it going, Kate?"

"Fine. The Japanese should get back to us any day."

"Feeling pretty positive then?"

"Yes. Very." At least she could act positive.

Welch twirled his heavy gold signet ring. "Good, good. I have every confidence. Now, Kate . . ."

Here it came. She braced herself.

"You know I don't pay attention to these things, but this thing in that supermarket tabloid, the *Exposé* . . ."

"What thing?"

"Well, frankly, this." He unfolded a piece of paper out of his jacket pocket. It was a picture of Kate and Larry hand in hand, the one the paparazzi in the park had snapped. The headline read, or, rather, screamed, SPORTS LEGEND AND MOM-TO-BE. HOME RUN OR FOUL BALL?

It was insipid and ridiculous. A two-line blurb gave her name and mentioned her title at *Finance*. Kate hadn't seen it before, but then, she didn't read the tabloids. Neither did Stanton Welch.

"How did you get this, Stanton, if you don't mind my asking?" She quickly added, "Not that it's any federal case."

He looked at the ceiling. "Let's just say someone alerted me to it. Someone who cares about the image of *Finance*."

Guardino.

"I don't see how this relates to the image of *Finance*. I'm just walking with a friend."

"Kate, it's the implication that concerns me. What you do in your life is your personal business. But when the *Finance* name comes up, we are talking about our brand franchise, and I have to get involved. I'm forced to. Kate." He tried to sound fatherly. "You are the gatekeeper here, the guardian of the *Finance* image. I just want to remind you that it's a conservative world out there. The Japanese especially might not understand." He inspected his cuticleless, buffed nails.

"The Japanese read this junk?"

Welch smiled softly. They both knew this was a game.

"Oh," she said. Of course. Guardino would have sent them a copy, too, spineless life-form that he was.

Welch raised his open palms, as if surrendering, then slapped his thighs with finality. "That's all. Nothing heavy. Just a little friendly reminder. I know you've got a lot on your mind. You know I'm a big supporter of yours, Kate. Don't give people things they can use against you. Especially not on a silver platter."

Kate ripped the picture into confetti and threw it at the wastebasket. Little shreds of paper floated pointlessly to the carpet. "Thank you, Stanton. I'll remember that."

Fourteen

Kate had never felt more leaden. Her legs strained upward, one step at a time, and if her apartment had not been at the top of the stairs, she would have made an excuse to turn around and leave. The stairs were on her Enemy List now. As were long car rides, from which she emerged with no ankles; cocktail parties, to which other women wore dresses with waists; and panty hose, which started the day under her armpits and ended up slung somewhere around her thighs.

Right now her panty hose were shimmying even lower—Kate could feel the elastic at crotch-level, her belly bowing above, the skin of her protruding navel scratching against her black-and-white-checked overblouse. For the first time in her life, Kate knew what it must feel like to be fat, to gasp for breath after even the shortest sprint, and, when you breathed, to suck in such shallow drafts of air that you wondered if the oxygen would even hold out until the next breath.

Kate made a supreme effort and extracted her keys from her purse. There were exactly twelve steps from the front door to the couch—she'd counted them. She figured she could make it. She'd lie flat on the couch until she could breathe again, remove the boa constrictor panty hose, and elevate her feet on a pillow. Then, when she felt up to it, she'd limp to the kitchen for some cottage cheese and a baked potato. That was her routine these days.

She pushed open the door and flicked on the light.

"Surprise!" yelled a chorus of voices.

The living room was draped in crepe paper and sports pennants. A life-sized poster of Michael Jordan was tacked above the fireplace. There were a pile of gifts and a cake on one table. Larry, wearing a warm-up suit and a towel around his neck, led Kate inside and handed her a champagne glass. "Cider," he said confidentially. "Organically grown and pressed."

CeCe rushed over. "It's a sports shower," she said. "Larry's idea. He planned the whole thing."

"She helped."

"Clair got me the phone numbers."

Clair waved from the ottoman. Angie sat on the floor, her little girl in a Snugli. Kate could see Janet in the kitchen, bustling about. Margo was mixing drinks, a sure sign of trouble. As far as Kate knew from working with Margo at *Childstyle*, she had never mixed so much as a glass of ice water. Kate didn't recognize the rest of the crowd, which consisted of a number of very large men, several attractive women, and two girls in Spandex Azzedine Alaia dresses. "Who are these people?" she asked, astonished.

"Boom Boom Kelly over there—Super Bowl starting lineup, three years in a row. Oh, helping your mother, that's Don Waggoner, a.k.a. King Neptune from the pro wrestling circuit. King's a lot of fun. He's been cracking up your mom. That's Jonie King over there, his wife. Shel Russo—he's an umpire. He's so tough, he once called a guy out four times on strikes on his birthday."

Larry pointed to a man who was seven foot two and hard to miss. "Carlton Ramis. Slam-dunk champion last year."

Kate dropped into a chair. "That's wonderful, Larry. But why are they here?"

"Consultants. The kid is going to need coaching expertise. We're starting early."

"Clam dip?" Carlton Ramis, a towel over his arm, leaned over like a tilted skyscraper, bearing bowls of chips and dips. One of the Spandex girls trailed behind, carrying cocktail napkins.

"Kate, this is Carlton and Mimi. Carlton and Mimi, Kate. Carl, tell Kate why you're here."

"Well, Larry said you were having a sports shower, and we decided it should be authentic." He handed Kate a videotape. "This is the three-point shot contest from the last All-Star Game."

"Carl was deadly from the outside," said Larry.

"Play this tape for the kid as soon as he's born. He'll catch on."

"Thank you, Carlton," she replied weakly. It was hard to take it all in.

Larry pulled Kate to her feet and took her around the room, introducing her. Boom Boom Kelly scrutinized her swollen ankles. "My trainer could tape them for you," he suggested.

One of the Spandex girls stepped up. "Gee," she said. "You look great." Her tone was not altogether convincing.

"So do you," Kate mumbled, moving quickly away. She had no desire to torture herself by standing beside this girl, whose figure was so perfect it fit into a dress the size of a Chiclet.

Her mother intercepted Kate from the kitchen, wiping her hands on an apron. It looked like a rented prop. Where did Janet get an apron, Kate wondered. In her entire life, she'd seen her mother in an apron about as often as she'd seen her in a decompression chamber. "Darling, isn't it *sweet*?" Janet enthused. "Sports, imagine it! But, really, there's no reason why we can't have a Wimbledon champion in the family, is there?" She pulled Kate aside. "Larry is so supportive. You never mentioned him."

"Well, he's been helping me through this."

Janet nodded. "So he said. He said he was your coach."

"My Lamaze coach. One of them. Matt is the other."

Janet covered her eyes. "Kate, even I, who know nothing about team sports, know that this will not work. I hope you know what you're doing, darling," she sang in a singsong voice. "Just ask them to knock you out. That's what I did when you were born. Then you're not responsible for your actions."

CeCe pulled on Kate's sleeve, dragging her away. "So this is the famous Larry who you've said so little about? He's wonderful, Kate. Look at what he's doing for you and the baby." She shook her head admiringly. "You are so lucky."

It irritated Kate that CeCe considered Larry to be her male fairy godmother in a sweatsuit, as if simply having a man in her life was the solution to all of her problems. Angie, who saw Kate's expression, stepped in. "Don't mind her, Kate, she's not being objective." She sized up CeCe, who had dashed back to help Larry pass out drinks. "Vulnerable," Angie pronounced. "Very vulnerable. Now, Kate, let's get down to business."

Kate plucked a miniature pizza from a tray that was being passed by Don "King Neptune" Waggoner. What was that around his neck? A huge gold chain with a forked trident with ten carats of diamonds? Weren't those tattoos of winged creatures on the backs of his hands? "I got a quiche in the oven," he said.

Larry leaned over Kate's shoulder and snatched away the remnants of the pizza. "How many pounds last month?" he whispered, then patted her on the head. Larry was always saving her from herself these days.

It was amazing, Kate thought, feeling better now that she'd had some food, to see her apartment swarming with huge men carrying silver trays, like a waiters' muscle convention. Larry stage-directed from the bar, behind which stood the shortest bartender Kate had ever seen. "Who's that?" she whispered to CeCe.

"Ramiro Gonzales. Triple Crown jockey."

Kate marveled at the scene. Larry had gone to so much trouble! What had she done to deserve all this? For a minute, she wanted to cry, but then she remembered that crying was supposed to be behind her, over with the first trimester. She didn't have to cry, she could just be happy about things. She sat there smiling.

"Darling, don't you look like the Mona Lisa!" Janet Harrison fluttered in for a landing beside her daughter.

Kate groaned, but she still smiled.

"So this is your new . . . friend."

"Larry? I guess so. Yes."

"I wonder how to introduce him," Janet murmured.

"How about, 'I'd like to introduce Larry Sedlacek, he's a sportscaster.' "

"Yes. Yes, I suppose so." Janet frowned and twirled her pearls as she struggled to rationalize a relationship that defied her etiquette training. "Hmm." Her lips moved silently, practicing.

Margo planted an air kiss on Kate's cheek. "God! It's so good to see you! We've missed you at *Childstyle*. You look great. Motherhood must agree with you."

"Let's not rush it, Margo. Less than two months."

Margo pulled a copy of *Childstyle* out of her purse.

"I brought you an advance copy of our latest," she said. "Hope you approve."

Kate flipped through the magazine. The cover was a little softer than she'd have preferred, and there was less color overall in the magazine. But Kate amazed herself by her lack of a strong reaction. In the past, she'd have gone wild. She'd assumed she'd remain attached to *Childstyle,* but she felt no emotional tug of war at all. It was just a magazine, one she looked at distantly and objectively. This baby was grown and gone. The cord had been cut, Kate realized; her focus was on *Finance*. The challenge was terrible, almost daunting, and maybe, she thought, that was exactly why she cared as much as she did. It was the challenge of the courtship, that thrill of the chase, the act of making it happen.

Across the room, Kate could see Larry stacking gifts for her to open.

Her baby would not be like some magazine, Kate lectured herself, as he underscored the thought by flutter-kicking the length of her side. There would be no moving on to the next challenge once the initial thrill was over; this would have to be the thrill of a lifetime, literally. But then, the child would evolve, grow, change, and in a few years, it all would be inevitable, with or without her. She would be both his captain and his passenger. There could be no jumping ship. *As there had been with Matt,* an uncomfortable voice from somewhere reminded her.

Kate readjusted her beanbag body on the cushions. This was a bad time to think of Matt.

"You know," Margo said, frowning intensely, "we have a cir-

culation war going here with *Mother and Child*. They're plaster-
ing over every kiosk in New York with their new posters. We're
onto a very inventive counterattack plan, and I'd like your
opinion."

Kate nodded. "Sure." But her head wasn't in it. "Margo," she
said suddenly, "I know *Childstyle* is doing great, thanks to you,
but—what if it didn't? What would you do? How important is
it to you?"

Margo looked shocked. "What do you mean? It means
everything."

"Not *everything* everything."

"Well, I've put my whole life into it; you know that."

Kate did know that. She had put her whole life into it, too.
Once. She wondered how she could ever have gotten to such a
place in her life. What did it mean?

Now Larry was leaning over her, touching her shoulder, massaging the back of her neck with two fingers.

"Having fun?"

"This is incredible of you. I can hardly believe it."

"Wait till you see the cake. The guys were excited to do it.
Believe it or not, we've never given a shower before. Or even
been at one, except for in a locker room, of course."

"How'd you decide on the guest list?"

"Well, I figured we should cover all our bases. Maybe he'll
have a good arm, maybe he'll be fast, maybe he'll be small. I
figured—be prepared for any eventuality. Here's the game plan—
we get these guys involved early on, he can always call on them
later. Maybe a little coaching, a little recommendation to Notre
Dame, whatever. We got the pipe laid. And CeCe helped me
with your friends' phone numbers."

Across the room, Carl was demonstrating a hook shot to
CeCe, using a wadded-up napkin and the chandelier.

"Time for the gifts," Larry announced.

He pulled Kate to her feet, propelled her to the gift table, and
eased her into a chair. Then he handed her a whistle on a chain.
"Blow this."

She did, stopping all conversation in the room.

"Attention, team. Kate has a few packages here."

The group attentively gathered around.

Kate unwrapped the first box. It was small, with teddy bear paper.

"Cassettes." She held them up.

"The audio history of football," called out Boom Boom Kelly. " 'Cause he won't be readin' for a while, and we want him to get a head start."

Everybody laughed.

The next gift was a large tube-shaped roll, tied with a red ribbon. Also from Boom Boom. Kate unrolled it. "Astroturf?" she said.

"Gets him used to the feel of the field. He can crawl on it."

"Thank you, Boom Boom. How thoughtful. And it's so . . . green."

Boom Boom nodded enthusiastically.

Kate opened the next package. "A book of horse pictures." She held it up. "And the racing form." She waved a thank-you to Ramiro Gonzales, who ran up with another tiny box. Kate pulled back the tissue paper to reveal a miniature purple-and-yellow jacket, size double zero.

"He's gotta have silks," said Ramiro. "Later, I'll teach him to ride."

Virtually every sport was represented in the huge pile of gifts. There was a mobile of little tennis racquets and balls, a pair of high-top Nikes for newborns, a set of miniature golf clubs, an inflatable bathing suit for swimming, a little catcher's mitt and Wiffle ball, a jump rope, even a pair of baby wrestler's boots.

"One more thing," said Larry, after the last package had been opened, and the apartment was a mass of crumpled paper. He ran out of the room and returned, pushing a wheeled crib. Or, at least, it resembled a crib. It was wood, with rails on the sides. Suspended from the headboard was a little basketball hoop. Mounted flush into one side rail was a miniature scoreboard, which lit up when Larry plugged it in. "Just like Diamond-vision," he pointed out.

The room went wild.

"Where did you get this?" Kate asked, hugging him.

"I made it. Been working on it since we went to that baby store. Remember, I told you to hold off on the crib."

Kate stroked her cheek on the nubby blue of Larry's sweater. "Thanks," she said. "Only you. But I hope the poor kid lives up to all this. What if he's uncoordinated?"

"Then he'll be an umpire. Or a line judge. Or a ref."

"Would that disappoint you?"

"Not if it doesn't disappoint him."

"He's a lucky kid."

"I know. He's got you for a mom."

"I'm a lucky mom."

"I know. You got me."

"Do I?"

"Nah. I make cribs for everybody I go out with. They all say, 'He's insatiable. First the crib—then the changing table!' "

Kate looked at Larry, serious now. "I don't get it. How come you never had kids yourself? You'd be the perfect father."

"Too busy, I guess. Finding the right woman, settling down, having a kid—it's a lot of work. Think of all the time you saved me."

"Instant Kid."

"Right." Larry swiped Carlton on the rear end with a napkin as he passed. "Sort of like sea monkeys. Remember sea monkeys? You ordered them from comic book coupons. They came in a kit in the mail. All you did was add water, and in three minutes you had real, live sea monkeys."

"Well, not quite," said Kate. She ducked as a huge cake, shaped like the Orange Bowl, complete with thousands of icing fans, candy cane goalposts, and chocolate wafer bleachers, swung by. "In a way, though, I wish *I* could just add water. It would make life easier, not to mention a less painful delivery."

"I'll mention it at Lamaze," Larry said.

"You do that," said Kate, laughing because she knew he would.

"Here, have an end zone," said Boom Boom, handing her a slice of cake, slathered in icing.

Kate took her fork, scraped off the entire length of the ten-yard line, and ate the cake.

216

Angie picked her way across the room, precariously balancing baby Emily, a plate of food, and a drink. Pulling back the Snugli, Kate could see the baby's tiny face, nestled like a petal on her mother's chest. Her little hands curled and uncurled, the tiny nails adorable.

"Can I hold her?"

"Practice makes perfect," said Angie, unclipping the Snugli. "She's down for the count. She won't wake up." She passed the baby gently into Kate's arms.

Holding Emily, Kate realized with a start that she'd really never held a baby for more than one or two minutes. She had no brothers or sisters, she'd never baby-sat, and the only babies she'd seen up close were CeCe's. Even then, she'd avoided holding them, in case they wet or threw up.

It was a strange sensation. She could feel the baby's head against her chin, soft and downy, and she felt the in-and-out shallow feather-breaths. Emily had a scent that was beyond baby powder; her skin was poreless, like the inside of a shell where the white melts into peach.

There was no hormonal surge, no wish that this baby was her own. Kate enjoyed the baby for what it was—Angie's child. She wondered how she would feel holding her own baby, a few weeks from now. It was still impossible to imagine. There was no preparation, Kate realized. Books, classes, talking, imagining—what were they beside the reality of another life?

The baby started pursing her lips and stirring. She opened her eyes and stared directly at Kate, blinked once and started to wail.

"Uh-oh," said Kate.

She looked for Angie, but she'd disappeared.

"Shh, baby." Kate bounced the child, who continued to cry.

She looked around the room. Suddenly everyone seemed deep in conversation. Angie must have gone upstairs.

The baby closed its eyes and stiffened, mew-crying like a hungry kitten.

Hungry. That was it. The baby was hungry. Kate rocked Emily. "Mommy's coming, sweetheart. Hang on."

The baby cried louder.

Where was Janet? Where was CeCe? Where was someone with some experience?

One of the Spandex girls leaned over, her long hair swinging. "Ooooh. Poor baby, do you have gas?" she cooed in a British accent, reaching out. "I'll take her."

The girl proprietarily scooped up the baby. Its entire body was longer than her dress. She patted it on the back and a moist belch emerged. The baby stopped crying immediately.

"You'll get the hang of it," she said as Kate stared. She expertly slung the baby onto her hip and sashayed across the room on four-inch spike heels.

Observing the scene, with its animated buzz of conversation, Kate felt oddly distant, as if she were floating outside all the activity, peering in through the upper panes of a window. The shower had brought her one step closer to the reality of the baby, and it was as if she were polarized to him, magnetized to his fetalness, floating as he did, suspended apart from this scene that was taking place around them. They were the visitors, even when the party was theirs. She wondered if the birth would bring them both back down to earth, or if she would be left, stranded without him, victim of a symbiotic hit-and-run.

Someone was waving good-bye from the door—the umpire. Kate tilted sideways and pulleyed herself up along the back of the couch. She could no longer bend from the waist. What had the umpire given her? Was it the kiddie cassette player and tapes of "Take Me Out to the Ball Game"? Luckily CeCe had been keeping a list.

"Thank you so much for the tapes and the cassette player," she said. "I'm sure he'll love listening to them."

"We can start now," Larry said enthusiastically, coming to stand beside her. "We'll put earphones to Kate's stomach and when the part comes about 'One, two, three strikes you're out,' we can sing along, so he'll already know the words when he's born."

Kate pictured Larry, rocking the baby to sleep, singing, "One, two, three strikes you're out." She knew he would, too. Just as Matt would sing the *Allelujah Chorus*. This child would never be short on stimuli.

Angie left next, and she handed Kate a fancy box. "This is my present," she said. "But it's not for the baby. It's for you."

"Angie! But . . ."

"No buts. This kid is fixed for life." She squinted approvingly. "You, I'm not so sure about."

Kate picked at the ribbon.

"I'll save you from the suspense. It's lingerie. Victoria's Secret. Borders on the obscene, but very, very pretty. I almost had to keep it."

Kate hugged her. "Thanks, Angie. I know I'll fit into whatever it is again. Someday."

"I figure it gives you something to shoot for."

Larry grabbed Kate's hand. "Your big present is over here," he said. "I saved it for last. For impact."

The room was almost empty now; there were no presents left, and very few people. Only Janet, CeCe, Gonzales the jockey, and his Spandex date, who towered over him—the redhead in spike heels who had picked up Emily.

"Well," said Larry, "there she is."

The girl pirouetted on her high heels.

"Who?"

"Fiona."

"Yes. We've met."

"Fiona is your gift."

"What!"

Janet Harrison looked horrified.

"I'm your new nanny," said Fiona, smiling.

Mary Poppins, she was not.

"Fiona's a cum laude graduate of that Lady Di Nanny School in London," Larry explained. "She's over here doing postgraduate work. I got her via our BBC affiliate."

"I thought you were Ramiro's date," Kate said, confused.

"No," said Fiona. "I'm his nanny. He and Eva have a two-month-old. But I'll be available next month, when they go back to Argentina."

Larry beamed.

"I must admit, you don't look like a nanny," said Kate, recovering from the shock.

"Neither did Lady Di," Fiona replied cheerfully. "I'm sure we'll get on. Next week, I'll ring you and we'll coordinate our dates."

"My goodness," breathed Janet. CeCe just shook her head in wonder.

"Larry," said Kate honestly. "I am absolutely overwhelmed. I don't deserve all this. But just tell me one thing. How does Fiona relate to the sports theme?"

He thought for a minute. "She kind of looks like a cheerleader."

"A British, size-six nanny school cheerleader?"

"Right. That's it."

Kate nodded. "That makes sense." Depending on who you were.

After the guests had left and the kitchen had been cleaned and wrapping paper and ribbon had been picked up, Kate sat in the rocker in the baby's room and watched Larry install the crib.

"Once he can get around, the scoreboard can be wall mounted, so he can't get at it," he said, over the whir of the electric screwdriver. He brushed his hands on his pants. "There. It's all set up."

"It looks wonderful." She stood and put her head on his shoulder as they surveyed the room. They were like any happy parents-to-be, except *they* were not the parents-to-be. Only she was. Kate wondered how she would explain Larry to her son, and how Matt would fit in as the real father. When her own father had gone, she remembered, he had gone forever. His place had remained, never again to be filled. There was no substituting for your father, your real father. Of course, in adoption, the adoptive father would fill that role. But could you have two fathers? Wouldn't it be confusing for an infant, much less a child?

Then again, Kate suspected not. There was no such thing as too much love, she thought, as Larry held her now, kissing her hair, and stroking the small of her back where it always hurt these days. Love was a concept that even a newborn could master, she was certain.

She kissed him back.

No, there was no such thing as too much love.

220

Fifteen

Kate handled the prototype as if it were a precious gem, which, in a way, it was. All these months of theory, discussion, argument, inspiration, and anguish had now materialized into these pages, which gleamed glossy and elegant. Helmut, the German designer, had outshone even Kate's expectations. This new *Finance* looked like no other magazine; unique, yet with a comfortable dignity, approximating the qualities of a beautifully manicured and appointed estate, or a world-class luxury car. The genius of the concept lay in the size, which was just slightly larger and squarer than the average magazine. As a result, each page was elegantly lavish with white space. Within the environment, ads floated airily, and editorial beckoned invitingly. There was none of the squeezed-together look of so many overstuffed magazines. *Finance* now had the aura, Kate thought, of a fine coffee table book.

Across the table, the editorial staff looked nervous, except for Helmut, who was planted confidently in his chair; the man knew he was brilliant. If Kate had said that she hated his prototype, he would have shrugged and walked away, confident in the tininess of her brain. As it was, she wanted to kiss him—not literally, of course, but almost. He had managed the most difficult of tasks—executing someone else's vision, and improving on it.

Kate looked up at him and nodded slowly. "Perfection," she said. "Absolute perfection." She laughed, rubbing her hair. "My God, this is gorgeous work! Congratulations, Helmut, and all of you. I know how hard you all have worked."

A large whoop rose from the group, and everyone started talking at once. The noise attracted Phil Moran, who was passing by in the hall.

"Is that it?" he asked, trotting into the room before Kate could cover the prototype.

"Yes," enthused Joel Weberling, the assistant art director. "Not bad, huh?"

Phil grabbed the prototype and flipped through the pages like a deck of cards.

"Whoa!" he yelled. "Wait a min-ute. No staples?"

"Staples?" Helmut's lips moved imperceptibly. "Why would there be staples?" Pinpoints of dust swarmed in the fluorescent light.

"We always had staples before."

"Yes, well, this is perfect-bound."

"Well, how you gonna handle my tip-in cards?"

"They will be slipped between the pages, like the subscription offer cards," said Kate.

Phil grimaced. "My clients aren't going to like that. They like a nice, strong staple. Other than that, I suppose it's okay." He tossed the prototype on the table like a used Kleenex and started to leave the room. Then he turned back. "Oh, one more thing."

"Yes, Phil?" Kate wished he would beam himself into somebody's Golden Parachute and disappear from her life, but rationally, she'd realized long ago that you had to deal with the Phil Morans of the world; there were always more of them than there were of you.

Phil seemed agitated. "You better run this by Guardino. Just a quick fly-by, you know?" He reached out a hand. "Give it to me, I'm on my way to his office."

Kate practically threw herself on the prototype, raking it toward her, her fingernails scratching on the mahogany tabletop. "It's fine, Phil. When we're ready, I'll handle covering off Roy. It's a little premature right now. I've only just seen it myself."

222

Phil nodded. "Yeah, I can see there's a lot of rough spots. All that white space. You gotta think of something to fill it in."

"What?" said Helmut, his voice a spike.

Phil pantomimed digging a ditch. "Filler," he said. "You know."

"Thank you for sharing your thoughts, Phil," Kate replied. "We'll keep that in mind."

"Maybe some eighth-page ads," said Phil. "A little more two-color. It's easier to sell. Cheaper for the client."

"Thank you, Phil."

"Filler?" Helmut repeated after he left.

Kate waved her hand. "Forget it. He's not a designer. We've considered his input, although I must admit we don't have to. Anyhow, the only adjustment I see here is this center spread. It needs more prominence. Otherwise, everything is right on target."

She stood up to cross to the other side of the table. Pushing her chair back, she looked down.

What was on her seat? Had someone spilled a drink when she wasn't looking—a dark, syrupy drink?

No. It was blood. Dark, spiderlike patches oozed across the fabric like a beached sea creature dotted with small rubies. Blood. Her blood. Perhaps her baby's blood.

For a second, Kate stared down in disbelief. Her next instinct was to bolt from the conference room, but she knew what the back of her skirt must look like, and, as the realization set in, she felt her knees shaking. Slowly and deliberately, she sat back down in the chair, covering the stain, feigning interest in the prototype.

"I'd—I'd like to look this over on my own, for a bit, if you don't mind," she said to the group. "I'll get back to everybody."

How serious was this? Kate wondered. Was she spotting? Bleeding? Losing the baby? She *couldn't* lose the baby. She wouldn't let it happen.

Don't kid yourself, said a rueful voice inside. *You couldn't control its conception; how can you control its life now?*

That had been different, Kate thought, suppressing panic as she watched the editorial group file out. Trying to get pregnant

223

was trying to control something she herself wanted. Protecting this pregnancy meant protecting her child. She would act now not for herself, but for him.

She would not let him down.

The trip up Park Avenue to the hospital seemed to take forever. The radio car alternated nauseatingly between stopping and lurching, while Kate, sitting on a bunch of wadded-up paper towels, wondered dully if she would bleed through the vinyl seats. Maybe she should have taken an ambulance, Kate thought, or allowed someone from the office to come with her. But she hated to admit the danger, and Dr. Warneke hadn't mentioned an ambulance. "It could be a placenta problem," he'd said seriously when she called him, her fingers clenching the receiver. "The condition can correct itself naturally. Or not. I can't speculate on the phone, so you'll have to meet me at the emergency room."

Was he telling her she was having a miscarriage?

Kate prayed it wasn't so. She'd read that many women spotted during pregnancy. What if this was just a bad episode of spotting?

Kate pulled her raincoat more tightly around herself. There was a phone in the radio car. She called Matt. According to his service, he was in Chicago, giving a speech. She couldn't face spending a half hour tracking him down on the phone—she could barely sit up. She wanted to save every ounce of energy for stopping the bleeding.

She squeezed her legs tightly together, although she knew it was a feeble gesture. *This couldn't be happening.* The baby was due in a month. Eight months, thirty-two weeks . . . The baby could live! She'd read that. Premature, but he could live. Providing the lungs . . . She tried to breathe calmly, to send him positive signals, but all that went through her mind, over and over, was one word.

Please. Please, please, please, please, please.

Kate lay on her back as the doctor squeezed the ice-blue jelly onto her stomach and scanned her womb with the ultrasound.

Straining to see the tiny screen, she couldn't make out anything except blurry shapes. "What is it?" she asked. "What's happening?" She felt no pain, strangely, but she could still feel the warmth oozing between her legs. It felt like being immersed in a warm bath. A blood bath.

"Is the baby alive?" she said, coughing with fear.

Dr. Warneke nodded. "So far, so good. Kate, it looks like a placenta previa."

"Something's wrong with the placenta?"

"No, not really. The placenta itself is normal. It's just grown into a position that's not the most desirable."

"I don't understand." Kate felt her throat tighten.

"Placenta previa means 'placenta first.' Your placenta is now very low in the uterus, almost covering the cervix. Frankly, the risk is greater for you at this point than the baby, this late in the pregnancy, if we can't control this bleeding. Of course, we'd like to see you carry to term, but we can't risk major blood loss." He pointed out a black-and-white picture of the baby's fist. "We'd prefer not to have to deliver the baby yet, if we can help it. So we'll admit you and monitor this thing. Hopefully, the bleeding will subside, but otherwise . . . well, let's think positively, shall we?"

"Admit me?" Kate struggled upright. "I have a major meeting on my new prototype tomorrow. Do you think I'll be out for it? I could push it back to the afternoon."

Dr. Warneke raised an eyebrow. "The world will go on without you, Kate. I guarantee that much."

Actually, Kate thought, she was afraid of that. But not as much as she was afraid for Max.

Max. Where had that name come from? Out of the blue, she supposed—a name when it was needed. Max. Her little Max.

Hang in there, Max, she thought. *Hang tight.*

Five hours later, wrapped in the standard, shapeless, flapping sack they called a hospital gown, Kate lay immobile on her newly assigned hospital bed. The bleeding had subsided to spotting, and the baby was safe, for now. But Dr. Warneke was exercising every caution, and Kate faced an exhaustive series of blood tests and total bed rest until the doctors decided she was out of danger—a period Dr. Warneke described as "maybe long, maybe not." One of the nurses had advised Kate to take up a hobby, like rug hooking, so she suspected she'd better get used to lying flat on her back like this.

It was dark now, and the hospital hall was quiet. Visiting hours were over, and patients were going to sleep. CeCe had dropped off an emergency suitcase that she'd packed herself, and left almost immediately to allow Kate to rest. She was alone.

She closed her eyes. She no longer had any desire to think about, much less attend, any meeting or even conversation. She was emotionally drained, her mind a sieve incapable of collecting thought. Was it minutes or hours later that she sensed that someone was sitting on the chair beside her bed, quietly, not reading, not speaking? A nurse? Groggily, Kate peered out from under her closed eyelids. It was Matt.

"How'd you get here?" she murmured.

"Chartered a plane," he said quietly.

"What do you think of the name Max?" she whispered.

There was a pause in the dark. "I like it." She felt his hand on the sheet. "Shh. Sleep now. It's going to be fine."

Maybe it was because Matt was a doctor and he had that kind of voice, but she believed him and, reassured, she went to sleep.

"Kate, is the baby all right? Are you all right? I'm worried sick!" Larry's voice boomed frantically over the phone.

"We're doing fine, for now," Kate said. "But we can't get up. Ever. I even have a bedpan." She wiggled with distaste.

"CeCe called and told me. She's here now; we're sweating it out together in the waiting room. We tried to visit, but they won't let us on the floor."

"Why not? Pregnancy isn't contagious."

"Your chart is marked 'immediate family only,' and those stuck-up nurses are enforcing it. The one that stopped me was a real battle-ax. I could've used her in my defense lineup. Obliterates anything in her path. Rita the Mower."

"I'm sure you count as family."

"Not immediate enough in a hospital where a certain influential skin doctor is on staff."

"Oh. I'll handle this."

"No. You shouldn't be handling one thing right now except you and the baby getting better."

"It's just a complication. I'm not sick, just immobile."

"Well take it easy, Kate. Everything's going to be okay. Remember, you've got us as messengers or errand runners or moral supporters."

There was a knock at the door.

"I have to hang up. I think they're here to take blood—if I have any left." She hung up. "Come in!"

It was Matt, with Kim holding his hand. Gregory followed.

"Hi Gregory, hi Kim." Kate tried to sound cheerful, but she knew she was forcing it.

Kim immediately burst into tears. Gregory hung his head.

"Kids," said Matt. "I warned you . . ."

"Oh, let them, Matt. They're probably scared. It's good to get it out in the open. It's all right, guys. The baby and I are fine. We just have to rest up. The doctor says all I have to do is lie in bed. Now won't that be fun?"

Kim looked relieved. "Yeah!" she said. "Slumber party!"

"You're lying," said Gregory, screwing up his face. "You're gonna die. The baby's gonna die." He started to cry.

"Greg!" Matt started to admonish, but the boy turned and threw himself, sobbing, into his father's arms.

"She's gonna die! I wished she was dead, I wished the baby wasn't happening, and now it's come true! I even said a Warlock curse from the seventeenth century. It worked!" he wailed. "I'm sorry! I didn't mean it!"

Matt held Gregory at arm's length and smoothed his hair. "It's all right, Gregory. Really, Kate and the baby will not die. Now, apologize to Kate."

Gregory shuffled over. "I'm sorry," he mumbled under his breath.

She reached out and took his hand. "You know, Gregory, I've wished bad things on people at times. Everybody does. But it's normal. It goes away. Wishing for something doesn't make it happen. You'll see. The baby and I will be just fine."

If only she believed that one hundred percent.

Gregory looked up, tears on his cheeks. "I didn't mean it, Kate. It's not you I hate, really. I hate not having my dad around all the time."

"And you thought a new baby would mean you'd see less of him?"

Gregory nodded. Matt moved up and put an arm around him, his other hand on Kim's head.

"That's not going to happen. You're always my son," said Matt. He ruffled Kim's hair. "And you're my girl."

Gregory rubbed his runny nose, searched for a Kleenex, and swiped at his nose with a corner of the sheet. "I'll make it up to you. I will. If you and the baby will just get better."

Kate pulled him close. "It's a deal, partner."

Kim ran up and waved a little pink bead bracelet at Kate. "I made this for you myself," she said proudly.

"Oh, how pretty." Kate slipped it on next to the plastic hospital ID band. *Well,* she thought. *I guess we're a family now, the five of us. Except we're not.* She looked at Matt as he sat on the edge of the bed. What exactly were they? Parents but not family? Family but almost not married? A couple but not together? There was no language for it. Whatever it was, however they felt, they shared something no decree or ceremony could change, a link that lasted longer than love, because it was stronger than love; it was life.

"Pretty slick, the immediate family rule," Kate said, with a smile.

"What?" Matt was all innocence.

He dismissed it with a wave. "Oh well, I agree with Dr. Warneke completely." He smiled back. "You need to save your energy. No unnecessary disturbances."

"You wouldn't have had anything to do with that, Doctor?"

"Hey, I'm not your primary physician here."

"But you are available for consultation?"

"Any time, Kate."

Matt had a way of getting things done, Kate had to admit;

effectiveness without fuss or fanfare. Larry was a crash cart and paramedics. Matt—he was a quiet hand in the dark. Kate readjusted her pillow, the only legitimate movement she was allowed. Men were one way or the other, it seemed. You spent your life as a female ricocheting from one end of the spectrum to the other, until you became a mother, and you had to be both yourself.

On her fifth day in the hospital, lying on her back, serviced by bedpans, meal trays, and nurses' call buttons, Kate knew the crisis was over. The bleeding had stopped completely, and Dr. Warneke had assured her and Matt that ultrasound and fetal monitoring showed the baby to be unaffected. And Kate herself only needed rest. They'd made it.

Well, she'd had her rest. Now she waited impatiently for Dr. Warneke to tell her she could go home, and, more specifically, back to work. Guardino was probably on the loose in the office with her prototype this very minute, she thought ruefully. In the race to the hospital, she hadn't even had time to lock it up, and Clair told Kate she hadn't seen it since.

Larry called several times a day—he and CeCe were still kept out of her room by the immediate family only edict. Surely, Matt was prolonging, if not behind, this. She could see no possible reason for it, now that the danger had passed. She meant to bring it up with Dr. Warneke, but then she also figured she'd be checking out before it would matter. At least Larry and CeCe were getting to know each other. They made a point of visiting at the same time to apply double pressure to get the nurses to bend the rules and let them see Kate. So far, their lobbying technique had failed, but at least they were company for each other in the waiting room. They were conspiring together, sending little notes and cute cards back to her. Knowing how lonely CeCe felt these days, Kate had even convinced Larry to take her to dinner one night.

Two lines on her phone lit up. Kate had arranged to have a three-line phone installed so she could work from her hospital bed. As a concession to hospital quiet, she had turned off the bell—otherwise it would have rung nonstop. Clair. The printer.

The sales department. Advertisers. The Japanese go-between. Everybody had a question or a problem—except Guardino, who had sent yellow carnations but not called, and was probably thrilled to see her sidelined. It was hard, Kate had to admit, to combine immobility with effectiveness. Still, she found herself attempting it.

Dr. Warneke walked in, studying her chart on a clipboard.

"Doctor, I'm so glad to see you. Now that everything has eased up and there's been no bleeding for three days, and the baby checks out fine, can I go home today?"

He nodded, but Kate noticed he wasn't smiling. "Home, yes. You can go home today."

She picked up the phone. "Great. Let's see, it's ten o'clock. . . . I'll call my office and tell them to expect me by noon."

Warneke held up his hand. "Just one minute here. Let's take this one step at a time. I said *home,* not office."

"But . . ."

"No buts. Kate, you can go home, but you must have complete bed rest. No office, no errands, no running around. You may get up to go to the bathroom. That's it."

"What! Why? I thought things were better." Kate was stunned. And worried. Her hands flew to her stomach.

"We've stopped the hemorrhage. You nearly required a transfusion, you know. But the placenta is still in the same position. It will remain there until the birth. With luck, you'll have a normal delivery. But to give your baby the best chance, I don't want to induce now, while the lungs are still a matter of some concern. Let's give the baby those extra weeks in the womb, as nature intended, to develop completely. That's always best."

Kate moaned. "Bed rest for how long?"

"Until you go into labor." He gave her a stern stare.

"What? But my work!"

"Work from bed, if you must. But nothing stressful. Kate, look at it this way. It's a chance to catch up on your hobbies. A little television, some reading. The time will fly."

Oh no! She'd already lost one week. This was unbelievable. And then there'd be the period after she actually had the baby. How was she going to explain this to Stanton Welch? If the doctor would only let her go back to work, she knew she could manage. "You know," she added hopefully, "I do have a very sedentary job. I'm not on my feet that much."

"Bed rest." The doctor was a broken record. "Now, will you speak to Matt, or would you prefer me to do it?"

"I'll do it. But what do I tell my boss?"

"Tell him you have a placenta previa."

"Great." Stanton Welch would think she was talking about a pasta dish.

It was going to be a long wait. But Max was safe, she reminded herself. Max was safe.

Tick Tick Tick Tick Tick. The sound of the clock was maddening, mocking Kate, reminding her, as she lay on the plump pillows of the couch, that she had all the time in the world and nothing to spend it on. It was like being at liberty to gorge on a ten-pound box of chocolates that all had mocha centers—when the only flavor you really gave a damn about was vanilla creme. She wanted to jump up and smash the clock, except she couldn't get up, much less jump.

Da Da Da Da Da Da Da. The theme song from "Jeopardy." One of the most irritating combinations of musical notes ever to assault the human ear. Kate punched the remote control buttons and flipped the channel before the first question got asked. She would have liked to have turned off the TV, but then the apartment was so devoid of human activity that she couldn't stand it.

Relaxation was not relaxing. Kate, who had not taken a vacation in five years, not even a honeymoon, felt like she was suffocating, not from the baby's proximity to her lungs but because of inactivity. What did people do all day if they didn't go to work? Or at least out? Probably what she did—pick the polish off their nails so they could reapply it, eat too much, memorize TV theme songs, go crazy.

From her daytime command post of the living room couch, Kate passed time by memorizing every sound and shape in the apartment. The loopy shadows cast by the leaves of the ficus tree onto the ceiling would be embedded forever into her memory;

fluted wall moldings might as well have been cast in plaster in her head.

At Kate's feet was a basket of colorful yarns—moss green, fern, apricot, rose, and ivory—and a rolled-up needlepoint canvas. Had she cared to unroll the canvas, Kate could have surveyed her handiwork—six stitches, after which she had stuffed the canvas back into the basket, where, at least, it gave the impression that she was working on something. On the floor were stacks of books and magazines, all of which she'd read, and the complete works of Proust, which she'd sworn to reread, but which was too daunting to begin.

Also on the table were her three-line speakerphone and portable fax machine. Occasionally, the office sent a fax, but Kate had quickly discovered that she had nothing to fax back. She had no secretary, typist, or editorial department at home. She could initiate nothing. All she could do was sit and wait for the work of others to drift by in the current.

There was a cooler on the floor beside the couch. Inside was Kate's lunch, which Carrie, her new housekeeper, always fixed before she left for the day: cottage cheese, fruit, and a pint carton of milk. Small bottles of Evian and apple and cranberry juice were also packed in the cooler. Tonight, Larry and CeCe would come over and they would all order out dinner. That was the one good thing about this confinement, Kate thought. It gave CeCe something to think about besides her divorce, an excuse to get out of the house. She'd noticed how CeCe had visibly perked up the past few weeks—she'd gotten some new downtown clothes, heavy on the black; adopted a dangly style of earrings; and started wearing makeup for the first time in years. Why was it that whenever a woman started a new life, or a new man, she made herself over, as if her old self didn't quite make the A-list at this new party? Kate vaguely wondered if CeCe's newly acquired sparkle could be attributed to a new man, but quickly dismissed the thought. She and Steve had only been separated for a few weeks, after all, and besides, she would surely have mentioned it. Right now, CeCe well knew, Kate was so starved for news that even the most microscopic tidbit of information was soaked up like a drop of water on the Gobi Desert.

Kate opened her filofax. There was one item in it: pedicure. Project Pedicure. This was to be her major activity for the day. She sighed and zipped open the brown-and-white-striped Bendel's cosmetics bag, which she had packed with polishes and polish remover pads last night. She was rationed to one trip upstairs per day, and that was to go to bed.

Kate opened the polish remover, peeled off a pad, and reached over. Her stomach stopped her about three feet short of her toes. Lolling onto her side, she propped her body with her elbow, pulled her leg up as far as she could, and stretched. Even in this contorted position, Kate could barely touch her ankle. It was hopeless. She flopped back onto the pillows, a trickle of sweat winding its way down between her breasts, and lay there listlessly, staring at "General Hospital." Somebody in Port Charles was confessing to something, and then there was a Crisp 'N Bake commercial. She watched with fascination as the chicken was covered in the crumb coating. People *ate* this? The next commercial was for an O'Cedar broom. She tried to envision herself on her feet, sweeping under her refrigerator, but the image refused to materialize. She picked up the needlepoint canvas, extracted the needle, still threaded with moss-colored yarn, and carefully made two more stitches. Slowly, she found the canvas dropping from her hand, and she fell asleep.

Half-conscious, Kate became aware of a buzz at the door. Larry? No, it was too early. She pried her eyes awake and activated the remote-control walkie-talkie that Larry had ingeniously rigged up to the downstairs entryway.

"Yes?"

"It's us, Kate. Can we come up?"

Gregory and Kim.

"I've hidden keys in the planter next to the door. Use the big key for the lobby door, and the little key for my door." Before she could finish, she could hear their footsteps racing up the hall stairs.

The door burst open. "Hi, Kate," said Gregory.

"We have a surprise," said Kim, beaming with the importance of her mission.

Gregory leaned out the door. "Okay, guys! One flight up," he shouted. Kate watched, fascinated, as two deliverymen hefted in a set of giant boxes. Under Gregory's direction, they then proceeded to uncrate a computer, a CRT screen, a keyboard, a laser printer, and some smaller boxes of software.

Gregory marched up to Kate. "Where do you want it?"

"Well, that depends what it is."

"It's a home office—a computer, a modem, a printer, and some terrific software. We've got Microsoft Word here, and Prodigy. You can make your own plane reservations from home."

"Or shop."

"Or find out the weather. And I can hook you up to the office today, with this modem. Thanks, guys." He peeled off a twenty-dollar tip for the deliverymen.

"This is too expensive, Gregory! Stop those men; we have to return it all right now. Your father would be furious. It's wonderful of you, but . . . this equipment costs a fortune."

Gregory patted her arm. "It's okay. I earned it myself. Liar's poker."

"Good grief."

"I chipped in my allowance," said Kim.

"Yeah, we wanted to do something really nice, but not, you know, sickening, like a get-well card." He mimed a gag-me-with-a-spoon motion.

"This is wonderful of you both, but you really have to return it."

"I can't. I think the stuff was hot."

"Gregory, I have to tell you, I have no idea how to use any of this."

"That's okay. It comes with forty hours of training. They train on-site, so, let's see, what if I book you for four hours a day starting next week? And I'll be available for tutoring." He rushed around, plugging in equipment, while Kim dusted the CRT screen with the hem of her skirt.

"Does your father know about this?"

"Well, we told him we were going to stop by with a gift." He studied a manual.

"Kids, 'gift' stops at ten dollars."

"Okay, so don't call it a gift. Call it a bribe."

234

"For what?"

"To keep Dad happy. To get back with him."

"He's not, you know," chirped Kim, pursing her lips, "happy."

Gregory sighed as he hooked up the components. "He's a case."

"Oh, I'm sure he'll manage." Kate was remembering the redhead.

"Shh. Let me just install Microsoft Word on your hard drive." His fingers flew over the keys. The kid had to type a hundred-eighty words a minute. Clair could barely manage sixty.

Gregory adjusted the various pieces of equipment, then spun around. "So, will you go back with Dad?"

"Gregory . . ."

"We'll pay you."

"Gregory, you can't buy love. It doesn't work that way. We do love each other, in a way, but not in that way anymore."

Gregory looked at Kim. "Pathetic. They're both just pathetic."

"I'm never getting married," Kim said emphatically. "Never, never, never."

So, Kate thought, she'd failed as a role model even before she was a mother. "Listen. We have you two, so does your mom. And there's the baby."

"Think about it," mandated Gregory. "Personally, I wouldn't want my only brother to be dealing with joint custody before he can even crawl. I know. I've been there." He took Kim's hand and yanked her toward the door. Kate heard him whisper, "She'll come around."

After the children left, Kate closed her eyes and thought about her baby. She'd have to resist the temptation to give him whatever he wanted. Otherwise, he would end up like Gregory, assuming anything could be bought, unable to cope with not having the world his own way.

But was it too much for a child to ask for, Kate wondered, the serenity of a happy marriage in his life? Parents? Stepparents? Was it too much, as a parent, to offer?

She could never go back to Matt simply from a sense of duty. What she'd told Gregory was true—she did love Matt. But there was much more than duty involved. It was complicated and difficult, but now, looking back and attempting to analyze her motives, she could not make sense of them. Her anger had faded to a shadow on the sidewalk, something she could stamp on with both feet, yet which could not be held accountable.

Sometimes now, in her solitude, Kate reached for the phone, dialing the familiar numbers she'd shared with Matt just to feel the pattern on her fingers. The phone would ring once, the ring she well knew, and she'd imagine the phones on the other end, in the library, the kitchen, or by the night table, waiting for the service to pick up, and she'd hang up before that could happen. Sometimes, very late, after she'd made her nightly trek upstairs, Kate's bedside phone would ring once and stop, and she occasionally imagined it was Matt, but then she would remind herself that this was New York, that weirdos routinely called you in the middle of the night, that strangers on street corners demanded your life savings, that people spilled out their stories to faceless seatmates on subways—but that men and women who had loved each other, made children together, could not be counted on to speak.

"Who writes these things anyway?" Kate held up her fortune cookie fortune. She really wanted to know. Then she could call the person up and ask if hers was a real flash from the fifth dimension or just computer-generated garbage. The fortune merited verification: "You will be showered with gold and good wishes."

"Mine says, 'You will take a long trip.'" CeCe crumpled it and crunched her cookie. "They all say that."

Larry was lying horizontally on the floor between CeCe and Kate, the cardboard carry-out boxes of rice, sesame chicken, and steamed vegetables scattered around him.

"This is one time in my life that I would really like to know the future," Kate said. "I wonder what my child will be like, where we'll be living."

"You'll still be working. I don't need a crystal ball for that," said Larry.

"I don't know. Maybe, maybe not."

"Pass me another egg roll, somebody," CeCe said. "Kate, Larry's right. You're the original workaholic."

"I'm not working now."

"Briefly and necessarily."

"I don't know, CeCe—you know, for the first time, I'm wondering if it's worthwhile."

"Thinking about the Mommy Track?"

"I like that," Larry said. "A race track for mothers."

"No, the Mommy Track, where you decide to take the lesser career path, as opposed to the fast track," explained CeCe.

"Is that what you did?"

"No. I got off the track altogether. I was in the stands, though, cheering."

Kate watched her plate wobble on her stomach. "I can't see that Mommy Track thing. It's like a holding pattern. Men don't do it. There's no Daddy Track."

"Men don't sit around naming things, they just do them," said Larry. "Bonding. Good Old Boys. Those are just terms women made up in a futile attempt to understand us."

"God, a closet chauvinist," said Kate.

"No way, Kate. I'm just saying there's no need to overthink this stuff."

"True," she said thoughtfully. "You just do what you have to do in the end."

"You're not thinking of quitting work?" asked CeCe suspiciously. "Some of this talk doesn't sound like you."

"No. But I can see why you did. I want time with Max, but eight weeks, that's it for my leave. And besides, who's counting? I've got to get back. I *want* to get back. It's just facing up to having to be two places at once."

"You're good at that," said Larry. He wadded up his napkin and lobbed it into the paper carry-out bag. "The same way CeCe's good at being a mom."

"That's a little ridiculous, Larry, and that's my point. Why does it have to be so either-or? CeCe's good at lots of things, not just being a mom."

"True. She bakes a mean peach pie."

"Peach pie?"

"Oh, Larry came by one afternoon and I had one in the oven for the kids," CeCe quickly explained.

"I told her she could do that for a living. This thing had a crust like a work of art."

"I'm thinking about it. Maybe getting into catering. The people I used to work with at the magazine have connections."

"I'll set her up with the network," said Larry enthusiastically, smiling at CeCe.

"That's great, CeCe," said Kate. "You'd be terrific at it."

"Well, maybe," said CeCe, lowering her eyes.

Larry unraveled his legs, stood up, and stretched. "We'd better let Kate get some rest."

"Give CeCe a ride home, will you?"

"Sure," said Larry, holding CeCe's purse for her. "Maybe she has some peach pie at home."

Kate wondered why this made her feel like less of a woman, but it did. So what if she herself had nothing with lard in it in the kitchen? So what if the only heat from her oven came from the pilot light? So what if her career involved type and layouts and business plans and travel? Suddenly she felt defensive, as she never had before she was pregnant. Every night, when she was with Matt, they ordered out or went out. There was never a pie in the house, peach or otherwise. Nobody cared. So why did she care now? What difference did it really make?

She told her hormones to shut up.

"That's looking real pretty, Kate."

"Thank you, Carrie. I think so too."

Kate's housekeeper stood back and squinted at the needlepoint apples and pears. The canvas was almost complete.

"You just have the border to do, as I see it."

"Yes, but I'm thinking of changing it from green to yellow. What do you think?" Kate held up two swatches of yarn.

Carrie nodded. "Yellow. I'm going upstairs now—do you need anything?"

"I'm fine for now, thanks." Kate smiled to herself. The needle-point pillow really didn't look too bad. Later, when it was finished, blocked, and made into a pillow, she'd tell Max how she'd worked on it before he was born. But, in a way, she was sorry she only had the border left to do. She'd come to welcome the soothing, undemanding repetition of the stitches. In and out, in and out. Until there was a pear, or a leaf, or a stem.

Kate hadn't heard from the office in a week, and she'd had no desire to call in. This morning, she'd instructed the answering service to pick up all her calls and turned off the sound on her phones. Her world had shrunk to this room, this baby, the peacefulness of the moment. The minutes were fat now, ripe as her belly, falling slowly through the hours.

A fax was coming in. Kate leaned over and pulled out the page. It was from Clair:

Couldn't get through on phone. Akito contacted us. Told him you were out but working at home. He wants to see you today at eleven. No further details.

Kate looked at her watch. Ten to eleven! Why would Akito come to her apartment? After the past incommunicado weeks, she'd all but written him off. She futilely straightened her over-sized sweatshirt top. There was no possibility of going upstairs and changing clothes. It was just three weeks till the baby was due, and she wasn't about to take any chances. One trip upstairs per day was her strict limit. She grabbed the phone and tried to call Clair, but the call jumped to the switchboard, which meant Clair wasn't at her desk. She called the service for messages: ten from Clair, saying please call the office immediately, and one from Fiona, the nanny, saying she was sorry, she was no longer available. Kate didn't know which was the greater emergency.

Before she could dial again, the buzzer rang.

"Carrie, could you please get that!" Kate swung herself upright. At least she could be sitting up when the man arrived.

Carrie went downstairs to guide Akito up, but the first thing that came through the door was a huge, cellophane-wrapped white wicker basket, brimming with stuffed animals, tied with a blue satin bow. Behind it was the unmistakable pompadour of George Haneda, Akito's consultant.

"Please forgive the intrusion, Kate," he said, carefully depositing the basket on the hall table. "But Mr. Akito wanted to congratulate you personally."

Kate looked closely. She didn't see Akito. "Is he coming with you?" she asked.

"He is in the car downstairs, waiting."

The next best thing, clearly, to a personal call.

"Why thank you, George. I hope you won't be offended, but I can't get up just now. You know how conservative some doctors can be. Won't you sit here, next to me? Carrie can get us some tea."

"Very kind of you," said George, gingerly making his way through the clutter of magazines and books that surrounded Kate. He sat down, looking like a small dark sparrow, manicured hands folded on his breast. Then he smiled. "Yes. Congratulations," he said again.

"Thank you," Kate repeated, wondering exactly what Akito had in mind. This was not a man who would fly in from Tokyo to drop off a layette gift. Clearly there was a business purpose. But what? The Japanese, she had found, were not as direct as most Americans.

Carrie materialized with the tea, and George poured deliberately and precisely.

"Mr. Guardino tells us you have taken a leave of absence due to concern for the well-being of the future child."

Kate tried to hide her disappointment. Akito was no doubt thinking she'd lost interest in her work, in the magazine she'd represented as her life's main focus. "Roy told you this?" she said.

"Yes. In fact, he said your child was now your priority."

"Well . . ." Kate conjured up some explanations, but it was obvious why she was home. There was no hiding an eight-month-plus pregnancy. "Yes," she said finally, calmly, because it was true. "Yes. My child takes precedence for just a little while, but—"

George nodded enthusiastically. "Of course! That is as it should be. The family must come first. All else will follow." He stirred his tea with precision. "We have been approached by many American organizations, as you know. But so far none of them has been a match. Mr. Akito prefers to go by, shall we say, gut feel, not, as so many times is the American way, by the bottom line. The person is important to Mr. Akito, not the deal points." He sniffed his tea. "Ah. Black currant. Very nice. Unfortunately I cannot linger. Yes, as I was saying, any business arrangement is only as good as the sum of the individuals involved. Mr. Akito asks himself—What kind of person is this? Do we see things similarly? Can we communicate? What values do we share?" He sipped the tea slowly, then patted his lips meticulously with one of the small linen napkins that Carrie had laid out. "Frankly, when we last met, Mr. Akito realized you are, first of all, the person we will need to deal with on your magazine's proposal, but second, I must admit he did require reassurance that you shared his values. Any woman, if you'll forgive me, who does not put her family first would be very hard for Mr. Akito to understand. He must ask himself—What kind of person is this? You have temporarily given up your business for your child for certain reasons. Mr. Akito applauds you. And he knows you will make ethical decisions. Therefore," George held out his hand, "he welcomes your partnership."

They shook hands. Kate was stunned. The moment felt unreal.

"Mr. Akito knows I am very committed to *Finance*," she said. "I won't let him down. Our product will be worthy of yours, I promise you."

"You are a resourceful woman. This I have seen."

He set down his cup. "Now. You must rest. Please forgive my intrusion. Our representatives will handle all details."

"I have the prototype, if Mr. Akito would like to see it."

"It will be sponsored completely by Hiro?"

"Yes, that's the concept."

"Then that is all he needs to know." George stood up and looked at his watch, which, Kate noticed, was slim and flat, on a leather band, not the prerequisite gold Rolex. Then he bowed slightly to Kate. "It has been a pleasure, but Mr. Akito is waiting. I will let myself out."

Kate listened to the muffled sound of his footsteps padding down the flights of stairs.

Kate waited to be thrilled, to feel the familiar surge of adrenaline, the pounding resonance of the win. Because she *had* won. The magazine, her vision of the magazine, was hers. She had won on her own terms, without compromising, without even being there.

But this is what went through Kate's head—an image of hours. All the hours it would now take to complete her vision, and all the hours it would take away from Max. The hours appeared to her as stacks of paper. The stack for *Finance* was very high and crisp. Max's was just a few crumpled sheets. Kate rubbed her eyes to erase the picture—not because she couldn't face it, but because she refused to allow it.

She stood up, and there was a warm, watery gush.

The baby.

Sixteen

She was bleeding again, she knew that much. And she knew that it was an emergency. The call to Dr. Warneke, his instructions to go immediately to the hospital, the blur of her departure with the help of Carrie, who, thank God, had not yet gone home, the frantic ride in the cab, Carrie patting her arm the entire way, the sting of the spinal anesthetic—all gave way now to a gnawing fear that something could go terribly wrong.

She could see it in the doctor's face, she could feel it in the electrodes attached to her belly that monitored the baby's life. And then: "The baby's heart rate has dropped a little bit. We're going to do a C-section right now."

"How much is a little bit?"

"From a hundred twenty to fifty."

"Oh my God!" Kate looked frantically around the room. Her legs were numb from the anesthetic. "Could somebody please call my husband and my—friend. I have a card with emergency numbers in my purse. And my mother . . ." She gasped with the hammer hit of the contraction and there was a sudden swirl of activity as she found herself transferred onto a cart and rolled quickly out of the room. There was no time.

As the ceiling tiles whipped by overhead, she heard Matt's

voice. He was running after the cart, calling her name. "Kate, I'm here." He grabbed her hand, running alongside.

"How did you know? I couldn't even call."

"Gregory. He stopped by to check out your new equipment and saw you leaving in a cab with Carrie. We figured this was it."

She had never been so glad to see anybody in her life. "Matt, I think the baby's in trouble. Or maybe I am." She felt totally out of control, swept along by the birth, a mere passenger. If the car crashed, she couldn't stop it.

"Kate, Kate!" Larry's voice boomed down the hall as he negotiated the distance like a fifty-yard dash to the end zone.

"This is an emergency," said Matt brusquely. "We are on our way to the operating room."

"I know. Carrie called me. I got here as fast as I could. Walked right out in the middle of the six o'clock news." He yanked off his tie.

"You'll have to stay outside, in the waiting room," snapped Matt as the cart careened around a nurse's aide pushing a mound of dinner trays.

Kate wanted to say something to Larry, but every time she tried, a fresh contraction erupted, and her body demanded her full attention. For a fleeting second, the irony of it occurred to her—now, when she weighed almost two hundred pounds, when she lay immobile, numb from the waist down, oozing fluids from every pore that existed in her body, her face a mask of sweat and tears, her hair matted and damp—two men were fighting over her. Or were they fighting over Max?

"I'm the baby's father."

"Biologically, yes. But this isn't the time to split hairs, my friend."

Dr. Warneke interrupted. "Gentlemen, who is the labor coach?"

"I am," said two voices.

"They both are," said Kate, her teeth gritted.

"I give up," said Warneke. "Put on gowns. I'll see all of you in the delivery room in thirty seconds."

With so much activity kaleidoscoping around her, Kate was acutely aware of only one thing: the ceiling. Basically, it was all she could see, but it was also all she wanted to see. She didn't care to focus on the fact that her belly was being prepped for surgery, that a screen of sterile blue drapes was being erected over her midriff, that someone was slicing the baby from her body. She felt—what? A finger being run across her abdomen?

At her left shoulder, holding her hand, stood Matt. On her right was Larry, blotting her brow with a sterile towel.

"Okay," said Matt enthusiastically. "Imagery! Concentrate, Kate. You're floating in a beautiful lake . . ."

"Hot-air balloon," said Larry.

"Somewhere in Wisconsin . . ."

"France!"

"You hear the waves . . ."

"*Wind.*"

"Get out of my image!" snapped Matt.

"Let's let the lady decide. Kate," Larry said warily, "whose image do you want here?"

"My own!" she panted. "The goddamn dressing room at Chanel, and men are not invited!" She squeezed her eyes shut, wishing they would knock her completely out.

Pushes, tugs, strange sensations, but no real pain from the surgery, and then—

"It's a girl!"

And her cries. Healthy, lusty cries, the most welcome cries in the world, swirling through the room. It was Max. Kate recognized the kittenlike cry as if she had known it all her life, and Max was here and healthy, and Max was a girl, a tiny *girl* now on Kate's chest, now in her arms, her little soulmate, her little shipmate. Kate's tears dampened Max's already damp and downy fair head as the baby calmed to her mother's heartbeat, and the men on either side of them, meeting the child in their blue gowns and surgical caps, could only look, smile, and, finally, reach in unison across Kate and Max, connecting with a fast high five.

"Yeah!" shouted Larry, spiking his mask to the floor.

Kate counted twenty-two flower arrangements and three baskets of fruit, which she could not yet eat, as she was still on liquids. When she had been in the hospital before, the awful time when she nearly lost the baby, people had held back, she realized, just in case; as she had, herself. Now the room was overstuffed, like an out-of-control flower shop. They said newborns had poor color vision, but she was sure Maxine Larra Weil could sense the opulent fragrance that wafted from so many dozens of gardenias, roses, and freesia.

Kate could barely walk, but she could hold the baby, which she did by the hour, acquainting herself with Max's intense navy-blue eyes, soft brown hair, the ears like miniatures of her own, with their shortened lobes, the mouth pink as a petal. Eight pounds. A good size. And already she had a good nature, as if the prenatal turmoil had prepared her for this graduate course of life. The wonder Kate felt was surpassed only by her complete and total adoration of her daughter. *Daughter!* It now seemed as if it could have been no other way—how could she have been so convinced that Max was a boy? As if reading her thoughts, Max stuck out a jellybean-sized tongue.

"Ballet, anyone?" Matt burst into the room and, with a flourish, presented Kate with a beautifully wrapped pink-and-white box. Inside was a tiny pink tulle tutu, size zero, pink satin newborn slippers, and a pink-and-white rose on an elastic ribbon designed to hold the rose in the absence of hair.

"Well," Matt said. "She's all fixed in the blue-and-white department. So I figured, how about at least one pink outfit?" He kissed Kate and then the baby. "She'll be dancing *Swan Lake* in no time."

Gregory raced in from the hall, trailed by Kim. Under his arm was a huge, rolled-up piece of paper. They unfurled it together. "It's a blueprint for her dollhouse," announced Gregory. "I did it with my architecture software."

"It has a media room and a convection oven," said Kim, pointing out the features.

"We'll subcontract the construction," said Gregory. "But I'll be the general."

"I'll decorate," said Kim, waving the blueprint at Max. "We'll share it when it's done."

"You girls had better not gang up on me," said Gregory, obviously pleased that he was still the only boy.

Kim, who was obviously equally pleased to have a new ally-in-training, smiled sweetly. Clearly, the day had finally come: she and Max outnumbered their brother.

Kate wished she could stay in the hospital forever. Here, life was a big bouquet. Here, there were no decisions to make; not even what to have for dinner, since she couldn't eat yet. Here, help appeared at the push of a button. Here, the world was just this room, the people in it, and one isolette.

Within a week, she and Max would be leaving—for what?

"Are you going back to the apartment?" Janet asked tentatively. Kate knew that what she really meant was: *Who* would she be going with, to *which* apartment?

Matt handed her the baby to breast-feed. "Greggie, ask Janet to take Kim and you to the gift shop for a minute," he said, and the kids skittered happily out the door with their grandmother, probably off to purchase and feast on an entire box of candy.

Kate and Matt were alone.

"Hi, Mom," Matt said.

"Hi, Dad."

Mom and Dad—was that what they had become? Was that enough? Then again, that was a lot.

"So. Who was the redhead?"

"What redhead?"

"The one in the park. By the boat pond. I saw you there, with Gregory. And a redhead."

"Oh, her. Does it matter?" He was trying to look nonchalant, something he was always too earnest to do well.

"No." Kate, on the other hand, was an expert at hiding her real feelings.

"Where's Larry?"

"Out celebrating. With CeCe."

"Oh?" He raised an eyebrow and paced across the room. "Well then, I'll use this opportunity to tell you: I'm goddamned jealous of that guy, and before he sets foot back in this room, I'm going to tell you what I tried to tell you the last time you were in the hospital, but I couldn't, because I knew he was making you happy, and I wasn't." He gripped the metal footboard. "Every time I wanted to try to make things up to you, I couldn't. Because I'd remember he was there, and you were choosing him. It seemed so pointless."

Kate clasped the baby closer, shaking her head. Was it possible they had misunderstood each other so badly for so long? So it seemed. Their self-defenses had caused the very thing they were defending themselves from: by assuming that Matt did not want her, she had intimidated herself into not wanting him. A typical Kate-ism: control the rejection and you can handle the pain.

"Listen, Matt." Her voice was weak, only partly from the birth. "Larry and I never—well, it never got that far."

Matt strode to the head of the bed. "Tell me now, Kate. Are you going home with him?"

"No," she said. "I'm not." How could she, she now realized?

She loved Larry, but in another way completely. Nursing Max made Kate realize how many dimensions love really allowed. Besides, she was not, in her own mind, the woman for Larry. Larry needed someone who understood peach pies. Who needed him, as she no longer did. Someone like CeCe.

He may have realized that already, Kate now saw. The dinners with CeCe. The excuses to meet. The looks they exchanged. She shook her head at her obliviousness—and theirs. Larry and CeCe. Of course. If they didn't already know it, they would soon.

Matt sank into a chair. "Kate, so many nights I wondered if he was there with you, sharing things that were my right to share. I would dial the phone, then hang up, because I didn't know what I'd do if he answered—probably run over there and then the guy would kill me, and Max wouldn't have a father."

"Then it *was* you? I did the same thing. I called, and hung up."

"That was *you*?"

They stared at each other, then Matt leaned over and put his arms around Kate and the baby. "I used to stand on your corner and look at the light in your room," he admitted. "Silhouettes on the shade." He dropped his head onto her chest until she was cradling it close beside the baby and she felt wet tears through her nightgown. "We have to do it," he said, his voice muffled by the sheets. "We have to try, and not just for Max. For me. Because I don't know what I'm going to do if you leave this hospital and it's not with me."

Kate stroked his head with one hand and held the baby with the other.

The great thing about birth and death—well, especially birth—was that they did put things in perspective. Why had they split? Kate had almost forgotten, as people told her she would forget the pain of labor. What remained was what mattered—a baby, a relationship. Commitment. Kate realized that she had come to the point where she could no more turn her back on a commitment born of love than she could on a child born of love.

"You know, Matt," Kate said, "when we split up, I really thought that was it." His arms felt good. They felt like home.

"It was. But now *this* is it. I don't know why I overreacted so much."

"Well, I overreacted too. I guess the pressure got in the way of everything else."

"It's still not going to be easy."

"I know, and I'm scared."

"Why is that, honey?"

"Because there aren't any guarantees—because I love you, but is that enough?"

"It is if you love me." He watched her carefully.

"I do, Matt—enough to say I'm sorry. So sorry for what we put each other through, for what happened to us." She closed her eyes, and he kissed them with a softness that soothed her to the soul, whispering totally unnecessarily that he loved her too, because she knew it.

"I'm taking a six-month leave of absence," she told him. She had considered and dismissed the idea of a three-day-a-week schedule, half days, a two-month leave, or other halfway measures suggested by Stanton Welch. She was not going to split her commitment again. And she knew where her priority was. In six months, she could reevaluate, but now she had a purpose to reestablish, a life to share, a new person who depended on her. The magazine was neither her partner nor her child; it was

249

work—she saw that now. Life was not a pie to be nibbled at, until you were left with a dry crust, and no cherries. It was better to enjoy a whole piece of anything, whatever you chose. Then you had something complete.

"The magazine is ready. We have a prototype." Thanks to Hal Radia, who had grabbed, hidden, and protected it in her absence, she had learned. "And our first sponsor. The others will fall in now. Hal and the group can handle it. I need to handle this." She touched the baby's cheek.

"No nanny?" he asked.

"No nanny." Kate was no longer panicked at this prospect; she welcomed it. She wanted nothing to come between her and this child. She wanted hers to be the first face Max saw in the morning, in the middle of the night. Any time she had a need, Kate wanted to be there for her. "We're going to get to know each other, you and me and Max. Max can sleep in our room for now. It'll be easier while she's nursing anyhow. '

"We don't have to keep the apartment," said Matt, stroking her forehead. "You always thought it was too big and empty."

"Not anymore," said Kate, because she knew for certain now that emptiness had nothing whatsoever to do with places. "Not anymore."

She kissed her husband like a lover she had not seen in a very long time. Because he was.